# Scattered Ashes

by

Maria Rachel Hooley

Scattering Ashes



Cover by Phatpuppy Art

# Chapter One

It was early one morning as August burned itself toward September's cooler glory that Jordan Carroway spotted a woman sitting at the middle of a wooden footbridge suspended high above a large river by rope and wire. Although she was completely still, the breeze swayed the bridge slightly, and the fact that she'd braved the height at all upped his estimation of her, considering the drop was a good thirty feet. Her legs were pretzeled beneath her, and the backs of her hands rested lightly atop her knees while she meditated.

Below, fish swam, their bodies burnished in the light, their tails flipping above the water, sending ripples on the surface. Dragonflies flitted, and a few isolated cumulous clouds scrolled lazily across the heavens. Still, in spite of all this beauty, he stared at her, at the way the breeze lifted strands of her long, dark hair, at the fullness of her lips as she pursed them in concentration. Mostly, he wondered at the way she could lose herself in a peace most people couldn't find.

He blinked a couple of times, waiting for her to move. Instead, she remained where she was, focused only on the moment. Doubtlessly, she didn't know he was there, watching, or she probably would have opened her eyes and given him "the look" most women gave guys who invaded their personal space.

He frowned and wondered if she came here often. Although he had grown up less than an hour away, this was his first trip here, and the only thing that had brought him at all was a required PE class, not that PE had anything to do with his graphic design degree. Then again, he knew that without this class, he wasn't going to be getting the diploma he'd worked the last four years to get. It wasn't that he minded PE; he just didn't see what this class could give him.

Although he would have liked to have stared at her all day, he forced himself to glance at his watch. He had about thirty minutes before class started, and that was more than enough time to take walk out onto that bridge.

"Why not?" he muttered, stowing his gear in the back of his Jeep. He started across the bridge without a clue what he planned to say. Then again, pretty much everything he had planned in his life had gone differently than he'd thought, so he didn't figure there was much use to expecting the future to mind him. It was like the egocentric five-year-old who never heard the word *no.* He should have thought about the fact he was getting married next month. It should have deterred him, but in the back of his mind, he saw the woman as more of a curiosity than anything and especially not a threat. Besides, what harm was there in talking?

He looked at her one last time, still awed by the way she seemed to lose herself totally in the private world she'd created. Sighing, he stepped onto the bridge and tried as diligently as possible not to move it enough to disturb her. He figured she would have felt someone there, stepping onto the wood planks, heading her way, but she didn't. She'd finally gotten up and turned to retrieve her bag  when he closer.

"Hey there," he said.

Time seemed to slow as she whirled, not realizing she was so close to the side of the edge. The momentum threw her off balance--and off the bridge, along with the ancient-looking camera which had been sitting there.

"Crap!" Jordan hissed. He eyed the water below, expecting her to surface, but in that moment, he thought about all the different plants that might be down there, the rocks, and the currents. Besides, he didn't have a clue how deep the water was. That all came from his lifeguard background.

When she didn't surface, he did the only thing he knew; he jumped feet first into an area near where she would have gone down, allowing her enough space so he didn't land on top of her. The rush of air didn't bother him. The cold water, however--that was another story, and found it deeper than he'd thought. Could she swim?

His first inclination led him to the river's bottom, and that's when he spotted her camera, which he grabbed before bobbing to the surface and found she was already there, treading water. She looked at him and shook her head. "You always go swimming with your clothes on?"

Shrugging, he said, "Just following your lead."

She laughed. "That wasn't a lead. That was clumsiness. What's your excuse?"

"You didn't rise quickly enough." He wiped the water from his eyes.

"You jumped in because you were trying to save me?" Her voice rose incredulously. "You don't even know me."

Reaching out, he offered a hand. "Let's remedy that. Name's Jordan Carroway."

She took a deep breath and shook his hand. "Nicole O'Roarke. Nice to meet you."

"I found this." He held up the camera.

She shook her head at the sight of water pouring off of it. "I don't think it's ever going to work again." She glanced toward the shore. "Now if you don't mind, I'm going to swim away. I've got a class starting in a few minutes." She thrust her arms in a tentative American crawl stroke, and he quickly kept pace with her.

"What kind of class?"

"PE  It's this weekend thing, if you want to know--not that I'm much for PE, mind you, but it's a graduation requirement."

Letting out a laugh, he asked, "Are you serious?  I think we're in the same class."

That stopped her momentum.  "Really?  Then you'd better get changed, too.  Unless you want to stay in dripping clothes."

"Good point."  He took the lead, and the two of them quickly made for shore where they parted company, the camera still in his hand.

Fifteen minutes later, Jordan stood back at the bridge, the only giveaways of his swim were his damp hair he'd raked away from his face and the squishy shoes which would have to dry on their own.  A white tee and khaki shorts had replaced his soaked clothes, and he stared out at the water spread below, a fluid covering of dark, mossy green the sunlight shimmered upon.

The sound of voices and laughter distracted him, and he turned to find more people—presumably other students—appearing.  Scanning the group, however, he didn't see the pretty brunette from the bridge. Then again, maybe she'd needed more time to dry off than he.

To his left, he spotted the instructor—a man in his mid-forties wearing a Mets cap, a navy t-shirt, and red swim trunks.  He climbed into a newer Ford F150 with canoes in the back.  Not long after the engine had growled to life, the man drove the truck down toward a much lower spot, where it would be easy to launch the canoes.

From Jordan's peripheral vision, he spotted a woman with long, auburn hair heading this way.  Instinctively, he turned toward her and found Nicole approaching, her hair just as damp as his as it fell in waves around her face.  She wore a black, one-piece swimsuit, the bottoms of which had been hidden by a pair of denim cut-offs with fringed edges. Jordan stared as she ambled toward a blue Honda Accord and stowed her bag in the trunk.

The instructor gestured for them all to come to him. Jordan fell in with the crowd and even though he no longer watched Nicole, he found himself drawn to her nonetheless.

The instructor waited until the twenty or so students had flocked around him before he spoke. "I'm Richard Harris, and if you've enrolled in Basic Outdoor Recreation, you are in the right spot." He pointed to a clipboard on the hood of the truck. "Here is a sign-in sheet. Please write legibly, or you might not get credit for being here. As you can tell by looking in the back of my truck, we are going to start today by getting our feet wet while canoeing. In addition to the canoes and paddles, there are also life jackets I expect everyone to wear. I don't care if you're an Olympian who medaled in swimming; you will wear the jackets. So grab a partner, a paddle, and a jacket while I unload the canoes." He pointed to two male students and asked them to help him with the canoes.

"Got a partner yet?"

Jordan turned and spotted Nicole standing next to him. Her hands were shoved in her cut-off pockets. "Nope. You?"

She shrugged. "I do now--if you're game. But I think we'd better sign in."

"Good idea." The two walked to the hood of the truck and printed their names on the sheet before grabbing paddles and jackets. As he turned toward her, the sun streamed through her hair, catching its red highlights. "Ever been canoeing before?"

"Nope. You?"

"Several times."

"Good to know." She put on her jacket, and when she was done, Jordan thrust his hands to his hips and smirked. Seeing his expression, she asked, "What? Why are you smirking?"

"Because that jacket isn't going to do you any good like that. You'd be lucky if it didn't come up over your head."

Although not adjusting the jacket right had embarrassed Nicole, she found she wanted to keep looking into his eyes, liking the way the sunlight caught the gold flecks there and turned them amber. She started to adjust the jacket and quickly realized she wasn't going to get far, not with the webbing stuck as it was.

"Here, let me." He stepped toward her and quickly grabbed the straps. At first his fingers seemed to slide on the rough fabric, but he just cinched harder, forcing the buckle to give. In a snap, he'd clicked the latches and stepped back.

"That should do it. You ready to get wet?" he nodded for her to help him carry the canoe toward the water.

"I thought the whole point was *not* to get wet."

"Guess we'll see."

The two carried the canoe to the water's edge where they set it down. They walked it out until the water came up to their knees, and Jordan nodded to her. "Go ahead and get in. Once I get it out a little deeper, I'll climb aboard."

"Aye-Aye, Captain. Wouldn't want to have to walk the plank." She stepped into the canoe and almost tipped it as she started to fall back. Jordan slipped his hand just below her shoulders and stopped her.

"Somehow I think this is going to be one wet ride." He grinned at her, helping her into the canoe.

"Nice way of telling me I'm super clumsy. So smooth."

"Glad you noticed." He waited for her to get in before he pushed the boat farther out so the current would catch and help propel it. Once he was certain the boat was out deep enough, he eased himself against the side, braced his arms on the rim, and lifted his body over the edge so he could slip inside.

"Nicely done. Care to try two out of three?"

"Didn't you say the object was to stay in the boat?" he asked, turning his attention to paddling.

"Yep." Nicole looked around at all the other pairs getting into their canoes or paddling out as they were. At least half of the people in the class were guys, and she noticed one interesting thing: compared to the rest, no matter what Jordan did, be it setting the canoe in the water or padding, there was a sort of masculine grace to his movements. It was as though every sweep of his arms were fraught with purpose so no energy was wasted, and the movements were fluid, as though he belonged wherever he was. Even when she shifted in the canoe and it wiggled, he didn't react. It was like a wash of calm assurance kept him in balance, and that amazed Nicole.

Of course, the canoe almost tipped once, and she turned back and looked at him. "What happened?"

He shrugged as they drifted beneath the branch of a low elm, forcing both to duck. "You switched your pattern, and I didn't realize it, so we were paddling on the same side. Definitely not a good idea."

"Something to keep in mind," she agreed. "So what's your story?"

She half peered over her shoulder to see him smile. "Oh, 'Hansel and Gretel.' Maybe *Peter Pan.* On second thought, definitely *Peter Pan.* Nothing like a wicked hot fairy who can only feel one thing at a time." He laughed.

"So not what I meant," she murmured as a flush colored her cheeks.

"But it's what you asked, right?"

She nodded. "Yeah. What I wanted to know is what's your major and all that stuff." She dipped the paddle deep in the water and watched a nearby turtle swim.

"Graphic Design is my major. Now, about all the other stuff you're going to have to be a bit more specific."

She laughed, kind of taken aback by the way he seemed so far removed from every other guy she'd met. Most wanted to talk about themselves. Jordan seemed comfortable no matter what, without the need to call attention to any of that. She was definitely intrigued.

"Okay, what do you do for fun?"

"Scare girls off suspension bridges," he smirked. "Next question?" he paddled a few strokes and looked near the banks where a raccoon scurried higher on the shore.

"No, no, no," Nicole said, shaking her head as she waved a dripping paddle at him. "You didn't really answer the first one, and you know it."

He finally nodded. "Okay. Guilty as charged." He frowned as though deep in thought. "What I do for fun. Hmmm. I like to go hiking and canoeing. Pretty much mostly outdoor stuff. Anything to do with water."

Her eyes lit up in wicked amusement as she dipped the paddle into the water and showered him with it. "Gotcha."

"All right. You started it." He laughed and dipped his paddle into the water to splash her. She stiffened and squealed in a way that made him laugh harder and want to douse her again, but he refrained.

"Oops," he said. "Didn't mean to get you wet."

For a few seconds, she sputtered as she reacquainted herself with the chilly water. Then she lifted a hand and tried to brush some of the water away. "Okay, Jordan, you are so going to pay for that!"

She got up and whirled.

"You're going to tip—"

The canoe lurched to one side, dumping them both into the river as it completed its half-revolution. As Nicole had known she was going to tip the vessel, she'd been prepared to swim from under it and easily bobbed to the surface, waiting to antagonize her canoe partner.

The canoe floated upside down next to her, and she waited

patiently, knowing he was going to surface at any moment, yet only the motion of her hands broke the surface. Frowning, she glanced around, knowing he had to be there somewhere.

"Jordan?" she called, edging around the canoe, looking for him. "Where are you?" She spotted the two paddles and grabbed them before the current swept them away.

He didn't answer, and that bothered her. She knew he hadn't been expecting the tip, but he was a good swimmer. He'd definitely proved that earlier when he jumped off the bridge after her. So where was he?

Could he have struck his head or something?

That thought panicked her. "Jordan! Where are you?" She circled the boat again, thinking she'd find him.

"Oh, no," she muttered, feeling a coldness sweep through her as she released the paddles. She dove, fingers groping, and even though she opened her eyes, the murky green of the river refused to reveal anything, only frustrating her more. She swam around until she felt her lungs would burst and broke to the surface, just knowing he would already be there.

Stillness. She was alone. For a moment, she tried not to panic, but it rose from deep inside of her into great waves, threatening to drag her under, and she spotted another canoe not far away. She was on the brink of calling out for help when she felt two hands grab her legs and drag her under.

When she resurfaced, she spotted Jordan floating there, a smirk on his face, and she wanted to throttle him, yet relief also flooded through her.

"Where did you come from?"

"There's a pocket of air under the canoe. I was hiding in there."

She waved a warning finger at him. "That was so not funny, Jordan!" She smacked at his arm and brushed the sodden bangs from her face, feeling stupid.

"Hey, you're the one who tipped the canoe, not me. Besides, I have to give you props. You don't panic easily--not that you should have panicked. I am wearing a life jacket which should have brought me to the surface. No drowning here."

That was it. His tone, so irritatingly cheerful, launched Nicole at him, intent on dunking him. Of course, as she came at him, he was prepared and quickly dodged, taunting: "What? What did I say?"

Although he thought he was out of reach, when she dove backwards, she managed to catch his shoulder. She had half submerged him when he whirled her around to face him and easily wrapped both arms around her, trapping her arms beneath his. "Sorry. This is a no-dunking zone."

"You're insufferable," she growled, trying to break free without getting anywhere.

"If I turn you lose, are you going to be a good girl?"

"I don't know how," she retorted, thinking she had almost gotten one arm free when he adjusted his grip and tugged into back in the confines of his own.

"Okay, if you can't be good, at least say it was your fault because you turned the canoe over." Nicole opened her mouth to say it but found herself staring into the depths of his dark amber eyes. Her breath caught in her throat, and she found she couldn't stop staring. Each breath came out shallow and unsettled.

At first, she told herself it had been the scuffle that had made her heart race, but she knew better. It was being so close to him, their faces only inches apart. The sunlight backlit his hair, burnishing its strands a dark auburn, and at first his mouth seemed set in a grin, but the longer he stared, the more it slowly straightened, as though he, himself, didn't completely understand what was happening between them.

"It was my fault the canoe tipped," she said at last, mesmerized. Although the water was cold, all she seemed to feel was his arms wrapped about her, keeping her close. “But it scared me when I couldn’t find you. I thought maybe you might have hit your head." She swallowed hard, finding it hard to take in enough air.

He chuckled. “Yeah, well, my mom might think that would improve things.”

Nicole found herself laughing, but she thought it might in part be because she didn’t know how to handle emotions running through her about a guy she'd only just met. She figured the best thing she could do would be to ignore them, so she turned her focus to the canoe. She reached out and tried to grab the paddle again, but they had drifted quite a ways in different directions.

"Uh oh," she gulped.

He laughed again. "You get one. I'll get the other."

Nicole started swimming until she reached one of the paddles, and by the time she got back, Jordan was already waiting for her.

“Well, what are we going to do now? I don’t think the canoe is going to right itself.”

“Nope. Probably not,” he agreed. Swimming to it, he gripped his fingers under one end and tugged it toward shore. Not sure what else she could do, Nicole swam after him.

“What’re you doing?” she asked.

“Taking the canoe to shallow water. It’ll be easier to flip.” He glanced over his shoulder. “You coming?”

“Right behind you.”

A few of the other students in canoes spotted them swimming with the overturned canoe. More than once, somebody chuckled, but Nicole didn’t feel so bad, considering the tip had been intentional. Once they'd reached water that touched just above the knees, Jordan held the canoe still and nodded at it.

“Get in. It’ll be easier in the shallow water. I’ll push us out. Again.” The last word came out with a smirk, and Nicole laughed.

"But you're so good at it."

"Umm-hmm." He waited for her to climb into the canoe and get settled before gently nudging the boat out deeper. Then he climbed in, sat, and grabbed his paddle. "You ready?"

"Sure. Why not?" She shrugged.

"We are going to stay in the canoe this time, right?" he asked, laughing.

"That's for me to know and you to find out," Nicole taunted, dipping her paddle in the water.

* * *

They spent most of the morning in the canoe before reaching the pick-up point, where the instructor waited for them, and once they'd finished their water journey, the two loaded the canoe into the truck and sat down amid the group to wait for stragglers.

The instructor must have also had an interest in photography because he was taking pictures of the students with an instant camera. He shot one picture of Jordon and Nicole sitting on the bridge, and Jordan had given it to her.

Three or four of the students who had arrived back first had been put in charge of grilling burgers and hot dogs. While Nicole didn't much like either, she had to admit to working up quite an appetite during the trip downriver. Her stomach growled in agreement.

"Was that you?" Jordan asked, looking at her stomach.

"Well, yeah," she finally said, feeling a flush creep into her cheeks. She looked at the massive tree they sat under, enjoying the soft breeze that rustled among the leaves, rubbing them against one other. Although she sat with her legs crossed and tucked toward her body, she leaned back, resting on her palms behind her. His knees were drawn to his body, and he rested his arms on them.

"Should I tell them to put a rush order in before you eat one of the canoes?" Jordan said helpfully.

"No, thanks. I think I can wait," she replied, shaking her head.

"Don't say I didn't offer."

"So, tell me more about you," she said, licking her lips and wishing she had some Chapstick. Then again, considering the way her shoulders were slightly red, she knew she'd probably wish she'd worn sunscreen even more by the time the day was through.

"Let see. I'm going to be a monk, and I like country music." He shrugged, wearing a serious expression, but she knew better. She leaned over and nudged him with her shoulder.

"You liar!"

"Oh, you wanted the truth. Well, why didn't you say so?" His eyes twinkled in amusement and he laughed, a warm, deep sound that suffused through her as the breeze gently lifted a strand of his hair and made it stand on end before it eased back with the rest of his dark hair. He took a deep breath.

"Let's see. I have a younger sister who kind of reminds me of you. Right now I work in a Best Buy selling computers, and in May I'll be done with my degree." He looked straight ahead as though suddenly lost somewhere else, and in that moment the smile died as though he were thinking about something he didn't particularly want to think about right. He turned back to her.

"Is that enough?" he asked, staring into her eyes as another strand of hair blew across her face. Before she could lift a hand to move it, he reached out and pushed it behind her ear.

Nicole took a deep breath, trying to figure out whether she were really going to ask the question at the heart of things, a question she didn't want to ask but that she knew she'd want to kick herself repeatedly for if she didn't, and it didn't appear that he was going to just tell her.

"So, what about a girlfriend?" she finally asked, reminding herself not to hold her breath and that no matter what, the answer wasn't all that important in the grand scheme of things.

"Girlfriend," he repeated, and as he spoke, the word almost sounded like it had been spoken in a foreign language. "Well," he continued, a frown tugging at his lips. "No, I don't have a girlfriend. I have a fiancé, which isn't quite the same thing." As he spoke, he stared off into space, distracted, and Nicole felt a flush coloring her cheeks. For the thousandth time, she wished she weren't so easily embarrassed.

"A fiancé. Wow. So when's the big day?"

He took a deep breath and released it. "The end of next month. Right now she's a maniac wedding planner, and it's just safer to stay out of her way, which is another reasons I'm here on this PE class. It'll keep me out of trouble."

Nicole nodded and tried to digest the information he'd given her, her mind frantically spinning at all the behavior cues she had read so wrong. Was he really just that friendly of a guy? She hadn't known him long enough to tell, but she was a pretty good judge of character, and he didn't seem like a jerk to her. He seemed pretty honest.

She unfolded her legs and mimicked his posture. "So how long have you known her?"

"Three years. We met when we were both freshmen." He kept staring ahead, and his voice seemed more tense than it had been, and Nicole wondered if there were a reason he seemed so uncomfortable.

Nicole swallowed hard and nodded. "That's great. I'm glad you've found someone who makes you happy."

"Thanks." Jordan slowly turned to face her. He'd tugged his eyebrows downward and wore a thoughtful frown. "And have you?"

Although Nicole started to answer, another guy in the class approached them and handed them each a plate with a hamburger on it. Both Nicole and Jordan accepted the offerings and said "thank you" in unison.

For a moment after, there was an awkward silence as they began eating and Nicole kept replaying the conversation up to that point. Finally, as she felt him staring, she said, "Not yet, not even close." At that, she mentally went through the list of guys she'd gone out with and now lamented. Although the list was short, it was far from sweet, and unfortunately none of them were anything like Jordan or perhaps she might have been able to see a future with someone. "And I've had enough blind dates to last a lifetime, thank you."

He nodded. "You say 'blind date' like it's a bad thing."

"Don't get me started." She waved her burger at him. "I've been down that road, and it never turns out well." Shaking her head, she took a bite and focused on eating, unsure where to go from here.

"So, aren't you going to ask me any of the usual questions, like 'How did you know she was the one?' or something like that?" He, too, took a bite.

Shrugging, she said, "Okay. I'll bite. How did you know she was the one?"

"I've never known that. We've just been close for years, and I thought maybe that was what was supposed to happen." Again, he stared off into space, suggesting he had gone somewhere she wasn't privy to.

"You don't sound so sure of things."

He shifted slightly so he could set the plate on his legs. "Maybe. I don't know. It's probably just a sign of cold feet or something."

She nodded but tried to tell herself not to think too much about the 'or something' she had started to feel. Still, she wasn't about to broach the topic. She didn't know why, but for some reason, she really enjoyed being around Jordan, and even if they were only to be friends, she didn't want to chance ruining that, not when he was so easy to talk to.

## Chapter Two

Once the stragglers had found their way to the group, they all finished lunch and prepared for a mountain hike. Harris guided them to the mountain in question and told them once again to pair off and stay on the trail. He also handed out a sort of scavenger hunt list of items to return with to get a grade. While Jordan figured it was more a way to make sure everyone was staying on task, he thought it was also a lousy way to earn grades. Then again, this whole weekend PE credit thing had not been his idea of a good time.

Until he'd met Nicole.

He didn't know what he'd been thinking when he'd approached her on the bridge. He'd figured she was probably just another pretty face, and he'd seen plenty of those. But whatever had drawn him to her had gone beyond beauty. He couldn't totally dismiss that even when he'd been watching her before he'd approached, there'd been something between them. Granted, it was something he didn't really understand, but it was there nonetheless. He knew, considering that he felt something unusual stirring, he should just keep his distance, but he kept telling himself that whatever was happening could be the start of a great friendship. For whatever reason, he couldn't seem to dismiss it altogether.

"So, you up for partnering off again?" Nicole asked, eyeing the mountain just ahead as she stood with her hands on her hips.

"Sure. Why not. At least there's no canoe to tip." He nudged her with his shoulder.

"Ooh, funny guy. Thanks." She shook her head and turned her attention to the list. "Looks like we've got about ten things to find to get the grades. You ready to get a move on?"

He gestured to the path. "Ladies first."

She laughed. "You just want me where you can keep an eye on me."

"That, too."

The two started up the trail, keeping their pace leisurely to let all the other, more dedicated students get a head start. Nicole figured if she were going to be forced to do this, she might as well enjoy her surroundings, and that sure wouldn't happen with other college students noisily tromping the grounds, shimmying to their iPods, oblivious to the natural world around them, one that existed far beyond the ten things they had to find.

Truth be told, Nicole preferred nature to people. Nature she understood. People were a different story. She licked her lips, feeling the sun burning down upon her and felt grateful that just ahead was an area where trees on either side laced together high overhead and shut out much of the glaring sunlight. She looked down at her shoulders and muttered, "Oh, crap."

Jordan's gaze followed, and he shook his head. "Let me guess. You have something against sunscreen."

She ran her fingers over the pink skin. "No. I just sort of forgot to bring some."

"Of course." Jordan shook his head and tugged his small pack from his shoulders. Unzipping it, he said, "Well, at least one of us didn't forget." He pulled out a small bottle and handed it to her.

"Thanks." She poured some into her hands and rubbed it into her shoulder. Of course, there was the problem of her back because there was no way she'd ever be able to reach it. Gritting her teeth, she knew she was going to have to ask for help even as awkward as it might seem.

"Could you put some on my back? I can't reach it, and I'm sure the sun has already burned it, too."

"Sure." Jordan swallowed hard and nodded as he took the sunscreen and squirted some into his palm. He looked at his hand for a second or two then lifted it to her shoulder and began rubbing it in. "Yeah, you're right about the sunburn. Something tells me you aren't going to be comfortable tonight."

"Lucky me," she muttered, unsure what to make of the feel of his hands caressing her with such a light touch. Of course, it definitely wasn't helping, considering this was supposed to be a friendship. Then again, there was that old saying about women and men not being able to be friends, something she'd never really believed before. It wasn't her fault Jordan Carroway was giving her doubts about everything.

What the hell was going on with her? She'd never reacted like this before.

"Okay. You should be good." She felt his hand lift and turned to smile at him.

"Thanks. At least this way my back won't burn anymore."

"True." He capped the bottle securely and shoved it back into his bag. The two started walking along the trail again. Jordan unfolded the list and began reading.

"So tell me something to look for," she said.

He scanned the page and finally said, "How about a sycamore leaf? Think you can handle that?"

"No problem." As they headed deeper into the shadows of the trees, Nicole meandered towards the edge of the path and glanced at the branches, searching for the telltale three-pointed leaf. While the trees nearest the path weren't sycamores, she did spot one farther back and immediately began trudging toward it.

“Ummm, Nicole—"

“Hang on,” she said and moved faster, determined to be the first to find one of the items on the list. “I’ve almost got it.”

“I really think—"

“I’ll be right there!” she called and reached down.

“Don’t touch that!” Jordan called. His tone was louder and firmer, causing her to turn abruptly.

“Why? The leaves are right there.” She pointed to the dead leaves littering the ground.

“Because you are standing knee-deep in poison ivy, and if you stick your hand in there, you’ll end up with it all over the place, which I really don’t think you want.” Jordan folded his arms across his chest and waited. He wore a bemused grin and arched an eyebrow at her.

Nicole looked down, and this time she focused on the plants jutting up around the shaded base of the tree. The obvious three-leaved ivy now stood out since it had been called to her attention, and as she looked down, she quickly realized her calves were brushing the leaves already.

“Now you tell me,” she muttered, trying to back away gracefully without touching the offending ivy any more than possible.

“I tried to tell you before you went in, not that you would listen because you were in such a rush to be an over-achiever and all.”

“I feel your sympathy and support, Jordan. I really do.” She kept stepping backwards until she’d extracted herself then turned to face him and noticed the smirk. Blushing, she waved a warning finger at him.

“Not funny.”

“That depends on your point of view, doesn’t it? Personally, I find it hilarious--and if you don't have trouble getting comfortable with that sunburn, I think this might just close the deal.” He shook his head and clicked his tongue as if to say, "Shame on you."

"Great. Now what do I do?" She looked down at her legs and felt helpless. Although they had already started itching, she figured that was just from her over-active imagination telling her they should be itching after being exposed to poison ivy. It was amazing what the power of suggestion could do.

Jordan nodded to the path. "I say we keep moving. I hear water moving somewhere in the distance, and we'll probably find the river soon enough. When we get there, you should rinse off your calves and hope that helps."

She smiled. "That's a great idea. You're a genius."

He shrugged and started walking. "Whatever you say, Poison Ivy."

"Thanks."

To the left, they spotted a large evergreen and beneath her majestic limbs, several pine cones lay scattered. Jordan pointed. "A pine cone is on the list. Since I don't see anything green beside the tree, you should be safe enough."

"I'll be right back." She veered to the left and darted beneath the tree to grab one of the cones, then returned. "Do you want to put it in your pack?"

"Works for me." He slid the straps from his shoulders and removed the pack so he could put the cone inside and zipped it.

As they resumed walking, he consulted the list. "One down, nine to go. Keep your eye out for a locust shell. You do know what they look like, right?"

She nodded. "I may be a city girl, but I do like the outdoors, smarty."

"Not surprising. You do look like you belong here more than the city." Jordan risked a glance at her, liking the way strands of her hair kept falling into her face and her constantly reaching to push them aside as though that would keep them out of the way. "So tell me what you want out of life."

She shrugged and looked at the ground. "Nothing I'm going to admit. It'll sound maudlin, and it's not supposed to."

"Why not tell and let me be the judge?" He looked up at the small swatches of the sky that appeared among the outstretched branches.

"Okay--no laughing though." She glared at him.

"No laughing, I promise," he said, nodding.

"I don't have a clue about most stuff. The only thing I know is I want to change the world. I want to make it a better place."

Jordan understood why she didn't want to say that. If anyone else had said it, he would have agreed it was trite and over-used, but something about the way she stared ahead, toward a future she couldn't see, her full lips parted in a wistfulness he could only imagine, told him she meant it. She really wanted to make a difference, and she knew that difference might not be easy to achieve but that mattered to her all the same.

"Aren't you going to say something?" Nicole asked, looking at him. He could tell by her expression she expected him to make fun of her.

"What's wrong with wanting to make a difference?" he finally asked.

She shrugged. "I don't know. Everybody says they want to change the world, to make it better, and maybe they mean it, but it seems like, for the most part, nobody does it, you know?"

"Yeah. I get that." He looked at her and marveled at how different she was from Alyssa, his fiancée. It wasn't that Alyssa was bad; she just lacked the blind optimism which seemed so inherent in Nicole, and while Alyssa had many good points, he knew the only way Alyssa would ever change the world would be by changing her expensive clothes. Of course, this was the first time he'd ever really thought about life in that context. Always before it had seemed that the bond with Alyssa had been enough. Then again, until there was a basis for comparison, how could anyone know what was enough?

"So you think I'll be one of those who makes the plans but never follows through?" She looked straight ahead, and Jordan didn't know why, but he sensed that his opinion mattered to her. Her lips formed a straight line, and her shoulders suddenly tensed.

"No, I think you're probably too stubborn to give in, no matter what. I think you'll follow through because it matters to you."

Immediately those lips curved into a warm smile and she flashed those dark green eyes at him. "Thanks. It's always good to hear I'm stubborn."

"Glad I could help." He shifted his focus back to the list. "Shall we find a new item of choice?"

"Sure." Nicole found herself smiling despite falling off a bridge and having a close encounter with poison ivy. Strange, really. How long had it been since she'd felt such happiness bubbling up inside her? So long it seemed unreal.

She scanned the area waiting for him to tell her an item to watch for when she spotted a large sycamore just off the path. Squinting, she scrutinized the ground around it was free of greenery, which it was. Without waiting, she veered toward it.

"Hey, where are you going?"

"To get something."

Jordan snorted. "You might watch for poison ivy this time."

"Got it covered." She bent, picked up one of the leaves, and whirled to show it to him. "How's this for a sycamore leaf?"

He nodded appreciatively. "That will do. Of course, I don't think we want to put that in my bag. It'll just get ruined."

"You've got a point," she agreed. "I'll just hold onto it."

"Good idea." He stared at the list for a few seconds and looked up, cocking his head to the left. “I think the river is close. He pointed to where he heard the sound of rushing water. “Let’s go that way so you can wash off your legs.”

Turning, he cut through the foliage, and she followed. About twenty feet ahead, they spotted the forest open up a bit as the land dipped into a recess where the river ran free. Although the water moved quickly, there seemed to be enough shore that Nicole would have plenty of space to wash her legs without falling in.

“Perfect,” she said, suddenly taking the lead. Although her skin had been itching since she’d tried to go for that first leaf, she’d forced herself to ignore it. Now the itching was worse, as though it sensed the water was about to wash it away forever.

Jordan followed at a leisurely pace. “So are you clumsy?”

“Depends on whom you ask,” she retorted, already at the water's edge. She hurriedly tugged off one shoe, then the other, preparing to just wade in.

“Well, you might not want to go in, then. The last thing you need is for Harris to be lurking around and fish you out of the river.”

Nicole waved dismissively at him. “This water isn’t that fast. I think I’ll be fine.” She set the leaf by her shoes so she wouldn’t forget it.

Removing his pack, Jordan stepped up and took her by the wrist. “Okay, so maybe I’m a worry wart. Just humor me.”

She looked at the way his fingers cinched around her wrist and felt a strange warmth suffuse through her. “Okay, since you put it that way,” she said, but she could tell her voice was off, distracted.

She stepped toward the water, and even once she'd set her foot down, she found herself grateful Jordan had anchored her upright. He’d been right to guess the water was moving fast, and had he not been holding her, she probably would have ended up falling in face-first and washing downriver. She tried not to give away how right he’d been but found herself wobbling at the sudden force of the water, and his grip tightened in response.

"You okay over there?"

"Peachy." She bent and began splashing water over her legs below the knees, trying to wash away whatever residue the ivy have left. More than once, she accidentally got Jordan, and he shook his head.

"Hey, I'm nowhere near your legs, Nicole."

She shrugged and stood upright. "Near enough--so sorry about that." She stepped from the river, slipped her shoes back on, and retrieved the leaf.

"You know, I was really dreading this class," Jordan said, shaking his head. "To me, it seemed pointless."

She traced the veins in the leaf. "Pointless--well, maybe, but the thing is, if you try to amuse yourself, sometimes even the pointless things get better."

"True," he agreed. "Then again, I think part of my surprise about this trip was meeting a friend who makes me feel I can talk about anything."

A flush dotted Nicole's cheeks, and she found herself floundering in the sudden silence, unsure what to say. It appeared some part of her had latched onto him as much as some part of him had latched onto her. Of course, although she found herself thrilled to have met someone she felt so comfortable with, it was difficult to understand the timing. Why couldn't it have happened before he'd been engaged.

"Yeah, it is nice to be able to pretty much talk about anything." She would have said more but wasn't sure what.

He looked at the list. "Okay. Why don't I look for a locust shell while you find some moss? Sound good?"

She shrugged. "Yep. So long as I stay out of the poison ivy, right?"

He smiled. "Leaflets three. Let them be."

“I’ll keep that in mind.” She started off to the left side of the path. As she walked, she heard his footsteps as well as well as her own and glanced over her shoulder at his retreating back, watching him walk. If her best friend Sarah had been there, she’d have been elbowing her and muttering comments about checking out his ass, but something about this went deeper than that. It felt as if she had known Jordan for so much longer than hours. She didn’t know why, and considering he was getting married, it probably didn’t matter, but some small voice inside her insisted that even if he were tying the knot next month she shouldn’t completely lose contact with him. She liked talking to him, and what harm could there be in that?

She was so lost in her thoughts she didn’t watch where she was going. She found it hard to concentrate on much besides Jordan Carroway. Of course, he’d probably just think she were stupid for being so fixated. More than once, she’d thought that herself.

The next step proved to be her Achilles' heel, and it had nothing to do with poison ivy, just one of the smaller areole of a monster cactus, most of which had been well hidden amid the tangles of underbrush, which is why she'd missed it. Her foot, however, stepped on the plant, and the spines shoved themselves through her shoe and impaled her foot.

Although she'd intended to scream from the excruciating pain, all that came out was a whimpering, hissing sound, and as she jerked her foot away, the spines free of the plant and remained in her.

She stumbled to the ground, and tears filled her eyes as she gasped from the fire blazing at the base of her foot. Hadn’t her run-in with poison ivy been enough? For a moment, she just sat there, steeling herself to look at the shoe and prepare for the idea of having to pull out the spines.

“Nicole?”

She heard Jordan calling her name and cringed at the

embarrassment. Normally, she was self-sufficient. Normally, she knew to stay out of poison ivy. Normally, she didn't step on cacti. There was no way in hell this was a normal day.

"Nicole?" he called louder, and she realized she might as well just fess up to her clumsiness and get it over with.

"Over here," she responded, still unable to look at her foot, not with the searing pain she couldn't acclimate herself to. Who knew a cactus could go through a shoe?

"Over where?" His voice was closer, but she knew she was still going to have to guide him.

"Keep coming. You're on the right track."

She heard footsteps on the earth and looked up to find Jordan there. "Umm, Nicole, I don't see any lichen around here."

She shrugged. "Yeah, well, I was sort of taking a break." Gritting her teeth, she moved her leg, starting to lift it so that she could look at the sole.

"Oh, my. You found a cactus."

"No shit," she muttered, looking at three large spines, the sight of which made her light-headed.

Jordan knelt and removed his pack. "Yeah, well, you look like you're about to pass out, so how about you not look at your foot right now and let me deal with it."

Nicole gladly looked away, feeling her cheeks burn with embarrassment. She lay back and stared at the sky, preferring that to watching Jordan. "Did I mention I wanted to be a nurse until I passed out giving blood?"

"Why does that not surprise me?" he muttered with his usual calm voice.

"Doesn't anything rattle you?" she snapped, suddenly more than frustrated by the situation.

"Well, this probably would if my foot were the pincushion. Then again, one of us has to be calm, and I don't think you're feeling it." He took a deep breath and looked closer. One hand, the one with the black watch band, gripped her ankle as he examined her. "Okay, I can't get the shoe off to look at your foot until I pull out the spines. You okay with that?"

"Great." Nicole gritted her teeth.

"Okay. Deep breath."

Immediately, she felt more pain as he tugged the spine out, and she held her breath, waiting for him to finish. The pain lingered for a few seconds then diminished.

"One out," he said and glanced at her. "Damn, you're pale. You aren't going to pass out on me, are you?"

If Nicole's foot hadn't been throbbing so hard, she might have laughed at the expression of horror on his face; instead, she shook her head and took another breath. "Nope. I'll stay conscious just for you."

"You have absolutely no idea how grateful I am." His words sounded almost like a sigh of relief. He regarded her foot again before glancing back at her face. "Ready to tackle the second one?"

"Sure. Why not?" She shook her head. "Basic outdoor recreation, my ass. This is not---OWWW!"

Jordan cringed as he pulled out the spine. He felt Nicole's ankle suddenly tense. "Sorry," he said.

She breathed in and out quickly and shook her head. "It's not your fault, Jordan. It's my own. If there's a cactus, I'll find it. If there's poison ivy, I'll find it. I'm lucky like that."

He shrugged. "Well, there's one good thing about the cactus."

"What?" she exclaimed in disbelief. "What could be good about stepping on a cactus?"

"A cactus spine was on our list." He waved one of them at her, careful to hide the part that had been bloodied from going into her foot.

"You're an optimist, aren't you?" she demanded.

"In the flesh." He looked back at her foot. "One more to go. You ready?"

"Of course. I'm always ready for pain."

He nodded and smirked. "Oh, you like those kinds of web sites. I get it. You really did do this for fun, combining the Japanese foot fetish with masochistic tendencies."

Nicole huffed up and threw some leaves at him. "I am not mas—DAMN! That hurts!!!" she screeched.

"Yeah, but it's out, and you were so busy yelling at me you didn't seem to notice the pain until the spine was almost free." He grinned and waived a particularly large spine at her.

"That was in my foot?"

He nodded. "Why do you think I distracted you? Sneaky, eh?"

She laughed. "Definitely.

"All right. Let's take your shoe off and get a look at that foot." As he leaned over, she spotted a gold cross dangling from a chain around his neck. It was kind of different, though, a Celtic design.

"Okay." She raised up so she could prop her elbows behind her and support her body as she felt Jordan untying and removing her shoe. Then he gently tilted her foot so that he could get a better look.

"Well, Bones, what's the verdict?"

He chuckled and in his best Deforest Kelley, said, "Damn it, Jim, I'm a graphic designer, not a doctor."

Picking up a bunch of leaves, Nicole hurled a handful at him, and more than a few got stuck in his hair. "Boo! That was terrible."

He wagged a warning finger at her. "You started it!" He glanced at her foot again. "You've got three punctures in your foot that need cleaning." He reached into his bag and pulled out a small spray container whose contents he quickly applied to her foot, and while she thought it might sting, all it did was tickle, and he fought to keep her still.

"This isn't getting the germs out, Nicole."

"It tickles!"

He shook his head. "Okay. That should be good." He also pulled out three bandages and put them on her foot before putting the sock and shoe back on.

Once he'd put the first aid items away, she pointed to his hair. "You have leaves in your hair, Jordan."

He nodded. "Of course I do. You put them there." He started batting at them, and all but one fell out. The last he actually had to pull free, and he looked at it as he tugged it loose.

"Hey! Good work." He flipped the leaf toward her and said, "Viola--moss. You just scored two points—moss sample and cactus spine." He slid his pack on and rose, lowered his hand to help her up.

"Yay, me." She grabbed it and got to her feet, but the first step she took on the wounded foot almost made her fall. Jordan quickly steadied her.

"You okay?" He nodded to her foot.

"Yeah, it just hurts like hell."

He pulled off the backpack. "I figured. Here, put this on." He held out the pack."

"What?" She reluctantly took the pack.

"Trust me."

Shrugging, she slipped it on, and he turned and bent for her to climb on his back. Blushing, she stepped away. "I don't need a piggyback ride."

"Okay, have it your way." Without warning, he hefted her over his shoulder. "Of course, it's probably going to be much harder to find things this way since the list is in my back pocket."

"Put me down!" Nicole said between giggles.

"Nope. You've achieved your disaster quota today. Could you kindly get the list and tell me what I'm looking for?"

Figuring there was no point in arguing, Nicole saw the edge of the list protruding from his pocket and eased it out before unfolding it. "You know reading from this angle isn't easy."

"But think of all the cactus and poison ivy you'll miss."

It took another hour to gather the last few scavenger items, and Jordan didn't complain about carrying her. She eventually did switch to riding on his back, figuring that if he were going to carry her one way or another, it might as well be the way that made her less dizzy. He spent most of the time telling her jokes or stories, distracting her from thinking about a humiliating day, and when they returned, she found herself sad, knowing the day was drawing to a close and that each of them would be returning to worlds that had nothing to do with the other.

After completing their final assignment, a quiz about what they had learned, Nicole found her foot able to withstand the weight of her body, and Jordan walked her to her car, where she reached into her glove box and pulled out a scrap sheet of paper which she jotted her name, phone number, and email address.

"I'd like to keep in touch, if that's all right. One can never have too many friends, if you know what I mean."

He laughed. "You just like me because I'm good with cactus spines." He looked at the information and tore away the lower half of the paper so he could jot his information, which he gave to her. "And you're right about friends."

He offered her one last smile, and she drove away, watching him standing there, staring at her car until she couldn't see him anymore.

## Chapter Three

"So, tell me all about your weekend class," Sarah said, eating her spinach salad as they sat in their apartment living room. Sunlight spilled through the Bohemian-style curtains, making the dark burgundy of the sofa and walls appear lighter than they really were. A soft, cool breeze wafted through the open window as Nicole stared at her own salad, suddenly not hungry.

"There's not much to tell. I went canoeing and hiking. That's about it." She averted her gaze, not wanting her best friend to see the mixed feeling buried there.

Mmmhmm," Sarah said, brushing the long auburn strands from her brown eyes. "Nothing happened. That's exactly why you came back with a nasty limp."

"You know I'm clumsy," Nicole said.

"So what happened?"

Nicole rolled her eyes and leaned back against the couch. "Well, okay. I stepped on a cactus and Jordan had to pull these huge spines out. They were so sharp they went into my shoes, if you can believe that." She took a bite of her salad, something to take off the nervous energy she felt. She hadn't talked to anyone about Jordan because she was still trying to sort out her feelings.

"Who's Jordan?" Sarah set down her fork and crossed her arms over her chest.

A flush heated Nicole's cheeks, and she shrugged. "Just this guy I met. We sort of partnered up for the canoeing and hiking, and he was nice enough to help me out with the cactus." She took another bite.

"And is he cute?

Nicole's shoulders sank. "It doesn't matter. He has a fiancée, Sarah. He was just a nice guy. A friend."

Smacking her on the head, Sarah lamented, "Of all the guys you could have met, you find the one who has a fiancée? What is wrong with you, Nicole?"

Nicole fidgeted with the salad a bit longer before setting it on the coffee table and staring off into space. "I wish I knew."

"But he was cute, right?" Sarah asked, smirking as she leaned back, her head close to Nicole's as though they were conspiring.

Nicole laughed. "Hell, yeah." Once the giggling had stopped, she turned to her best friend. "Besides, he seems like a wicked cool guy friend, if you want to know the truth." She pulled the scratch paper out. "And I got his email and cell number just to, you know, keep in touch."

Snatching the paper from Nicole, Sarah unfolded and read it. "Jordan Carroway." She arched her eyebrows at Nicole. "Why am I picturing a guy that is about 6'2" with dark brown hair and amber eyes?"

"Because you know me too well, that's why." She took the paper back and wished the blush would leave her. She didn't even have to close her eyes to see him--the way his lips turned into a smile, and the sound of his robust laughter. She could remember well how his hand had felt around her ankle. Even the pain of the spines hadn't overcome that sensation.

Sarah frowned and scrutinized Nicole's expression before sitting up straighter and pasting a serious expression on her face.

"You know, if you think you have feelings for this guy, you could just be honest. What could it hurt?"

Nicole launched herself from the chair. "What could it hurt? Are you kidding?" She paced the living room, her arms folded across her abdomen. "He's getting married next month, Sarah. He's planned a life with somebody, and if he's happy, he deserves to have that happen." She gritted her teeth.

"But what if he's not happy?" she argued, taking another bite of her salad. "What if he's just been confused into thinking he's happy and years down the road you both regret not admitting how you really felt?"

Nicole shook her head and pointed accusingly at her friend. "You always do that. You want to believe every guy is a romantic. Just because Jordan gave me his number to call him as a friend, it doesn't mean anything. Pulling cactus spines out doesn't mean he likes me. It means he's considerate. The last thing I need is to say that maybe I have feelings for him and provide everyone lots of conflict and sleepless nights. It's better if I just keep my mouth shut and move on."

Nicole stormed out of the room, and Sarah sat there, still holding her fork. She winced at the sound of a bedroom door slamming and shook her head.

"Yeah, well, Nic--if he's anything like you, I don't think anybody is going to move on any time soon." She looked down at her salad and took another bite.

* * *

Jordan sat in the back yard of his rental house and watched the sun slowly sink toward the horizon in a fiery burst of orange and pink clouds. He leaned back in the lounge chair, enjoying the soft breeze stroking his skin, and even though his gaze turned toward the sky, his mind drifted back to yesterday and a weekend PE class that had once seemed trivial.

Of course, yesterday, before he'd met Nicole, everything had focus and he'd known what he wanted, but everything had blurred afterward, and now he wasn't sure. He'd talked to Alyssa a couple of times since and pretended nothing was wrong.

Had she not been so wrapped up with wedding plans, she might have been able to tell his tone was off, but somehow she'd missed it, and he was grateful. He watched the sky burn itself toward darkness and felt the night inside him already. Part of him wanted to call off the wedding, if for no other reason that one PE class shouldn't have been able to twist him around so much, but that made him angry because nothing should have been able to derail something he'd worked so hard to build, something he so believed he wanted. He didn't understand.

Jordan reached into his pocket and pulled out one of the more resilient leaves Nicole had thrown at him. What a strange thing to keep. He couldn't explain it. He just wanted something physical to remind him of the trip--or at least that's what he told himself about the stupid cactus spines he had in his room.

He looked over at the water-damaged camera sitting on the table beside his chair. Granted, Nicole hadn't been particularly attached to the camera, but he thought that perhaps it might be worth fixing up. Maybe, if he managed that, he could even get it back to her. He didn't really know because he hadn't had the chance to find out what he'd need to get it fixed.

His cell phone rang, and he pulled it from his pocket to check the display. Alyssa's picture popped up, and he let it ring once more before he flipped it open.

"Hey, baby," he said, brushing his fingers across the leaf. He listened to her babble about her dress fitting and ordering the wedding cake, but deep inside he felt hollow and unsure. Still, he smiled and said, "That's great. I'm glad everything is going well."

She mentioned that a few more RSVPs had come in and he pretended to be interested, but he kept thinking back to Nicole and the day before. Whatever else Alyssa might have said blurred, and he was glad to hang up.

He heard footsteps from behind and turned to find his dad standing there. David Carroway was a little shorter than his son, and even though he was only in his mid-fifties, his hair had turned grey, or at least what was left of it. Nonetheless, time had not diminished the intensity of his blue eyes.

"You and those sunsets." David sank into the other chair.

Jordan shrugged. "You know me, Dad."

For a moment, the two grew silent. Then Jordan asked, "What brings you here?"

"You missed dinner, and your mom was worried."

Jordan's shoulders sank, and he shook his head in frustration. "I can't believe I forgot about that."

"You do have a few things on your mind," David said, "what with the wedding and all. How's that coming, by the way?"

Jordan tucked the leaf into his pocket along with his cell. "Alyssa's been planning like mad." He shook his head, not wanting to even think about the mania that seemed to have lain claim to her once he'd proposed.

"You don't sound thrilled," his father said, peering at his son. "Any reason for that?"

*Try a million*, Jordan thought--*and start with Nicole O'Roarke.* He shrugged and realized he really did want to talk about this with somebody, and even though he and his father hadn't always seen eye to eye, he knew enough to respect his dad's opinion.

"Did you ever worry that when you proposed to Mom you'd made the wrong choice?"

His dad's gaze shifted from Jordan to the sunset. "Sometimes. I mean, if you take the vows seriously, it's kind of intimidating making a promise you plan to keep forever." David's hand drifted to his wedding ring. "You've known Alyssa for years, and before now you haven't seemed to flinch at a future with her. Is there something going on?"

Jordan couldn't find the words, then he realized it wasn't so much about finding those as it was about admitting to them because his dad was right: it wasn't Alyssa who had changed.

"Son?" David prompted. "Did you meet someone else?"

*Oh, great*, Jordan thought, knowing that no matter what he said his father would know if he were lying. Parents were pretty intuitive that way. "It's complicated," he said. "I mean, no, I haven't been dating around on Alyssa. I just met a girl who was different, and even though she's just a friend, it made me wonder if I were making the right decision." He raked his fingers through his hair, waiting for his father to explode.

David didn't. He merely sat there for a moment, probably thinking about what Jordan had said. "I know you want me to give you some sort of wisdom here—a way of knowing whether marrying Alyssa is right--but, Jordan, there aren't any guarantees. The only thing that's going to give you any kind of answer is time."

Jordan took a deep breath, feeling a little better because, while his father hadn't given him an easy way out, he had at least listened. Talking about his concerns with someone else had made things more bearable.

"That's probably not what you wanted me to say, was it?" David asked.

"What else could you say?" Jordan responded, sitting up a little straighter. "I kind of figured that even with all your experience, you didn't have the answers, either."

"So what do you want to do?"

Jordan frowned and watched the last of the sun ebb toward the horizon. "I'm not sure it's about what I want but what I should do. I mean, how can I throw away years with a woman who has been my best friend because I'm having a few doubts?"

"Yet how can you live without knowing?" David countered. "That's what makes this life difficult. There's always a choice and they're consequences for that choice." He rose slowly up and headed back to Jordan's back door.

"Tell Mom I'm sorry and that I'll be there next weekend."

David nodded. "I'll tell her." He gave his son a parting wave and stepped inside.

*So what* are *you going to do?* Jordan wondered as the last of the light vanished, leaving him with a sudden darkness he couldn't shake. He reached into his other pocket, pulled out the scrap of paper, and ran his fingers over the dried ink. He knew it wouldn't help.

## Chapter Four

Sunlight poured through the stained glass windows, shading the beige carpet in front of Jordan with rich jewel tones of blue and green. Although the air conditioner was on, the room was hot, especially with this black and white tuxedo. He tugged at the tie, trying to loosen it, but it refused to give.

The door squeaked open, admitting his father into the room where Jordan waited. "So how's life in a monkey suit?" David asked, standing next to him.

"Hot." He shook his head and paced the room. When he'd first entered, he had thought the room big, but now, after having paced it repeatedly, it felt as though the walls had been closing in, and now he couldn't breathe.

"How are you?" David asked, scrutinizing his son, looking for something that would clue him in about the vows he was about to undertake.

"I'm here." That was the best Jordan could manage. Although things had returned to normal and he knew he still had feelings for Alyssa, memories of Nicole had seemed to linger just beneath the surface, waiting for something to trigger them. He kept thinking they would pass, but he couldn't be sure they would How could anyone ever be sure of anything?

"I can see that." David looked at his watch. "And right about now, I'm thinking we should probably head to the front of the sanctuary because Alyssa is going to be walking down the aisle to meet you."

Jordan nodded and looked at the windows, focusing on the Virgin Mary holding Jesus that had so colored the world at his feet. It was beautiful, and given another time and place, he might have found peace in it, but the river running through him was anything but calm. It felt turbulent with an undertow he couldn't see and violent twists he hadn't--couldn't have --expected. He'd once come close to calling the wedding off, but something wouldn't let him. He liked to think it was something deeper than just his blind arrogance to make things happen as he'd promised. Perhaps it all went back to the stupid notion that, even if something didn't feel right, he could make it right through sheer determination.

"Are you ready?" David asked, staring as though he must have felt the dangerous undercurrents in his son. Jordan had never been easy to sway, and the fact that this one encounter was giving him so much difficulty troubled David. Had he believed in omens, he might have said something, but David honestly believed a man made his life. If this were the path Jordan took, surely his son could arrive at the correct destination, right?

"Yeah," Jordan finally said, looking up at his father as though he'd just broken free of a trance. He followed David down the hall that led to the side entrance of the sanctuary and then slipped inside. Although he tried not to scan the crowd in front of him, he still felt way too many sets of eyes watching him and had to look nonetheless.

In that instant, he felt ashamed and confused, as though he were making all the wrong choices but had been unable to change the course his life had taken. How could meeting one person have so derailed things? He shook his head and focused on the organ music as a distraction. He had promised Alyssa this day, and he was going to do this, one way or another. Besides, doubts were common. He just needed to shake them off and keep going. Everything would work out somehow.

He kept trying to keep his emotions on the level, right up until the organ started playing the processional and the flower girl started coming toward the front of the church. Then he saw one bridesmaid and finally the maid of honor before Alyssa, adorned in a spaghetti-strapped dress, slowly headed down the aisle, accompanied by her father.

In that instant, as he saw her long veil and ornately braided blonde hair, in addition to the beautiful smile he'd known for so long, Jordan stopped allowing his doubts to railroad him. If there were any reason to believe a relationship could work, it was this moment as he stood there, waiting for his best friend to make it down the aisle so they could promise each other the same things they had been giving each other for years.

Perhaps memories of that weekend PE class and Nicole would always be there, but he could move past them, and he wanted to, for Alyssa's sake. She deserved that, and he would find a way to make it happen.

Jordan kept watching as she drew closer and closer, stealing his breath with her beauty, and when she'd come to the front of the sanctuary and the priest had joined their hands, he smiled, telling her he meant this, all of it. And yet, even as much as he tried not to think about Nicole, he glimpsed the setting sun burning through the sanctuary's stained glass and wondered if he would always feel this horrible pressure.

He felt himself shaking as the ceremony began, and even though Alyssa probably wore at least two-inch heels, she still only came to his shoulders. He tried to focus on the words the priest spoke, but it all seemed fuzzy and out-of-focus, as though he were seated on a ride that had spun out of control. That was probably the worst fear he had, and even beneath the calm of this day, as gift-wrapped as it seemed, he was smart and intuitive enough to sense something amiss. He just wished he knew how to fix it.

For the last three hours, Nicole had been on the blind date from hell. She wore a black cocktail dress, and they were sitting in this fancy Italian restaurant. The guy in question was a little more jock than she usually liked, but the whole evening, he had been nice enough. He definitely had manners, probably because he was a senior in college and still living at home where his mother could knock some sense into him if necessary.

She couldn't quite put her finger on where things had gone south. It had probably started when she'd asked him if he enjoyed reading. He didn't. He'd confessed he hated college, and he was only persisting at it because his parents had insisted. Who in their right mind had something against learning? She couldn't fathom it.

Of course, as they sat near the fountain and drank wine, the truth of the matter finally came to her: whether she wanted to admit it or not, thoughts of Jordan Carroway still flitted through her mind, and while most of the time she could distract herself with other things, a memory of him surfaced every so often when she wasn't focused on something else. It was as though an impression of his face had been embossed into her mind, and now, no matter what she did, he was always with her.

Granted, she would have liked it better if he hadn't been engaged and ready to walk down the aisle, but her heart had never been wise, and at least she'd known the score going in. *Still*, she thought, taking a sip of the wine, *I wonder if he ever thinks of me?*

The answer she always came up with was that maybe she made him laugh from time to time but that really there was no reason for him to think of her. She had passed through his life, and he had passed through hers. There was nothing to be done about it, and no matter how hard she wanted to, she could change nothing.

Still, later that evening, as her date kissed her goodnight, Nicole thought of Jordan again and wondered what it would be like to kiss him. The thought actually shocked her because both of them had tried so hard to keep things on a "friends-only" basis.

After the kiss, she'd headed inside, and Sarah was sitting in front of the television with a huge bowl of popcorn watching *Willie Wonka and the Chocolate Factory*. For a moment, Nicole just stood there, shaking her head then asked, "What is up with that movie?"

Sarah straightened and shook her head, throwing a popcorn kernel. "Nothing is up with this movie. I just happen to like it, Nic. What's up with you and married guys?"

Gritting her teeth, Nicole strode into the kitchen, calling back, "Not much, apparently." As she pulled out a soda, Nicole rather wished she'd never told her roommate/best friend about Jordan. It had provided incessant amusement for Sarah, but all it had done for Nicole was remind her of how things hadn't worked out and how much she wanted them to.

"So how was this date?" Sarah asked, slipping into the kitchen to grab a can of soda from the fridge. "Was he cute?"

Plunking down at the table with her drink, Nicole shook her head. "He was okay, I guess--a jock, which is so not my type." She reached up and drew out the bobby pins holding her hair in its ornate twist and enjoyed the feel of the strands falling about her shoulders.

"So are you going to call him?" Sarah persisted, sitting in the chair across from Nicole.

"Let's see. I hate football, and he's a quarterback. That's a no."

Sarah waved dismissively. "No, not Jock Boy. Cactus Geek."

A flush crept into Nicole's cheeks and she leaned over and tapped her forehead repeatedly against the table. "Don't you have any of your own boyfriends you can abuse with horrible nicknames?"

"Nope. I live through you, Nic." She lifted the soda and took a sip. "So, are you going to call him?"

Leaning over, Nicole pulled off her pumps and shook her head. "Why would I do that?"

"Oh, I don't know. Because you're dying to talk to him." She drummed the table right in front of Nicole. "And don't even bother to tell me you aren't."

Nicole knew lying was pointless. Sarah knew her well enough so that no matter what she said, the truth would eventually come out. "He's probably married. Why would this be a good idea?"

"Because maybe he'd enjoy talking to you as well, not that you'd ever admit to finding a guy who is attracted to you." She shook her head and went back into the living room. "I'll just visit the chocolate factory while you give somebody a little call.

For a moment, Nicole simply stared off into space. She heard the familiar dialogue of the movie, so her best friend must have canceled the pause. Although a little voice told her it probably wasn't a good idea, she pulled out the paper with Jordan's information on it and pushed his number before she'd run out of courage. On the first ring, she felt a little panicked, the second ring her get up and start pacing, and the third actually made her nauseated. She didn't get to the fourth ring, however, because a deep male voice said, "Hello."

"Oh, hey," she began, already hearing a tremor in her voice. "Is Jordan there?"

"Speaking. Who is this?"

"You might not remember me, but it's Nicole." She stopped walking and stared outside as fireflies darted around like pricks of light here and again, hovering above the ground.

"Oh, hey, Nicole. I remember you. You were taking body piercing in a whole new direction, right?"

She laughed as the blush on her cheeks deepened. "Yeah, that would be me, all right."

"So how's your foot?" he asked.

"Good. It healed really well." As she stared through the glass, she noticed her own reflection superimposed over the fireflies, and she could see the hope and fear in her eyes yet didn't understand why, at that moment, she looked more alive than she ever had. What was it about Jordan that made her feel this way?

"I'm glad to hear that. I was hoping you'd let me know."

"So what's going on with you." She slowly walked over to the chair and wondered what he would say.

"Well, I got married a couple of weeks ago, and I've been busy between classes, work, and remodeling the house."

Part of her sank at the mention of him getting married. Then again, she had known it was coming. It shouldn't have been a surprise. Her hair slipped into her eyes, and she brushed it back. "Oh, wow. Sounds like you've really been busy. No time for canoeing, eh?"

He laughed. "Nope. Besides, what fun is there in canoeing if you don't have a partner who is willing to tip it over for the hell of it?"

His voice was warm, and she could almost see him at the other end, standing on his front porch, maybe, and smiling as though the moonlight actually had touched him as much as it had her.

"I guess you have a point." She wanted to say something else, but nothing came to mind, and the silence between them felt interminable.

"Is everything all right, Nicole?" he asked softly, all traces of laughter leaving.

"Oh, yeah," she said, plastering a fake grin on her face. "Everything is just fine. Really. More than anything, I just wanted to wish you a great marriage and say thanks again for helping me on the PE trip."

"Thanks, Nicole. And if you need something, just give me a call any time, okay?"

"Yeah." She nodded as she disconnected the call and sank into a seat, both feeling a warmth streaking through her from talking with Jordan and an emptiness from feeling as though he were lost again. She didn't know how long she had sat there, staring into space and replaying the conversation, but she jumped when Sarah ambled through the doorway, her eyes scrutinizing Sarah for clues to the conversation while she sat at the table by her best friend.

"You called him, didn't you?" she asked, offering Nicole a wicked grin.

"Yes," Nicole said.

Sarah immediately scooted her chair closer. "Okay then, out with it--inquiring minds want to know."

Nicole got up and opened the fridge. She definitely wasn't hungry after the lasagna, but she felt empty and figured that maybe seeking some comfort from her misery might make things feel easier.

"It wasn't that big of a deal. We just had a low-key conversation. It wasn't any big thing, if you want the truth." Of course, if it weren't anything big, why was her heart hammering in her chest as though it were going to break out? Why did she feel so lightheaded and excited? It had nothing to do with the blind date. She knew that much.

"So why are you all flushed as though it was important?" Sarah asked, propping her elbow on the table to support her head. "I mean, you look really guilty of something."

"It's nothing, okay?" Nicole chewed her bottom lip and tried not to think about the exact thing Sarah was pushing so hard for her to focus on.

"Look, sweetie," Sarah began, setting her hand atop Nicole's. "I'm not stupid. I know you really like this guy. Even though we both know he's married, your heart doesn't seem to be getting that message. It's just not ready to hear it. But you can't just sit around and compare every guy to Jordan. Your date will lose every time to somebody you can't have."

Nicole swallowed hard and nodded. "Don't you think I know that? It's not like I want things to be this way. They just are, and I don't know what to do about them."

Sarah picked up the scrap of paper from Nicole and said, "Put this away. Maybe someday you'll be ready to just be his friend, but I don't see it happening any time soon, Nic. I know you never expected to fall head over heels in love. You never have before. But it's written all over your face."

Sarah touched her cheeks and felt the flush burning there. She wanted to argue with her best friend, but she knew Sarah was right. Instead of arguing, she held out her hand for the scrap. "Okay, you win. I'll put it up somewhere so I won't be tempted to call. Happy?"

"It doesn't matter if I'm happy," Sarah said, handing back the paper. "You're the one who's so stuck on this guy."

Nicole stood and headed to her room, where she tugged open the closet and stared up at a column of photo boxes. She used a stool to pull down the top box, and without stepping off the stool, set the paper inside. Of course, she knew it wouldn't change anything. The number was in her phone, and she wasn't about to tell Sarah that. It would be one thing if Jordan were just a minor distraction, but there was nothing minor about him, and that was the problem.

She looked over at the canvas where she'd started a new painting. Although she had barely gotten much of the landscaping in, there, in the center of the canvas, she'd taped her inspiration--that picture of her and Jordan on the bridge. She sighed and gently set the easel into the closet, figuring she'd work on it when Sarah wasn't around to ask questions Nicole didn't have answers to.

## Chapter Five

"You're awfully quiet," Alyssa said as she lay in bed, an open book she paid no mind to propped in one hand. Her long, blonde hair spilled down the front of her nightgown, and her face, freshly washed, shimmered in the soft florescent glow.

"It's kind of been a long day," Jordan said, sitting on the side of the bed to pull off his shoes and socks. He drew his shirt over his head. Not only did the air caress his bare skin, but he also felt Alyssa's fingers gently stroking the center of his back with her fingernails.

"Is everything okay?" she asked softly, staring in hopes his dark eyes would meet her light blue ones.

"Sure," he said, turning toward her. "Why wouldn't it be?"

He reached out and took her hand.

"I don't know. I just keep getting these weird vibes that seem to say something is off between us, and it worries me." She chewed her bottom lip nervously.

"You're worried?" Jordan kept a straight expression despite the discomfort he felt. Although before the wedding Alyssa had been so distracted with all the details, now she seemed to pick up on the subtlest nuances of his every mood, and she could feel something amiss within him. Hell, *he* could feel that same something rocking his world, but he wasn't about to admit it was a problem. It was a distraction, yes, but not one capable of real harm, of that he was sure.

Not knowing what else to do, he turned his body to face her and held his arms wide. Smiling she fell into them so her head slipped beneath his chin as he wrapped his arms around her, drawing her ever more tightly to him.

He closed his eyes, willing himself not to think about Nicole but instead about the woman in his arms, the same one he'd promised to love forever. He wanted to believe his feelings for Nicole had been just a test and that they would pass in time. They had to.

"So what are you worried about?" he asked softly, kissing the top of her head.

"You just seem so distant, like even though we're in the same room, you're a million miles away."

He laughed softly, but the amusement never touched his eyes. "Alyssa, I'm right here. With you. How much closer can I get?"

She drew back slightly and studied his face. "You think this is about physical distance, but it's not. You just seem to stay lost in your own little world, and sometimes I feel like you're doing that because I can't possibly reach you there."

He brushed the hair from her eyes and caressed her cheek. "There're always a million things going on between work and school. You know that. There's nothing to be worried about. I promise."

She gave him one last, long look before slowly falling into his arms again and resting there. His hand crept up and down her back, and the feel of the silken nightgown caught his attention.

"Have I mentioned how good you look in red silk?" His voice was deep and rough as desire suddenly overtook him.

"No," Alyssa giggled. "I really don't think you have."

Jordan leaned closer and brushed his lips across her throat. "You definitely look good enough to eat." He slightly nipped her neck slightly.

Long after the two of them had made love and curled up for the night, Jordan lay in bed, still awake, watching moonlight filter in around the curtains. The sound of crickets to filled his senses, and he looked at Alyssa, his hand resting on her shoulder as her body spooned against his. In the moonlight, her hair appeared a dark gold, like wheat, as it slipped across her face, and her slow, steady breathing should have comforted him. At one time, he would have thought this enough, that if every evening unfolded as this one had, he would be a lucky man.

Unable to take the stillness anymore, he eased himself from his wife's embrace and stood. The night air was warm against his bare chest, and he tugged on his boxers and pants before he slipped from the room, headed for the office.

Raking his fingers through his hair, he slipped into his rolling chair. Although two of his textbooks lay spread open on the desk, he wasn't interested in doing the homework. He'd do that later. Instead, he turned on the computer and waited for it to warm up so he could surf the net. He sorted through a few of sites before realizing that research, which had always been a sort of panacea for all kinds of worries, wasn't going to help him sleep this time.

He took a deep breath and let it out before leaning back in his chair and opening the desk drawer where he found the leaf and one of the cactus spines. He knew there were strange things to keep, but in some ways he felt that if he hadn't saved something from that weekend, it would have seemed only made up as his mind blurred the details, rather like the dreams he'd had in childhood. Sometimes it seemed difficult to know which were real and which were created anymore.

Why did he keep coming back to Nicole? It had only been a weekend PE class, for crying out loud. He toyed with the cactus spine and closed his eyes. Without warning, he found himself back in time. He could feel her resting on his back as he carried her, laughing at his jokes. He'd thought that by getting married he could diminish the memory, but it had remained with him, and he was beginning to doubt anything would get rid of it.

No, he hadn't told Nicole how good it had really been to hear from her when she'd called, but he'd thought it. He twirled the spine in his hand, remembering the timbre of her voice. There was something soothing and earthy about it. Perhaps that was the problem. Alyssa was a city girl, always had been and always would be. He sensed Nicole was something different, and that intrigued him beyond measure.

"What are you doing up?"

He glanced up to find Alyssa in the doorway, her body leaning against the frame as she clutched it with both hands.

"Just having a little trouble winding down," he said, casually dropping the leaf and spine into his drawer and then closing it.

Alyssa offered a sweet smile as she slowly eased into the room and walked to the back of his chair. Setting her hands on his shoulders, she began a gentle massage. "I think this is probably just what you need."

He closed his eyes and savored the feel of her hands kneading his muscles. "Mmmm. I think you might be right."

"Why don't you come back to bed with me?"

"Okay." He looked at the closed drawer and tried to push Nicole from his thoughts, telling himself yet again it was just a friendship the two had shared, nothing more. As Alyssa stretched out her hand, he took it in his and eased himself from the chair. Arm in arm, they exited the office and headed back toward the bedroom next where he lay on the cool cotton sheets and felt his wife gently curl up to him, her head tucked beneath his chin.

Smiling, he drew the covers over them both and let his eyes acclimate themselves to the darkness. He tried to sleep, but once again, it refused to come. What did come, however, was a small list of things he planned to get tomorrow to work on that camera. he still wasn't sure he could fix it, but there wasn't any harm in trying it.

"Okay, I won't be party to this moping you're doing, Nic. It's just not working for me." Sarah stood before her with her hands on her hips.

"Moping?" Nicole muttered, leaning back on the couch. "I'm not moping."

"Aren't you?" Sarah sat beside her on the couch. "Your body might still live here, but it's as if you've gone to wherever Jordan is. And how long has it been since you've been on a date, anyway?" She patted Nicole's knee.

"Last month I went out with that stupid jock, Theo Watkins. I think that was enough dating for a while. He was all over me." She shuddered at the memory and knew that no matter what, every guy she tried to go out with, or even those she *thought* about going out with. were quickly compared to Jordan, and they always came up lacking.

"Okay, so you still hate jocks. We both knew that. Why don't you pick another guy to unleash your devastating charm upon? If you haven't noticed they're all over the place, just waiting for your attention."

Nicole shrugged and looked out the window where a robin sat in the tree. "I'm not into it right now."

Sarah quickly stood and threw up her hands. "You see? That's the exact answer I suspected. Now if Jordan were here, I can damn well believe you'd be wanting to go out with him in no time, right?"

The bird flew away, forcing Nicole to pay attention to her best friend. "Why do you keep bringing up Jordan?"

"Because he's here no matter what we say or don't. We might as well acknowledge that he's the invisible elephant in the room." Sarah folded her arms across her chest. "There was a time you never thought you'd fall in love. Now look at you."

Nicole felt her cheeks getting hot and forced herself to get up and carry her glass into the kitchen, where she filled it with more water. "I'm not in *love* with Jordan Carroway. I barely *know* him."

"You know enough. Let's at least be honest about that, Nic."

Nicole took a drink and turned to Sarah. "You're obsessed with this."

"I'm obsessed?" Sarah touched her finger to her chest. "I'm obsessed. I don't think so. You're the one who's always thinking about him. It doesn't matter what you say. I know you, and I know exactly where you're going with this. You fell in love, and you're not willing to admit it. I'd give anything to know if it happened to him, too."

Nicole took a sip. "He was already in love. It just wasn't with me. And he's married, by the way."

Sarah grabbed Nicole by the shoulders and shook her. "That may well be, but you *aren't*. You're alive and breathing in a world with guys who would probably love to go out with you, and you're oblivious, so we're going to fix that." She pulled her hands back and turned abruptly.

Not liking the ominous way that sounded, Nicole frowned. "And what exactly did you have in mind, Sarah?"

"Something that's is going to take all weekend, and because I'm your best friend, I don't want to hear any arguments." She started to walk away, but Nicole grabbed her arm.

"Sarah, I'm not going out on any blind dates. I know what your tastes in guys are, and, well, no thanks. I can make my own mistakes whenever I feel like it."

"Funny, Nic." Sarah shook her head. "This weekend won't involve any blind dates. I can promise you that, but don't push for anything more. Consider it an early birthday present." She touched the doorway.

“My last birthday involved massive amounts of alcohol and lots of strangers. Did I mention I hated that party?” Nicole sat at the table and glared at her best friend. “Are you insane?”

“Certifiable. Then again, you already knew that.”

Nicole glared at Sarah’s diminishing backside and pulled out her cell. For a couple of moments, she just stared at the dark screen, her fingers hovering over the buttons as she saw her reflection in the glass. She wanted to argue with Sarah, but something inside her knew better. Her best friend knew her too well, and she would win this fight because no matter how much she wanted to deny having feelings for Jordan, she knew it wouldn’t feel like this if he were just a friend. That definitely caused just a few problems because he wasn’t exactly someone she could ever date, no matter how much she might like him.

Besides, even if Sarah’s idea of a good time didn’t match hers, she did have to admit that it had been a while since they’d really done something fun together. Lately it had pretty much been about academics. That tended to happen with the senior year at college. Sarah might just as well bring on the mischief for her to enjoy. Telling her no wouldn’t do any good, and maybe a little distraction was in order.

Still, maybe it wouldn’t hurt, she thought and dialed Jordan’s number. The phone rang twice before she heard him answer, his voice resonating deeply within her, bringing back memories of the day they’d met. She might even have said something, but in the background she distinctly heard a woman speaking to someone. Inhaling sharply, she snapped the phone shut and slid it onto the table.

What could it hurt? Her, that’s what. Nicole just wished she knew why.

* * *

“Okay, now I know you're truly insane,” Nicole muttered, watching Sarah load two duffle bags with clothing and toiletries into her old blue convertible. The sun was beating down, reminding them that, even though it was close to the middle of September, summer wasn't over yet, and the way her skin radiated in the heat told Nicole she might be sorry if she didn't pack sunscreen, so she hurried inside to grab a bottle.

When she came back out, Sarah leaned against her car, her long, blonde hair spilling down the front of her shirt. Although Nicole could guess at her expression, the large sunglasses hid her eyes. Still, her folded arms suggested she was ready to go. Patience had never been one of Sarah's strong points, which was why they got along so well.

"Are you done yet?" Sarah asked, shaking her head.

"I had to get sunscreen. Ten to one you didn't pack any," Nicole smarted back, walking around to the passenger side. She stopped before grabbing the door handle. "Maybe I should go get a couple of textbooks to work on my projects." She started to go back into the house again when Sarah blocked her.

"That's a 'no'. We're going out of town to have fun, not get smarter. You can resume that plan of study when you come back, Sunday night."

Nicole tried to step around her, but her best friend matched her. "But my project is due--"

"When it's due." Sarah grabbed Nicole's shoulders and turned her so she faced the car. "So get in and let's hit the road before I'm so old, I forget how to drive." She stubbornly waited until her roommate had belted in before she headed for the driver's seat.

"You're being a pain, Sarah," Nicole said, leaning back.

Sarah backed down the driveway. "Yeah, well, maybe I am, but you'll thank me later, when we've left this little town in the dust and found much more interesting scenery."

Figuring she might as well just give in to Sarah's latest whim, she pulled the sunglasses from her purse and slid them on. "Okay, Thelma, where're we headed?" She closed her eyes and savored the way the wind wildly blew their hair to and fro, for once not caring that when the car finally stopped she was going to look like the bride of Frankenstein.

"Not over a cliff. I can promise you that."

For two hours they drove, heading far from Bristol, Oklahoma, towards Oklahoma City, and while Nicole suspected Sarah would have a great time, she, herself, much preferred hiking in the mountains to the flash and dazzle of nightclubs. There was definitely something to be said for knowing what was real and what wasn't. Even the cactus spines going through her shoe and into her foot hadn't dissuaded her from loving nature and hiking. They had just made her more conscious of where she walked and what she might step on.

Nicole peered at the tall hotel and shook her head. The Marriot would definitely be a welcome respite, but she had a sneaking suspicion getting any rest wasn't on Sarah's list of activities. Sarah was more a I'll-sleep-when-I'm-dead sort of person, and she tended to drag those around her with her until somebody collapsed, usually Nicole.

"Did you make reservations?" Nicole asked as they got out of the convertible. She peered into the rear-view mirror, trying to bat her hair into some kind of shape, but the long, wavy strands weren't playing nice.

"Of course I made reservations. I'm not an idiot." She hefted her purse indignantly over her shoulder.

"No, but you like spur-of-the-moment things better than most people." Nicole brushed the hair from her face and tucked it behind her ears. "You've always been impulsive, and you know it."

"You say *impulsive* like it's a bad thing," Sarah muttered as they headed into the air-conditioned bliss of the hotel where a short brunette with a name tag that read "Amy" looked up at them.

"May I help you?" Amy asked.

"Yes, we have a reservation for tonight and tomorrow." Sarah gave her a smug smile.

"Okay, let me check." Amy side-stepped to the computer where she quickly tapped a few keys. "And what name is the reservation under?"

"Middleton." Sarah pulled out her credit card, and even though Nicole started to reach into her purse to get some money, her best friend tapped her on the hand and whispered, "No, I've got this. It's your intervention, remember?"

Shaking her head, Nicole wondered exactly what Sarah was intervening her from that wouldn't still be there when she returned. If Sarah thought Jordan were going to go away like a flu bug or something, Nicole seriously doubted it--not that she knew why, exactly. It was more of a hunch.

"Umm, I'm sorry, Ms. Middleton, but we don't show any record of your reservation. Did you call or perhaps make the reservation online?"

"Yes, I did it online," Sarah snapped, and when she caught sight of Nicole's huge grin, she smacked her best friend. "This isn't funny."

"Sure it is. You couldn't plan your way out of a wet paper bag, and you know it."

"Could you double-check that, please?" Sarah asked, beaming a huge smile.

"Of course." Amy tapped a few more keys as the door opened and admitted a family of four, obviously on vacation by the dad's loud Hawaiian shirt. Amy scrolled through a couple of screens and shook her head again. "No, I still don't see any reservations. I'm sorry."

Sarah tapped her credit card against the counter as she frowned in concentration, trying to come up with a contingency plan. "Do you have any available rooms?"

"No, I'm sorry. There's a Bon Jovi concert tonight, and we're completely full."

"Just my luck," Sarah muttered as they turned and headed out the door.

"So now what do we do?" Nicole sat in the passenger seat while Sarah slid behind the wheel.

"We troll for a hotel. There's got to be one here somewhere."

Of course, after driving around most of the metro area, they quickly realized that not only was there a massive rock concert in town but also that tourism was booming. No rooms were available, and no amount of cursing on Sarah's part was going to change that.

Together, they sat in the convertible, mulling over their options. "Maybe we should just drive home," Nicole finally suggested, more than dreading another two hours in the car. She could already feel her muscles stiffening.

"No!" Sarah snapped. "We both need a break, and we're not turning around and driving back so you can bury your nose in a textbook and I can go stir crazy in the apartment. We came here to have fun, and by God, that's what we're going to do, no matter what it takes!"

Sarah saw the Bricktown area just ahead and slid into a parking spot someone else had just eyed and would have pulled into had traffic not stopped him. As they got out, they both heard the mad honking of a horn, and the driver, a teenage male, flipped them off.

"I'd say he was just a little ticked," Nicole muttered and looked at her best friend, who's perkiness had slowly diminished, like a balloon with a slow leak. "So what are we doing now?"

"Going to walk around the canal. It's beautiful over there."

"That doesn't solve the hotel issue," Nicole said, shaking her head. "We need to find a place to stay."

"And we will--right after we walk out some of the kinks in my butt." She grabbed Nicole's arm and dragged her toward the canal.

Although she figured the walkways would be packed, there weren't many people out; probably, most of them were getting ready for the Bon Jovi concert so it was kind of nice to stroll around without worrying about running into people.

It seemed that stretching Sarah's legs had done wonders for her perkiness, because before, long she was chatting about everything under the sun, and Nicole did what she always did, pretended to listen but really focused on the world around her. That was when she spotted him.

He wore a forest green Henley and Bermuda shorts. The sunlight toyed with his hair, casting a red glow on some of the strands as he headed toward a deli. At first when Nicole saw him, her stomach knotted, and her feet stalled. She felt like even breathing was tough. Then, as she realized she was about to lose him to the corner just ahead, she broke into a sudden run, desperate to catch him.

"Nicole? What are you doing?" Sarah called from behind. "Wait up!"

Nicole pretended not to hear and managed to get right behind him before he rounded the corner, then forced herself to slow and say, "Excuse me."

The man turned, and while she had expected amber eyes and a Michael C. Hall smile, the features were all wrong--foreign. It wasn't Jordan.

"Yes?" the man said, frowning.

Nicole stumbled backwards a step. "I'm sorry. I thought you were someone else." She averted her eyes in embarrassment and turned away.

He gave her one last look, shook his head, and walked off, just as Sarah caught up with her. Even though she had stopped running, she was breathing hard, suggesting just how out of shape she was.

"What the hell, Nic? You know I don't run or jog."

Nicole stared out into the deep green water of the canal, and her eyes took on a far-away look. She didn't seem even to hear her best friend speak.

"Nic? What's wrong? What happened?"

Nicole swallowed hard, trying to come to terms with the excitement that had so quickly turned to disappointment. "I just thought he was someone else."

A knowing expression filled Sarah's face. "No, actually it wasn't because you thought he was someone else. You wanted him to be someone else, didn't you? You wanted him to be Jordan, right?" She touched Nicole's arm.

"It doesn't matter," she said, pulling away.

Sarah was about to argue when a stranger zipped up behind them both, wrapped his fingers around Nicole's purse straps, and jerked at them. Nicole's eyes widened, and she tried to hold on. She might have been able to had the thief not used the strap to slam her face-first into the brick wall. Nicole groaned, and the world seemed to blacken instantaneously.

"Somebody help me!" Sarah yelled. Nicole could hear her best friend even beneath the warped blackness that now tried to wash her away, and she wanted to tell Sarah just to be quiet so the pain pounding in her brain would leave her alone, but she couldn't muster the energy.

"What happened?" This voice was different—masculine and deep.

"Someone took her purse and threw her against the wall. She's bleeding."

*I'm bleeding?* Nicole thought. Then blackness washed everything away.

# Chapter Six

"Miss? Can you hear me?"

Pain radiated through Nicole's head, and she just wanted to be left alone. "Head hurts. Go away," she mumbled, trying to push away the hand she felt touching her forehead.

"I need you to open your eyes," that same deep, calm voice said.

"Is she going to be all right?" Sarah's voice sounded anything but calm, almost like she were going to burst into tears at any moment.

"We need to get her awake," the guy said. "What's her name?"

"Nicole O'Roarke."

Figuring if she didn't force open her eyes, Sarah was going to go off the deep end and this guy would never leave, Nicole blinked…and was immediately rewarded with pain.

"Damn!" she swore and clenched her eyes shut.

"Well, I'd say the chances are good she'll be all right," he said, chuckling. "Nicole, I need you to open your eyes again, please."

"It makes my head hurt," she said, trying again to get away from him.

"I know. But I need to see your pupils so I know whether we need to call an ambulance."

The thought of having to go to the hospital got her attention, and she forced open her eyes in spite of the pain. At first, everything was blurry. She could tell by the shapes where both Sarah and the guy were.

Sarah hovered in the background while the stranger knelt beside her, leaning close.

"Well, her pupils are normal-sized, so that's a good thing."

Nicole lifted her hand to her head, but the stranger stopped her. "Easy there. You cut your forehead on the bricks."

"Must be why it hurts," she muttered and blinked, trying to get the world to come back into focus. It worked. The guy's dark hair took shape first, and when she could finally see his eyes, she realized just how brown they were, much darker than Jordan's. She chewed her bottom lip not only to distract herself from the pain splitting her head but also to try and make things seem less foggy.

"Are you a doctor?" she asked, puzzled at how he knew so much about caring for a head wound.

"Nope. Used to be an EMT. Now I'm just a lawyer." He turned to Sarah. "Do you think she broke anything?"

"I don't think so," Sarah said, chewing her nails as she anxiously watched him check out her friend.

The guy turned back to Nicole. "Do you think you can sit up?"

*If it'll keep me out of the hospital, you betcha,* Nicole thought, taking a deep breath. "Probably. Could you at least tell me your name?"

He chuckled, and Nicole found irritation in it. "What's so funny?" she asked.

"I only tell people who are standing so if you can get to your feet, I'll let you know." He winked at her.

"Funny guy." She gritted her teeth and started to sit up in spite of the way it made everything fuzzy and unbalanced. She was grateful when the stranger slipped his hand to her back and gently helped her upright.

"You okay?" he asked softly, the sudden smugness gone as he watched her.

"Of course I'm fine. It's just a little bump on the head."

"I wouldn't…." he started to say when Nicole found herself falling, with only his arms to keep her from hitting the pavement.

"I'm okay," she said. "Just a little dizzy."

He lifted her hair to peer at the wound on her forehead. "Be that as it may, I think maybe we might want to take her to a hospital, and we need to call the cops to report that guy."

"No hospitals," she spat, "and I really don't feel like talking to the cops. I didn't have much money and no credit cards in the wallet. I just want to rest." She tried to step out of his arms, but he refused to let go.

"Stubborn, aren't you?"

"Yes. Now will you tell me your name?"

The grin returned. "Michael Adams at your service." He looked around. "Do you live in the city, or are you staying at a hotel?"

Sarah said "Hotel" at the same time Nicole muttered "We live here." He frowned, looking from one to the other before shaking his head.

"Okay. You two need to get your stories straight. Which is it?"

This time, Nicole said "Hotel" and Sarah replied "We live here." They looked at each other in horror as he started laughing.

"How about the truth this time?"

"Neither," Sarah finally admitted, a flush creeping into her cheeks. "Our reservations fell through, and we live two hours away, in Bristol." She folded her arms across her chest and leaned against the wall, almost looking like she were about to burst into tears.

"Okay, that settles it." He slid Nicole's arm around his neck and wrapped his arm around her back. "Let's go."

Nicole tried to plant her feet, but she was still so dizzy she could barely walk. "Where do you think we're going?" She tried to sound condescending. Instead, her voice only wavered weakly.

He nodded toward the hotel just ahead, the one right on the canal. "My hotel. You need to get comfortable, and you aren't going to be able to do that in a car or with all these people watching."

Sarah stepped into his path. "We're not going to your hotel. We don't even know you."

"Good point. Then again, I do have an extra room that you can use with no strings attached, and I don't think you want to find a bed for her at the hospital, so if you would just humor me, I'd appreciate it." He looked from one to the other, waiting for more arguments, and when none came, he started walking again.

Although Nicole would have preferred to make it on her own, she knew she couldn't. As it was, she leaned heavily against Michael's chest, aware he was just a little taller than she was, but it felt good to know his arms were keeping her standing. More than once, she felt herself drifting toward blackness. Michael must have sensed it, too, because he would then shake her back to wakefulness, saying, "Your head just hit the wall, which means you need to stay awake--unless you want me to take you to a hospital."

That threat worked wonders at keeping her conscious. It just seemed to take a long time to walk to the hotel, and her head was splitting. Once they'd finally arrived, Michael slipped his plastic key into the lock and propped open the door. Sarah swept in behind them.

"Here we are."

Sarah and Nicole studied the room and the way he had neatly arranged his belongings. The maid had obviously been there, as the bed was made and the trash empty. "You're very neat," Nicole muttered, feeling more light-headed than ever.

"Interesting thing for you to notice. Let's get you to the bed." He eased Nicole down on it and waited until she was settled before warning her. "Remember, no sleeping for a while, okay?"

"Got it," she said, gritting her teeth as he walked over to one of his suitcases and pulled out a bottle of Tylenol he handed to Sarah. "This might help with the pain. He thumbed toward the next room. "I'm on a business trip with a friend, and he unknowingly booked a room with two beds. I'm going to go see if he's in there, and I'll move my stuff out."

Sarah reached for her purse. "I can pay you for the room."

He shook his head. "Don't worry. It's paid for. Just take care of Nicole--and like I said, I'll be rooming next door if you need something or she gets worse."

As he grabbed a few of his things, Sarah caught his arm and said, "Thank you. So much."

"It's the least I could do," he said and headed out the door. "I'll be right back to get the rest of my stuff." He glanced at Nicole. "And remember not to let her sleep. I'm serious about that."

"Yes, Mother."

Sarah waited until he was gone before breaking the silence. "Well, that was interesting." She wandered over to the bed and sat down as Michael came back from the other room and grabbed another load of his things. He scanned the room and said, "Well, one more load and I should be done." He disappeared into the hallway.

"What was interesting?" Nicole asked, raising her hand to her head. Sarah saw what she intended to do and grabbed her best friend's hand.

"Everything. And you probably still don't want to touch that. I should go down to the store and get some peroxide. Will you be okay by yourself?"

Forcing herself to open her eyes, Nicole finally nodded. "Yeah, I think I can manage. I just won't be getting up from this bed because the room is still spinning."

She watched Sarah cross her arms over her chest and frown. "You sure you don't need to go to the hospital? You did hit that wall pretty hard, you know?"

Nicole waved her away dismissively. "I'm not going to the hospital--and don't you have some peroxide to get?"

"All right. I'm going. You stay put." Sarah slipped her purse straps over her shoulder and headed out. A moment later, Michael returned. He glanced around the room, looking for Sarah.

"Where's your partner in crime?"

Nicole forced her eyes open and started to sit up. That, of course, really got his attention.

"You should stay put," he said, moving closer as he eyed her. "Otherwise, you just might end up on that floor, and it's not nearly as soft as you might think."

"You trust my balance so much," she muttered, sensing he was right.

"Oh, I know you're unbalanced," he replied. "I could sense it about you a mile away. Then again, it usually takes one unbalanced person to recognize another." He walked to the chair and sat, still watching her carefully.

"You know, you really don't have to babysit me. I can stay out of trouble."

He laughed loudly and shook his head. "Somehow how I doubt that." He watched her glare, and the laughter slowly died. "Besides, I'd rather just sit here until your friend—"

"Sarah," Nicole interjected.

"Okay, until Sarah comes back. So I guess you're just going to have to suffer my presence until then."

The longer Nicole stared at him, the more his features—the wide face, blunt chin, and perfect teeth—grew on her. It wasn't that any of those features by themselves were particularly attractive; it was what happened when all of them came together, and when you added the smile to the mix, he was devastatingly handsome.

“What are you staring at?” Michael asked, leaning forward as he braced his elbows on his thighs and waited. His gold watch gleamed in the late-afternoon light.

“Nothing,” she muttered, embarrassed and looked away.

Another laugh. “Okay, now I *know* you hit your head hard,” he muttered.

“And why is that?”

“You were checking me out, and women don’t do that sort of thing.” He raked his hand through his hair. “Obviously it has to do with the brain damage you’ve suffered. Maybe you need a CAT scan.”

Nicole gripped the blanket, feeling her head throbbing a little too much. She just wasn’t sure if it were because of the cut or being slammed into the wall. Did it really matter, she wondered. “And why do you think women don’t find you attractive?”

“Are you saying you do?” he asked, offering a smirk as he leaned forward even more.

“I didn’t say anything. I asked a question, if you remember.” She felt herself blushing and hated that feeling, particularly in this case, because she did think he was attractive—not that she wanted him to know it.

He nodded slowly. “So you did. My mistake.”

Tired of lying in bed like an invalid, Nicole moved to sit up, which made him rise quickly from the chair and step toward her. “I don’t think you should be doing that.”

She nodded and gritted her teeth. “I got that the first fifteen times you said it, Michael.”

He laughed again, but that didn’t keep him from hovering. “You remembered my name. That’s definitely a good sign.”

She glared at him. “Sign of what?”

“Not having a severe head trauma?” he suggested hopefully. “I have no clue what you were thinking--unless it had to do with staring at me."

"You're insufferable," she snapped and got to her feet, which was the wrong thing to do. Immediately the world started spinning, disoriented her, so she closed her eyes. She could feel herself falling until Michael wrapped his arms around her again. Once she'd stopped feeling so dizzy, she opened her eyes and found her face just a few inches from his, and she was right. If she thought he was attractive from a distance, up close was worse, but at least he wasn't smirking. Instead, he frowned and stared at her as though he were mentally trying to check her out. For a moment, they just stood like that, his arms wrapped around her. Her heart was racing, and she couldn't seem to pull her gaze away from his dark brown eyes. Her eyes seemed to hold the same lure for him.

Finally, he asked, "You okay over there? I told you standing wasn't a good idea."

"You're right," she whispered, yet she couldn't seem to move.

"Am I interrupting something?" Sarah asked from the doorway, her eyes alight with amusement.

Michael glanced that way and shook his head. "Nope. Your friend here decided she was going to try and stand, and she almost ended up taking a nose dive." He looked back at Nicole. "You ready to lie back down so I can look at your head?"

Nicole blinked a couple of times, and although she wanted to argue, her head hurt, and she hoped that if she did lie down, the room would stop spinning. "Yeah. I am."

"I'm following your lead," he said, and as she started moving back toward the bed, his hold eased and his hands actually just hovered there to guide her as she rested back on the bed. "Could I have the peroxide?" Michael asked, looking at Sarah as he waved for her to come closer.

"Sure." Sarah still grinned as she stepped toward them and handed him the bag.

He reached into it and pulled out a small bottle of peroxide and a little bag of cotton balls, then peered deeper to find a box of bandages that he left in the bag. "Okay, let's get you fixed up."

He proceeded to clean and bandage the wound. The whole time he worked, Nicole kept her eyes tightly closed as she tried to ignore the fizzing of the peroxide. She'd never liked that sound, and it usually made her feel sick to her stomach--yet another reason being a nurse had quickly been scratched off her list of future plans.

"You okay?" he asked softly as he pressed the Band-Aid into place.

"Peachy," she replied, gritting her teeth, wishing this whole thing were over. She hated being the center of attention, and for whatever reason, Michael Adams had taken a personal interest in her. Part of her was flattered, the other unnerved as hell.

"Okay, she's good to go." Michael rose slowly from where he'd sat on the edge of the bed. Giving Nicole one last glance, he turned and grabbed the rest of his stuff.

"Let me know if you need anything," he said, heading out the door.

"Will do." Sarah waited until he'd slipped out the door and then closed it, scurrying over to the bed. "Whoa, baby--was he hot or what? And I think he really likes you."

"That's ridiculous," Nicole sputtered. "He used to be an EMT, and those old reflexes probably kicked in."

Sarah quickly perched on the bed and smirked at her. So, are you going to try and tell me you don't think he's cute? You'd have to be blind to miss that. And a lawyer? Wow--what a combo. If that doesn't take your mind off Jordan, I don't know what will."

"Why do you keep bringing up Jordan?" Nicole asked, raising her hand to touched the bandage on her forehead where the soreness persisted. "And could I get some of that Tylenol? My head is throbbing."

Sarah rolled her eyes. "I'm talking about a really hot bachelor who seems to like you, and all you can think about is Tylenol. This is the exact reason you still don't have a boyfriend, Nic. It's called *priorities*."

"We'll see how well you drool over guys when you get your face bashed against a brick wall, okay?" Nicole muttered, glaring. "Now give me the damned drugs."

"Boy, are you testy." Sarah twisted open the bottle and dumped two in Nicole's palm before she walked to the bathroom and filled one of the plastic cups. She paced back and found Nicole sitting up, reaching for the cup.

"Here," she said. "That should do you."

Nicole took the pills, popped them into her mouth, and washed them down before lying back down. "Maybe you should go enjoy yourself instead of staying in this boring hotel room with me. I don't think I'm going to be up for your mad night of partying and drinking. Sorry, Sarah."

"It's all right," she said, sighing.

Nicole shook her head. "You really should go and enjoy yourself. I'll be fine here. Promise."

Looking at her watch, Sarah frowned. "I don't know, Nic. I mean, on one hand, I'd love to go out because it seems like it's been forever, but you really shouldn't be left by yourself."

"I just bumped my head. No biggie--and I think I can call you if something happens, so there's no reason you have to waste your weekend watching me when you could be meeting single guys."

Sarah shook her head doubtfully. "I dunno, Nic."

Nicole raised her hands and waved around the room. "Where exactly am I going to go? I think I'll be fine, and there's no reason for you to waste a weekend babysitting me."

“Are you sure?” Sarah asked, frowning.

“Positive. Now go get ready and let the madness begin.”

Sarah pulled her keys out of her purse. “I’m going to go get the car and move it to the parking lot. I’ll be back in a few. Stay put.”

“I can do that.”

Nicole watched her friend leave and shook her head, lamenting how things had turned out despite their best intentions. Oh well, at least Sarah wasn’t letting it hold her up, and Nicole could always use the time to catch up on some television since she wasn’t allowed to move around, not according to Michael.

## Chapter Seven

Sunday afternoon, Nicole stood before the easel, working on her painting. The landscape was much fuller, and it seemed as though she was going about this the wrong way, filling things in from the outside. She had yet to put herself or Jordan on that canvas, and she wasn't sure why. Maybe it was just the idea of getting it wrong somehow. She didn't know. She wanted to blame it on the heat--September and still no sign of a cool front. Fascinating. But even though she was sweating, as some moron in apartment complex management had made the money-saving decision to shift from air to heat, she knew better. Her thoughts kept returning to Jordan.

The doorbell rang, and she called, "Hey, Sarah, can you get that?"

No answer.

The doorbell rang a second time, forcing Nicole to move. Although she wasn't still dizzy, thank God, she did have a small headache. Still, she could live with that, she thought, walking to the door. As she passed the hallway, she heard the distinct flow of the shower and realized that was probably why Sarah hadn't answered.

When she pulled open the door, a huge bouquet of red and white roses greeted her—that and the flower boy's body. The bouquet was so huge it seemed to hide all of his head so that it looked like a strange mutant rose guy stood on the doorstep.

Weird. She shook her head, thinking, *These must be for Sarah.*

"Ms. O'Roarke?" The delivery boy/mutant rose guy said.

While she doubted he could see it, she nodded and said, "Yes."

"Here you go," he said and held out the roses. Instead of taking them, she stepped back, puzzled.

"Perhaps you're really looking for my roommate, Sarah Middleton? She's in the shower, but I can take them for her." She smiled at him, thinking, *Who would send* me *flowers? This has to be a mistake.*

"Nope," he replied smugly as though glad to get the massive bouquet off his hands as he shoved them toward her. "Not unless she also goes by the name Nicole O'Roarke." He stared at them expectantly, but Nicole just stood there, stunned. "Look, Miss, these flowers are heavy. Could you just take them so I can get on with my other deliveries?"

"Okay." She edged forward and gently took them. "I don't understand. Who could they possibly be from?"

Grinning, he tapped the envelope attached to the flowers. "Maybe you should read the card," he suggested helpfully and abruptly turned away, headed for the parking lot.

"Gee, thanks," Nicole said, shaking her head as she stood there for a moment longer, still in shock. The delivery guy had been right. The bouquet was heavy and very expensive. Whoever had sent it had extremely good taste.

Chewing her bottom lip, Nicole backed slowly away from the door and shut it before turning and setting the ornate crystal vase at the center of the dining room table. She stepped back to admire it. Had Jordan sent it? Why would he?

"I thought I heard the doorbell," Sarah said, stepping into the room. Her long blonde hair curled down the front of her tank top, and her shorts were just a little shorter than acceptable for public.

"Oh, you did." Nicole crossed her arms over her chest, not sure she wanted to read the card. It was one thing to want it to be from Jordan, and while it was sitting there, still unopened, she could believe that, even if it weren't true. It was another to find out the hard way Jordan hadn't sent it.

"Oh, my!" Sarah exclaimed. "These are gorgeous."

Nicole nodded slowly, unsure what to do. "I thought they were for you."

"For me?" Sarah turned back to her. "Not likely. I'm between boyfriends at the moment, and the ones I've dated recently aren't so fond of me for some reason--maybe because I broke up with them. Hmmm." She bent low and smelled one of the blossoms. "Okay, so who are they from, and please don't say Jordan!"

"I haven't opened the card."

Making a growling noise, Sarah straightened and set both hands on Nicole's shoulder to shake her. "What is wrong with you? I'd have ripped open the card before the delivery guy was even out the door." She plucked the card from the stand nestled among the flowers and leaves. "Here. Put me out of my misery, please."

*Who's going to put me out of mine?* Nicole thought, slowly taking the envelope. It seemed to take her forever to pull the card free, and it didn't help that her best friend kept staring at her.

She'd barely scanned it when Sarah already started jumping up and down. "Well? *Who* is it? The suspense is killing me, and since no guy is going to send me flowers, I'm living through you."

Nicole looked at the signature: Michael Adams. Okay, things were definitely getting a little wonky. Lawyer guy wasn't just a good Samaritan? Oh, boy.

"Nic, come on! Who are they from?" She folded her arms over her chest.

"Michael Adams." She avoided looking into her roommate's eyes, knowing Sarah was going to have a field day with this. She was sure of that. Instead, she focused on what he'd written above his name.

Nicole,
I'm going to be at the Red Lobster this evening at 7:30. I know this is short notice and you may not be interested, but I thought I'd ask, anyway. If you'd like to join me, I'll have a table waiting. No muggers will be invited.
Michael Adams

"Michael Adams! The lawyer guy?" Sarah exploded. "Holy cow!" She tried to bustle close to her friend and get a look at the card, but Nicole hid it against her chest. "C'mon, Nic, what does it say? I'm your best friend. You have an obligation to share."

"All right," Nicole muttered and handed over the card before she looked at her clock. It was two now, so she did have time, if she wanted to go out with him, and that was a big *if.*

"Wow!" Sarah exclaimed, dancing around the room. "You've got a date, woman! And it's not even a blind date! Woo-hoo!"

"I didn't say I was going," Nicole said, plunking down at the table. She couldn't for the life of her sort out her feelings with her friend doing a mad dance around her like that. Part of her was disappointed they weren't from Jordan. Part of her was thrilled Michael had seen something besides the head wound and a dizzy woman who acted like she was blonde. Part of her just wanted to bury her head in the sand.

"Oh yes, you are!" Sarah said, abruptly whirling on her and marching her down the hall.

"Where are we going?" Nicole snapped, trying to slow her best friend down, not that it worked. Sometimes Sarah was a blonde Tasmanian devil. Or Tigger. Either way, Nicole didn't stand a chance.

"To find you something to wear."

"But I'm not sure if I'm even going," she muttered again.

Sarah pointed a finger at her. "And I said that you were, no excuses. The guy is sweet, hot, and wonderful, not to mention being a lawyer. It's a dream date, and you know it. The only problem in your eyes is that he isn't Jordan. Well, nobody is Jordan except Jordan. And Jordan is very married, so deal."

"You're impossible!" Nicole snapped as they arrived in the bedroom. "Completely and utterly impossible. Just so you know that." She plunked on the bed as Sarah strode to her closet.

"It's duly noted, Nic. Now let's get to work."

* * *

By the time Sarah drove Nicole to Red Lobster, she felt foofed up beyond measure and couldn't remember when she'd last played dress-up like this, not that it would have been a good memory. Nicole had always liked jeans and sweaters. She was a tomboy at heart, and this black cocktail dress, with its v-neck and the thigh-length hem, made her feel naked. She wasn't, of course, but that didn't stop her from *feeling* it.

Then there was the make-up and the hair. Sarah wasn't going to leave her alone until, like some kind of mounted Barbie head, both of those were perfect. Of course, perfection required her to wear her hair to one side to hide the bandage. The length of it had been swept up—Sarah's choice, not hers. And these heels. What the hell had her best friend been thinking? Who wore these? And why? Wasn't she clumsy enough without trying to be some kind of sex kitten? Really!

"Go get him, Nic," Sarah said, as Nicole stepped out into the full parking lot. She scanned the cars, wondering which was his, not that it mattered. She wasn't sure anything mattered at this point except the violent butterflies in her stomach. Now those *definitely* mattered.

The lobby was crowded, and she excused her way to the front to talk to the hostess with dark hair and eyes. In her own way, she reminded Nicole of Michael. Then again, Nicole was probably just imagining it. "I'm supposed to be meeting a Michael Adams here."

The hostess nodded and said, "Yes, we've seated him. If you'll follow me." She led the way through the crowd and headed into the restaurant proper as Nicole wondered how the hostess remembered Michael so well. Interesting.

The hostess led her around the tables and back to a corner, where only two tables sat. One was vacant. Michael sat at the other. He was looking at the menu when Nicole approached, and as he glanced up, she saw him smile.

"Well, well--looks like you made it," he said, rising.

"Yeah," she replied. "I did."

He gestured to the seat across from him, and she nervously sat. Then he pushed it toward the table for her, making her all the more nervous because she really didn't think many guys still had those kinds of manners. She'd actually thought they were extinct.

"What would you like to drink?" a waitress asked, appearing right beside her.

Nicole looked at Michael's glass. Wine. Oh, boy. "I think I'll have what he's having, thank you."

"Certainly." The waitress nodded and disappeared.

"I almost didn't recognize you," he said, taking a sip.

Nicole laughed and waved at her hair. "Yeah, I know. It's up, and I'm dressed like a lady and all that. Still the same me though." She averted her eyes, unable to take the constant staring.

"No, that's not what I meant. I knew you were beautiful, but tonight you're absolutely stunning."

Nicole licked her lips and tried not to think about being nervous. *Yeah, and skunks might start spraying perfume,* too, she thought. "I hope you haven't been here long. I think I'm a few minutes late."

He smiled and nodded. "Yeah, but I would've waited even if you had been later."

"That's never a good thing to tell a woman," she whispered, shaking her head.

"Yeah, I know, but you didn't ask me why I would have waited, either." He took another sip as the waitress brought Nicole's glass and a menu.

"Thank you," she said, then looked back at Michael. "Okay, why would you have waited?"

"Because it's my little sister's first day on the job as hostess, and I wanted to sit back and watch her work, maybe give her a little grief from time to time."

"That's how she knew who you were," Nicole said, taking a small sip. She didn't usually like wine, but she figured it might help loosen her up.

"What did you think? It was magic?"

"I don't know." She frowned and thought a moment. "You don't by chance live around here, do you?"

"Yep. Fancy my surprise when I found you in Oklahoma City. I've lived here most of my life, and I hadn't run into you before now. What were the odds?"

"You are devious! That explains how you were able to find my address."

His grin broadened. "Yeah, but you like it. You might as well admit it, Nicole. Besides, I'm a lawyer. Sometimes it's my job to find people."

She nodded slowly. "Yeah, I guess I do like it."

The waitress arrived to take her order, but Michael held up his hand. "She may not be ready to order. I don't think she's even looked at the menu."

"Some of us don't need to look at menus," Nicole corrected before turning to the waitress. "I'll have the popcorn shrimp, please."

The waitress asked a few more questions about her order and proceeded to take Michael's. Although Nicole didn't feel comfortable staring at him while he seemed to be unaware, catching him off guard was another story. He seemed at ease with the world around him, and it amazed her. In fact, this whole thing amazed her. She still wasn't sure she could actually believe it was happening, not completely.

The diner passed pleasantly, and even though Nicole felt the effects of the wine, it was as though a mild calmness had spread through her, making things easy to enjoy and temporarily wiping Jordan from her thoughts. Even though she'd been trepidatious about going out on the date in the first place, as the evening went on, she grew more and more glad she had been willing to get out, not that she really expected this to go anywhere. Then again, she hadn't expected Michael even to remember her after he'd left. Sometimes, things were a lot different than she thought they would be.

Although she wasn't sure what would happen when they left the restaurant, once Michael realized she hadn't driven and would be riding with him, he suggested a walk around a nearby pond to enjoy the evening. A rejection was on the tip of Nicole's tongue, but she found herself quickly agreeing in spite of it.

Walking through the parking lot, she scanned the cars again, wondering which was his. The answer came quickly enough—a dark blue Lexus—as he opened the door and waited for her to sit before closing it. Nicole allowed herself to wonder if she'd made a mistake. She didn't know Michael all that well, but a little voice in her head told her that unless she let a few more people in behind those walls she'd erected, she was never going to know anyone that well, so she might as well start with Michael.

Dusk was setting the sky and pond on fire as they pulled up. Once again, Michael opened her door. She watched the geese scatter into the sky as the two of them started along the walking trail. Michael shoved his hands into his pockets and looked at the heavens. The light danced off his hair, illuminating the auburn highlights throughout.

Finally, he turned to her and asked, "So--how's your head?"

"Still attached," she said touching the Band-aid that her hair had kept hidden.

"Thanks, smartbutt. I'm serious. How's your head?" He bent and picked up a stone, and with a flick of the wrist cast it across the water.

She shrugged. "I still have a headache, but it's better. And thanks, by the way."

"For what?" he asked softly, picking up another stone and skipping it across the placid pond.

"Everything--especially the hotel room. Sarah said she'd made reservations, but I don't think she did."

He shrugged. "You're welcome. Glad I could help."

As they walked around the pond, they conversed quietly about future plans and the lack of significant others in both their lives. Although Nicole thought about Jordan, she also remembered he was married. Besides, even though she'd begun to accept that Jordan would always have a place in her memories, she knew she had to move on. Michael was offering her that.

It was late when Michael drove her back to her apartment. Always the gentleman, he walked her to the door. For a moment, both stood there awkwardly, looking at each other before he gently took both her hands in his and stepped closer.

"I had a great time tonight, Nicole," he said softly. "And I'd really like to go out again."

"Me, too." Their eyes met, and she felt the burning in his as he leaned close and brushed his lips across hers, driving away all thoughts she might have had, as well as any form of reason.

"I'll call you tomorrow," he whispered, giving her cheek a slow kiss before he walked away and she slipped inside, where her best friend waited, sitting on the couch and eating popcorn while watching a movie.

"Well," Sarah said. "How was it?"

Nicole leaned against the closed door, wanting for just a moment or two to replay how the evening had gone and how much she'd enjoyed Michael kissing her. It didn't seem possible.

"Nic?" Sarah set the bowl aside and stood. "You are blushing, woman! What happened?"

Nicole started laughing, and it came out in such a rush she could hardly breathe. Sarah grew frustrated and started shaking her, which didn't help much.

"Nic, come on! Tell me what happened? Do you like him?"

Nicole nodded, and when she'd finally caught her breath, she said, "He is so awesome! Really amazing--and he lives here, close by!"

"Yes!" Sarah said. "I knew it was meant to be."

Nicole nodded and pointed to her bedroom. "I'm going to go get ready for bed."

"Okay. I'm finishing this movie."

The two women parted company as Nicole headed to her bedroom. She reached into her purse to look at her cell phone, still grateful that it hadn't been stolen with her other purse. By some miracle, she'd put it in her jeans pocket.

She scrolled through the display options and saw she'd missed a call. "Crap," she muttered and saw it had been Jordan who'd called, leaving a message.

Gritting her teeth, Nicole played it and waited, holding her breath.

"Hey, Nicole, It's me, Jordan. I just wanted to see how you were doing. Things are great here. I just miss having someone to talk to. Have a great evening."

For a moment, she just sat there with the phone resting in her open palm. She wanted to talk to him, and she knew she probably shouldn't call, but she couldn't seem to help it. She pushed the contact button and selected his number. For the first couple of rings, she tried not to wonder where he was and if he were happy. For whatever reason, there was an attachment between them. It would have been nice to have discovered that under different circumstances, but there was nothing to do about that now.

On the third ring, a woman answered, taking Nicole aback. She almost dropped the phone before she could close it, and long after the call had been disconnected, she stared at it in horror. It was one thing to know he was married but another to hear his wife's voice.

She must have listened to the message ten times before she set the phone aside and tried not to dwell on it. What else could she do? She wasn't sure. All she knew was that even with all the happiness she'd felt as a result of her date, her last thought before drifting to sleep was of that suspended bridge and Jordan

## Chapter Eight

Over the next year and a half, Nicole spent a lot of time with Michael, and although she hadn't forgotten about Jordan, she felt as though her world didn't revolve around him anymore, and that was a good thing because she knew their paths were headed in different directions. If she spent much time at all thinking about might have been, it was only because the heart wants what the heart wants. It didn't seem to understand that sometimes things are beyond its reach.

She'd even gotten to the point she spent the night at Michael's more often than not, and nobody, especially Sarah, was surprised when he proposed. He'd brought her to the Red Lobster again, more for the sake of reminiscing than because the food was the best in town. It wasn't. But this was the place they'd had their first date.

Nicole had sensed what was coming when he'd slipped down on one knee and offered her the ring. The whole restaurant had broken out with cheers, and she'd found herself giving him a "yes" even though Jordan yet lingered in the back of her mind and in her heart. Perhaps that should have been a warning, but she did know one thing: Michael was a good man who loved her. He would treat her right, and they could make a life together. Part of her knew it wasn't the life she sought; it never would be, no matter how much she might want things to be different.

After making love until almost dawn, she called her mother from

Michael's bedroom as she heard him in the shower getting ready for work. He hummed randomly as always, and Nicole found comfort in that.

Her mother answered on the second ring. "Hello?"

"Good morning, Mom," Nicole said, trying not to grin so much. Her mother would definitely pick up on that.

"Nicole? Is that you?"

"Yeah." She ran her fingers through her hair and tried to pat it down. That was one of the good things about having long hair.

"Is there something wrong? Shouldn't you be getting ready for classes?"

Nicole laughed at her mother's worried tone. If there were anything to frown over, her mom would find it. "Everything is fine. I just had something I wanted to tell you. Michael proposed last night."

"Oh, my baby."

Nicole could hear the emotions running high in her mom's voice. "Are you crying?" she asked, incredulous.

"No, of course not. Is this what you want?"

Nicole paused, and an image of Jordan floated through her thoughts. He wore the same clothes as on that weekend PE trip, and he smiled and waved at her like nothing had changed--like *she* hadn't changed. She nodded, even though her mom wouldn't be able to see it. "Yeah, Mom. I love him. I really do."

"Then you need to come over this weekend so we can plan the wedding, and I won't take "no" for an answer. You hear me?"

Nicole stifled a giggle. "Yes, Mom."

She hung up as Michael slipped back into the room. He wore a white dress shirt and a navy Armani suit with suspenders underneath. As he leaned over to kiss her, she caught a whiff of his aftershave—Obsession. Their lips touched, and he lifted his head to look at her.

"Good morning, wife-to-be." His hand stroked her cheek lovingly.

"Good morning, husband-to-be."

He peered at her and shook his head. "Aren't you supposed to be getting ready for class?"

She stretched lazily. "What time is it?"

He consulted his watch. "Almost 8." He walked over to the closet to get his dress shoes.

"Crap!" Nicole snapped, immediately throwing the covers back and climbing out of bed, searching for her clothes. "I have a test this morning."

Michael watched her via the bureau mirror. "Yeah, well, you'd better get something on, or I'm coming over there, and we're both going to be late because what I'm thinking right now is going to take all morning."

She threw on her clothes and finger-brushed her hair before flying out his front door as he laughed and called, "Your shirt's on backward!"

"It's a new fashion trend!" she yelled back. "See you tonight." She ran to her vehicle, and as she started driving, she glanced down at her shirt and noticed Michael had been right. "Damn it."

* * *

Jordan sat at his desk, staring out the window. At any other time, he would have noticed how beautiful spring was, but not today. The house was quiet, emulating the stasis in their marriage. It had been two years since they'd taken their vows, and he wasn't sure what had gone wrong. Perhaps most of it had to do with the miscarriage, but even that couldn't bear the whole weight of this…silence...which seemed to have settled in their marriage. He didn't understand it.

He stood slowly and looked around the room, unsure what to do next. He had take the day off to try to clean the house and get a nice dinner ready to shore up some of the stress which had been eating at both of them lately, but he wasn't sure that was going to do much.

Still, he started some laundry and picked up before checking to make sure he had all the ingredients for a wonderful dinner  steaks, potatoes, and such. As he headed out to start the grill, he spotted one of their wedding pictures on the mantle. It was the first thing Alyssa had set in the house when they had moved in, and he marveled at how he'd never really looked at it, had never really looked at any of the wedding photos. He'd always intended to, but the days had just kept blurring past, and he'd been so focused on getting a job there had it been enough hours left to do everything.

Perhaps that was the key—more time with Alyssa? She'd been cold since the miscarriage, and he was running out of options. Sometimes he wanted to just call one of her friends and ask what was happening, but he doubted even that would prove useful. Alyssa's friends hadn't really gravitated toward him, just as his friends hadn't breached her outer circle, but he had foolishly believed their friendship would be enough to tether them together.

Perhaps he had been wrong?

He didn't know where to turn. He'd tried talking to her, but she'd refused to get past the surface level, leaving him in unfamiliar waters.

Without thinking about it, he pulled out his cell and dialed Nicole's number. Okay, maybe she wouldn't have any insight, but then again, maybe she would. He didn't have any other options. Talking to members of his family or hers was out. They didn't even know about the pregnancy or the miscarriage.

The phone rang twice before she answered. "Hello?"

"Nicole?"

"Yeah," she said cautiously. "Who is this?"

"Jordan. Jordan Carroway. Perhaps you don't remember me?"

There was a pause before she quietly said, "I remember you, Jordan. It's just been a while. How are you?"

The two launched into small talk, at least until Jordan felt comfortable enough to talk about Alyssa and what had happened since taking their vows. For a moment, Nicole said nothing, leaving Jordan to hold his breath.

"She's just hurt, Jordan. A miscarriage is a big deal, and she's probably wondering if she's ever going to be able to have a baby, which is only going to make her want one more. Just be there for her and keep trying to talk things through. It'll turn around if you give it enough time."

He'd been pacing the room and finally sank into a chair as he raked his fingers through his hair. "God, I hope so. I can't take the tension."

"Just hang in there," she urged, and then they talked for a few minutes more. She told him she was getting married, and while she expected some kind of enthusiasm, his silence didn't qualify. How strange.

"Really? Who's the lucky guy?" he finally asked in a tight voice.

"Michael Adams. He's a lawyer."

A lawyer? He wanted to tell her he couldn't begin to imagine her with that sort, yet he sat in stunned silence, unsure why things even felt worse than before. Still, he knew that wasn't the response Nicole had expected, so he said, "Well, that's great. Congratulations. How long have you known him?"

"About a year and a half."

"Huh." It was all he could come up with. Nicole was a grown woman who had decided to marry. What was wrong with that? He didn't have a clue, but the tightening inside told him he really didn't like this Michael Adams, even though he'd never met him.

At one time Jordan had wanted to ask her if she had ever felt something the way he did, but he knew that was a bad idea if he were going to follow through with his promise to Alyssa. After all, what did her answer really matter if he were going to promise his life to someone else?

The closest he came was blurting out, "Do you think I made the wrong choice in getting married?" Jordan hadn't meant to ask, but he couldn't seem to help it, even though he knew Nicole couldn't answer. Even he couldn't answer it.

For a moment, Nicole said nothing, and Jordan tried to imagine what she was thinking at the other end, but he couldn't. His mind was blank. Except for wondering who Michael Adams might be. When she finally did speak, her voice was quiet, kind of shaky.

"I wish I knew the answer to that. You've just got to keep faith that somehow it's going to work out. We all do." She paused for a moment, and he could hear lots of people in the background before she spoke again. "Look, Jordan, I hate to cut this short, but I'm on my way to class. I've got a test that I can't miss. Otherwise, I'd be glad to keep talking to you. I'm sorry."

He shook his head, imagining the expression crossing her face right about now. "It's all right, Nicole. This isn't your problem. It's mine. Thanks for giving me your input, and good luck."

"Bye."

Taking a deep breath, he closed the phone and leaned back in the chair. He'd hoped calling Nicole would give him just a sliver of peace. No dice. Suddenly he had a whole lot more to think about than he'd planned, including Michael Adams. Then again, why should he bother Jordan? Nicole had the right to marry whomever she chose. He just wondered if she were making a mistake, just as he was beginning to suspect he had.

Nicole snapped her phone shut and lingered in the hall outside the classroom. She knew she had to go in, but right now her heart was ramming in her ears, and she was shaking. *It shouldn't matter that he called*, she thought. *I'm engaged to Michael, and he's what matters.*

She looked up at the clock and gritted her teeth, feeling her stomach suddenly tied in knots she didn't have a clue how to untie. She had five minutes before class, and she reached into her purse and fingered her cell, thinking about calling Sarah. The only thing that stopped her was the knowledge that, while Sarah might be able to give her wonderful advice, all the things her best friend would tell her would be the same things she was trying unsuccessfully to tell herself. There was no one, Sarah included, who could change what was going on in her heart.

She forced herself to go inside, all the information she'd studied seemingly having flown out of her head with Jordan's voice, but she didn't care. She just kept replaying what he'd told her.

*You can't do this*, she thought, setting her books below her desk to prepare for the test. *Besides, having problems with a wife isn't the same thing as available, and do I really want to wish his marriage to come crashing to the ground like that?*

The instructor stepped to the front of the room and started giving instructions for the test, but while Nicole watched his lips move, she y didn't really hear a world. She just kept hearing Jordan repeating the same words over and over until she'd wished she'd been deaf.

Nicole completed the test as best she could, feeling as though her mind were in a fog, just like it did when she was sick. It was like a million puffs of cotton had been tucked into her brain, making her thoughts slow and jumbled. When she'd answered all the questions, she packed up her stuff and turned in the test, even though she'd only been there half the class time and probably hadn't answered half of them right. Then again, she knew it wouldn't matter how long she kept the test with her mind so distracted. There was nothing to be done about it.

Although she had an English class after this, she headed back to her car and drove home. More than once, she had picked up her cell, thinking of calling Jordan, but she managed to keep from doing it somehow, despite the conflicting emotions. As she pulled into the parking lot of the apartment, she was glad Sarah wasn't there. She needed a of chance to think.

As if *that* were going to help.

She rushed inside, thumped her book bag on the table, and headed for her laptop. Carrying it to the table in the dining room, she set it down and turned it on. She grabbed her phone again and thought about calling one more time before she forced herself to pretend she was just checking the time before setting the cell on the table next to her book bag.

What did the time have to do with anything?

Once the computer was ready, she logged onto the internet and did something that, up until this point, she had managed to avoid. She typed Jordan's full name into Google and did a search. Although there were more than one results, only one seemed to have anything to do with her Jordan.

*Her Jordan?* Where had that come from? For a moment, she cradled her head in her hands. She wanted to laugh about how absurd this whole thing seemed anymore. And talk about timing. How was that possible? Couldn't he have had his misgivings before she'd met Michael? The whole thing just left her aching inside as though she'd been involved in a car wreck and everything had been bruised on impact.

She lifted her head and looked at the screen to find the one entry that applied. Moving the mouse, she clicked on the link, and what came up really wasn't something she'd been prepared for—a wedding announcement and an image of Jordan and his bride, Alyssa.

For a moment, Nicole couldn't say anything. She just stared at the happy couple, focusing on the strawberry blonde to his left. The woman was so different than Nicole--so petite and perfect. And Jordan struggled with her? How was that possible, considering in their wedding photos they had looked so perfect, almost like a storybook couple.

"What are you doing?" Sarah asked, setting her keys on the counter.

Nicole tried to shut the computer, but Sarah grabbed the screen and stopped her. Since she couldn't seem to distract her that way, Nicole asked, "What are you doing home right now? Don't you have class?"

"I could ask you the same thing." Sarah gave her a knowing stare. "In fact, I will. What are you doing here? And please tell me you aren't looking at a picture of who I think you are." She peered more closely at the screen.

Nicole gritted her teeth. "I guess that depends on who you think I'm looking at, doesn't it?"

Sarah turned the laptop so she could scroll down the screen and read the announcement that went with the photo, her eyes widening as she kept reading. When she'd finished, she glanced at her best friend.

"What?" Nicole blurted, wishing her best friend would just get on with the lecture. She knew it was coming.

Shaking her head, Sarah walked to the fridge and pulled out a soda. "I don't get it, Nicole. You and Michael seem happy enough and yet you're still looking up photos of him online. What is your deal?" She closed the fridge, popped the tab, and took a sip.

Nicole closed the computer. "He called me this morning. Apparently his wife was pregnant and miscarried. The two of them are having some…issues...it would appear."

Giving Nicole a frown, Sarah slowly slid over to the table and sat down. "Oh, great--that just gives you more reason to think about him? He's still married, Nic, and if he's the kind of guy you think he is, that won't change without a lot of pain, and I don't think Michael is going to wait around forever for you to make up your mind."

Eyeing Sarah's soda, Nicole stood and got one for herself. "And that brings us to the next problem. Michael has proposed, and I said yes." Her voice trembled, and Nicole realized she didn't even sound like herself, just some stranger.

"He what?" Sarah stood, her frown immediately changing to a brimming smile. "Nic, that is soooo awesome." She flew to Nicole and wrapped her in an embrace. "You so deserve this kind of happiness!"

Even though Nicole smiled, she felt torn and uncertain. "But what if this isn't right? What if the marriage fails?" She looked at her best friend, hoping for answers Nicole knew Sarah didn't have. No one would have them, she realized.

"Is that why you're looking up pictures of Jordan?"

Nicole reluctantly nodded, and the two of them walked to the table. "Yeah. I was on cloud nine last night, and then out of the blue Jordan called this morning with that news. It shook me--I mean really *shook* me."

Sarah reached out and set her hand on Nicole's to comfort her. "Look, I know some part of you is always going to feel connected to him. I get that. I really do. But you can't live your life as though some random chance is going to come your way. It's not. And if it does, it won't be any time soon, Nic. I think, deep down, you know that."

Although she wanted to argue with Sarah, Nicole knew without a doubt her best friend had a point. Granted, it wasn't a point she wanted to hear, but that didn't matter. She just wished talking about this would somehow make her feel better instead of worse.

## Chapter Nine

The church was cold, and Nicole shivered, dreading pulling on the long-sleeved wedding dress she had picked out. Granted, the top did have a sheer overlay studded with numerous pearls. But she suspected the cold air would just seep right through the thin fabric, and it was so darn tight that it was hard to breathe.

"How are you doing over there with your make-up?"

Nicole turned to Sarah and shrugged. "I guess I'm almost done." She looked back at her eyes and applied shadow to her lids, followed by mascara. Every time she looked at her reflection, she felt unexplained panic rising inside her. She didn't understand. The only thing she knew was that she couldn't seem to control it, no matter what she did, and being here, in this church, waiting to walk down the aisle with her daddy only made her feel worse, not better. Was this about having cold feet?

No, it was about having cold everything. She shook her head. "Are you cold?"

Sarah plugged in her curling iron. "Ummm, nope. It's actually pretty hot in here."

*She would say that*, Nicole thought in disgust. "I'm freezing."

"Umm-hum," her best friend said, double-checking her makeup, which made Nicole think she could probably have said the moon was made of grey tapioca and Sarah wouldn't even have blinked. There was something about weddings that made everything but the ceremony seem unimportant because everyone was so busy getting ready that things constantly fell by the wayside. Imagine that.

Of course, as Nicole looked at the intricate braids the stylist had woven into her hair, the thing which kept crossing her mind was that the ceremony was just the top layer of her world, and she felt tremors shaking beneath. She tried to calm her nerves by touching her hair, but doing so did nothing to allay the fears that maybe, like Jordan, she was making a mistake. What if she was supposed to be with him?

She stopped toying with her hair and stood, walking around the room until she'd come to the wall with all the windows on it. As she looked out into the full parking lot, the butterflies in her stomach suddenly turned into frantic hummingbirds beating their wings against her insides.

Nicole's breath sped up and she clutched at the folds of the dress to still her trembling hands; she felt like she couldn't breathe, no matter how hard she tried. All those people here to watch her take vows she wasn't sure she would ever be okay with. Her body turned rigid, and she muttered, "I don't know if I can do this. I really don't."

From her peripheral vision, Nicole noticed Sarah still busily curling her hair. She even hummed some kind of song, probably a Tom Petty tune because those were her favorites. So strange. She could feel the fear building and wanted to scream, but she was stuck with all this silence that gnawed at her until all she could do was breathe--barely.

"Sarah?" she said pointedly, turning slowly toward her best friend.

"Yeah." Sarah eased a curl from the iron.

"What if this is wrong?" She spoke softly, still clutching the dress.

"What do you mean?" Sarah applied the iron to a new strand of hair.

"What if marrying Michael is wrong and I'm making a mistake?"

At those words, Sarah's eyes widened as she set down the iron down and stepped toward her. "Mistake? How do you figure that? Michael is gorgeous. He's a lawyer, and he's going to make you one happy woman. Face it, you are about to get your happily ever after, girlfriend."

"I don't feel that." She took a deep breath and folded her arms across her chest. She wanted to be happy and sure about everything, but she wasn't, and that just frightened her all the more. "Maybe I should just call this whole thing off. Maybe that's the right thing to do." She could feel tears rushing to her eyes, and she knew if she opened her eyelids, they would flood down her cheeks and ruin the makeup she had so carefully applied. If that weren't an omen, she didn't know what was.

"Nicole, sweetie--are you all right?" She felt Sarah gently wrap her arms around her and draw her close. "This isn't like you, and I don't know where this is coming from."

For a moment Nicole clung to her best friend as though she were the only secure thing in the storm whirling around her. She didn't know where this was coming from, either. It felt good just to stand there, but she knew that the hands of the clock were going to keep moving, and that no matter what she would have to make a choice.

Trying to gather strength, Nicole slowly pulled back. Her whole body ached, and she felt as though she were going to break under the weight of her heart.

Sarah frowned and put her hands on Nicole's shoulders. "Nicole, you need to talk to me. We don't have much time before you're supposed to be walking down that aisle. Your makeup is a mess, and I worried."

"What if he's not the one I'm supposed to be with?" Nicole asked softly.

"This is about Jordan, isn't it?"

Nicole didn't say anything but the tears streaming down her face said far more than she ever could.

"Nicole, he's just a part of your past, someone you met once and left behind. That's the way it's supposed to be." Sarah wiped at the tears. "You've got so much ahead of you, and you have to keep that in mind. Jordan was one day of your life. That's it. How many days has Michael been by your side?"

Nicole also dabbed at her eyes. "I know. I know. But some part of me always feels like he's the one. I don't get it either."

"Are you ready to throw your whole future away on someone who is still married? Is that what you want?"

Nicole shook her head. "No."

"Then let's get you ready to walk down the aisle and meet the future where you do belong," Sarah said and led Nicole back to the mirror so she could clean up the makeup the tears had blurred. Once the black smudges were gone, Sarah quickly reapplied the makeup and smiled.

"Okay, your face is beautiful, and your fiancé is going to fall head over heels in love with you all over again when he sees you. Now I have to finish getting me ready."

Even though Sarah turned back to the mirror as she started curling the last of her hair, she watched Nicole, a worried frown tugging at her lips. "Are you okay?"

Nicole nodded. "I'll be fine."

"For a few minutes, I thought I was going to be like a woman on a TV show who had to go out to the crowd and tell them a wedding had to be canceled, not just any wedding, but the wedding of my best friend, who deserves all the happiness about to come her way."

The door suddenly opened, and both women turned to find Nicole's father standing there, a huge smile on his face. "And how's my baby girl?" he asked, stepping toward Nicole. His smile deepened when he saw her in the dress. "Don't you look beautiful? Just like your mama."

Nicole felt relief rush through her as she fell into her father's arms and lingered there like when she had been small and skinned her knee. Maybe her father couldn't make the situation any better, but at least him being around was comforting.

"Everything all right?" he asked, gently pulling away.

"Oh, she's just got a few butterflies," Sarah said, coming toward Nicole with the veil. "She'll be fine once the ceremony starts."

Glancing at her father, Nicole wanted to believe everything would be all right because she'd never seen him so happy, as though this one thing were all he'd wished for her and he were thrilled it had come true. He looked at his watch and back at his daughter.

"I should probably head to the back of the church." He offered them both a parting smile and saw himself out.

"We should get this on you," Sarah said, nodding to the veil.

"Yeah." Nicole took a deep breath and sat in a chair so that Sarah could adjust it properly and pin it to her hair.

"Nic, don't take this the wrong way, but I don't know why you think you're in love with Jordan. You barely know him."

Nicole shrugged and looked at the carpet. "I don't know, either. There's just a connection there, something I can't imagine my life being without."

"And could you imagine it without Michael?"

Nicole stiffened, hating that question. "Of course not," she snapped.

"Just checking." Sarah touched the front of the veil and stepped back. "Looks like you're good to go." She eyed the clock. "We should join your dad so we can get this show on the road."

"Yeah," Nicole agreed, still feeling those hummingbirds. It should have helped that she'd made a decision about the wedding, but it hadn't. Then again, what had she expected?

The two of them headed into the hallway and turned in the direction of the sanctuary's back end. Even as they passed the closed doors of the sanctuary, Nicole could hear the organist playing "Jesu, Desire of Man's Heart," a piece she'd always loved. She clenched her teeth, thinking about the moments when she'd picked the music. She would have liked to have been able to say Michael had picked the music, too, but her fiancé had been on the road a lot. Most of the wedding had come about through Nicole's sheer determination, and she tried to tell herself that it wouldn't be as difficult when they had married.

But what if it were? What then?

She took a deep breath. *This isn't getting you anywhere, Nicole. Just focus on the ceremony.*

She brushed a stray hair from her face as they arrived at a room just off the back of the sanctuary and her father looked at them and smiled again. Above his head, the clock said they had just a few moments before Sarah would start down the aisle and Nicole would follow. She knew this was her last chance to change her mind, but she couldn't seem to make herself do that, not anymore. Somewhere in all this she wanted to believe she had fallen in love with Michael, but it all felt as though she were standing waist-deep amid a powerful river, where the current all but knocked her down, and if that happened, she'd never be able to regain her footing. At times she had let the current push her along because it kept her standing, but she wasn't strong enough to go against it.

The soft strains of music started, the song they'd rehearsed as a cue for Sarah to begin walking down the aisle. She turned to her best friend and wrapped her arms around her. "Guess that's my cue. Keep your chin up and think happy thoughts, Nic."

Sarah pulled away, picked up her bouquet, and headed toward the front of the church, where Nicole's father turned to her. "Are you ready?" he asked, offering his arm.

"I guess so."

Nicole stepped to him and took his arm, trying to ignore the panic she couldn't seem to drive away no matter what she did, and just before she thought she might have it under control, the processional started, and without warning, her dad started leading her into the full sanctuary. She kept telling herself to walk and keep calm, but even that didn't work.

Finally, instead of meeting the gazes of those guests, she looked at her intended groom. Although she'd picked out his black tux, she hadn't yet seen him in it, and in that moment, Michael's smile reminded her of why she'd fallen in love with him. She almost stopped walking, but her father kept leading her, his gaze traveling to her face as the only indication he felt her faltering steps.

At the front of the sanctuary, her father gave her away, and while she tried to remember what was being said, her mind blurred as she looked at Michael. He squeezed her hand once or twice, and she returned it. Somehow they both got through their vows. The next thing she knew was that the preacher had announced they were married and Michael gently kissed her before they turned and faced the guests his hand lingering in hers.

Hours later, they lay naked in a hotel room wrapped in each other's arms. Although both verged on drifting to sleep, Michael absently twirled a strand of Nicole's hair around one of his fingers as she rested her head on his chest. The sound of his slow steady, heartbeat comforted her immensely, and she felt as though she could spend the rest of her life in this position. Wasn't that what happiness was?

"Are you asleep, Nicole?" Michael whispered, brushing his lips across her temple.

"Mmm," she said, her voice lazy with exhaustion. They'd been together for a while, but knowing that they were married somehow made it so much better. Could it be that Sarah had been right--that her misgivings were just shot nerves and fatigue? She tried to look at him, but her eyes were so heavy it was a struggle to open, them which must mean she was exhausted.

"I just wanted to tell you what a beautiful bride you were and how lucky I am." His whisper was rough silk, and he gently nibbled on her earlobe.

She could feel herself falling down the rabbit hole toward unconsciousness. She wanted to tell him something but couldn't remember what, so she settled with, "I love you, too."

That's when she felt the darkness sweeping her away, so she snuggled closer against him to maintain the warmth, and in response, his arms tightened around her. Nicole tried, in that moment, , trying as hard as she could to hold on to its magic even if it meant exiling all the memories of Jordan into the dark corners of her thoughts.

## Chapter Ten

Three years later

Jordan leaned back in his seat as he sat in the driveway, dreading going inside. Through the windows, he could see Alyssa setting the table for dinner, and he tried to remember the last time a meal hadn't been a battlefield, with each of them sitting on opposite sides.

"Damn," he muttered, unknotting the tie from around his neck and pulling it free so he could undo the first button of his shirt. While that made him a little more comfortable, it did nothing to allay the sweltering summer. Sweat beaded on his forehead and ran down his temples until he wiped the runnels away, and he took a deep breath, forcing himself to get out and head inside, knowing it wasn't going to get any easier. It never did.

By the time he'd slipped into the dining room, Alyssa had finished setting the table and already put the food out. Their lives were running on the timetable they always did, but it no longer brought him comfort. Still, he reached out and stroked his wife's back as he'd done a thousand times before.

She stiffened at the feel of his fingers and edged away enough so he moved his hand back. It lingered in the air as though waving before he finally lowered it and stepped into the kitchen to grab a bottled water from the fridge.

As he sat at the table, he spotted the wine bottle—Alyssa's usual drink of choice, which had never appealed to him. He silently waited for her to finish setting out the breadsticks to go with the spaghetti. The two wordlessly filled their plates, and even though Jordan hoped tonight there would be peace between them, he knew it was an empty desire. It had been empty for the last year and a half and would continue until something Jordan had no control over suddenly changed.

Or Hell froze over. He wasn't sure which would happen first.

"How was your day?" he asked, twisting open the bottle and staring at anything besides Alyssa's expression. Everything else was safe.

"How do you think it was?" she asked in an icy tone. "How is it ever?" She toyed with her noodles, pushing them around on the plate but hardly eating. She rarely ate anymore.

Jordan, too, pushed noodles into the sauce and tried to concentrate on eating. Still, he made the mistake of looking at her and realized she required an answer. "I've told you that if you don't like your job, if it makes you that unhappy, maybe you need to find a different one. You don't need that kind of stress, and you know it."

She set her fork in her plate and pointed at him. "You always want to blame everything on my job. I actually like teaching."

"I didn't say you hated teaching. I think it's all the administrative crap you can't deal with, and that makes you…." His voice died away, and he realized he'd started something he shouldn't have. It definitely wouldn't be going the way he expected it would.

Alyssa rested both hands on the table and glared at him. "That makes me what, Jordan? You might as well go ahead and say what you're thinking." Her tone was low and angry.

He leaned back and looked out the window at his neighbor mowing the yard. For a split second, he wished he were that guy--anything to get him out of this. "Look, Alyssa, I didn't mean anything. Really. It's just that when you come home, you're upset--really, really upset--and I don't know how to help you. I wish I did."

"Once again we're back to that." She gritted her teeth and got up, carrying her glass with her as she strode to the kitchen.

"I didn't mean anything," he said, forcing himself to get up and follow.

She'd just made it into the kitchen when she whirled abruptly. "Of course you didn't. You never mean anything, do you Jordan? Nothing that matters, anyway."

He closed his eyes and took a step back, wondering how they'd come to this road. He'd known they both wanted children. He just didn't know how desperate Alyssa was for them and how angry being unable to have them would make her.

"Please don't," he whispered, reaching to take her hand, but she jerked back suddenly.

"Don't you get it, Jordan? Keeping silent about this isn't going to make it better. Ever. You can't just ignore it." Her blue eyes glared at him venomously, and she straightened her back sharply.

"I'm not trying to ignore anything," he snapped, thrusting his hands to his hips. "You act like none of this bothers me, like it's so easy for me to watch."

"It is easy for you," she spat, the hand holding the glass trembling so badly the wine threatened to spill.

"What the hell do you want from me? What more can I do?" Although he'd meant to keep his voice down, he couldn't take the way she looked at him, everything about her so accusing that even breathing seemed wrong.

"I want you to be understanding! I want you to think about the reason my job is so difficult!" She leaned toward him, and some of the wine spilled onto her bare foot and yet it never registered. All she could do was glare at him as though everything in the world were his fault somehow.

“I do understand!” he shouted and reached out to grab her shoulders. “This isn’t just about you, Alyssa. This was supposed to be about us, remember? Or don’t you get that anymore?”

“You son of a bitch!” she yelled and slapped him, spilling the rest of the wine on his leg and the floor.

Jordan immediately let her go and took a step back, feeling himself boiling with a rage he couldn’t seem to keep under wraps. He stood there for a moment, watching tears spring into her eyes as she threw the wine glass against the wall, watching it shatter.

At one time, he would have gathered her into his arms and said all the right words, but he didn’t know the right words anymore, and he didn’t feel anything but rage. He balled his hands into fists and whirled, heading toward the door.

“That’s right. Just pretend this never happened like you always do!” she shouted as he strode toward the office to cool down.

No such luck. Alyssa followed him.

"You can't just hide from this, Jordan."

His back stiffened, and he wished he'd never come in. He'd known this was coming, but like a fool, he'd thought he could fix it somehow.

"You can't ignore me, either." Alyssa picked up the camera, and as Jordan gauged the wild look in her eyes, she was about to throw it so he caught her hand.

"Fine. I'm not ignoring you. I'm leaving." He jerked the camera out of her hand and rushed out the door, slamming it. For a moment he just stood there, trying to keep standing despite the frantic turmoil of his world falling apart. He strode to his car and drove away.

As he headed away from the house, the sky opened up and rain spewed down upon the car so hard he could scarcely see. Despite the anger, he felt tears seeping into his eyes, and they quickly spilled down his face, blurring his world even more.

“It wasn’t supposed to be like this,” he muttered, seeing a red light just ahead and easing the car to a stop. As he sat there, he forced himself to look anywhere but the mirror. Right now, he didn't think he could take looking at his reflection, afraid he just might see what his wife saw.

Looking around, he spotted a woman walking through the deluge. Her long, brown hair seemed familiar, and in that instant, he thought of Nicole and a day that had seemed lost until now. His heart sped up, and he veered to the left so he could park the car in at the corner. Jerking the key free, he shot out of the vehicle and ran after her, trying to ignore the violent rain hurtling from the sky like ice.

"Nicole," he called, rushing after her.

She didn't respond, so he kept running, thankfully gaining on her. At last his fingers curled around her arm and turned her. Immediately she jerked free of him.

"Let go of me!"

Although the long, brown hair was right, the eyes were blue, and her nose longer and skinnier. From a distance, she might have looked like Nicole, but not up close, not by a long shot.

Jordan held up his hands and stepped back, blinking to try to clear the rain from his eyes. "I'm sorry. I thought you were someone else."

She glared at him for a moment longer before striding away. More than once, she glanced over her shoulder to make sure he didn't follow. Closing his eyes, he stood there, letting the cold rain wash over him until his body was wet and numb. He needed all the distraction he could get, and when he realized the rain could never fully take away the pain drumming through him, he turned slowly and headed back to his car, feeling more empty than he had before he'd gotten out.

He damn sure couldn't explain why he always seemed to "find" Nicole without even realizing he was looking for her. They hadn't seen each other in years, but somehow, whenever things felt tough, he often thought of her and wondered how things were in her life. She'd probably be married by now and have kids, and as usual, he had no place in her life.

Of course, he realized, sitting behind the wheel, that he sometimes spent more time than he should wondering what would have happened had he chosen not to marry Alyssa and instead gone with his gut feeling that Nicole was right for him. Would he still be sitting in the rain, trying to put his world back together?

Chilled, he started the car, more to turn on the heat than anything. He wasn't planning on driving, but it was as if his body and mind weren't on speaking terms as he drove without knowing where he was going or why. At times, the rain fell so hard he had to pull over and give it a few minutes to ease up; the wipers couldn't keep up.

Then, at other times, the drops barely spattered the windshield, and even if he didn't know exactly where he was headed, he did understand that he needed to go somewhere--that sitting here, staring at nothing wasn't allowed.

The silence seemed to wrap itself around him, suffocating him, but he kept driving, promising himself there were answers somewhere. He simply needed to find them. He needed time to face Alyssa because he couldn't do it like this.

He looked at the camera in the passenger seat and frowned. No, he still hadn't gotten all the parts. Some of them were proving incredibly difficult to find, but that didn't stop him. He would fix it. Hell, it might be the only thing he could fix, at this rate.

He'd arrived before he'd realized it, and even though he'd thought he was driving at random, he now recognized the parking lot. Yes, some of the landscaping had changed a bit, but not the thing he'd seemed to be headed for all along—the rope bridge just ahead, the same one where he'd met Nicole and thought everything had already been so mapped out that nothing could happen to drive him away from Alyssa.

Despite the rain, Jordan parked the car and slowly got out. As he hadn't dried off from his previous excursion, the cold didn't bother him much. The only thing that really distracted him was how the rain kept falling into his eyes, blinding him.

He gritted his teeth as he reached the seam where the concrete path ended and the bridge began. For a moment, he just stood there, remembering how, the last time he'd stepped across its threshold, things seemed to change, and he wondered if perhaps, by crossing again, he could force another change. The question was, if that did happen, would it be a change for the better or one for the worse? He shook his head, and rain sprayed around him from his sodden hair. Never mind. He couldn't imagine things getting much worse than they were right now. He didn't even know if there were even a way to go back to his former idyllic bliss. He wanted to, God help him, but he was wise enough to know that Alyssa had to want that as much as he did or it would never work.

Then again, it was just a bridge, and there was no point in being superstitious. It's not like taking another step would force anything, like anything could simply force happiness. That was like a dragonfly. Some people just got lucky enough to have one light on their shoulders for a while. Catching it, however, was out of the question.

That's when he did edge his right foot atop the first wooden plank. The left followed, and he kept on until he'd reached the center of the bridge, roughly where Nicole had sat when they first met. At that moment, the rain abruptly died away and a ray of sunshine broke through the overwhelming grey overhead. To his right, he saw a perfect unbroken rainbow and smiled. Had he been superstitious, he might actually have believed this an omen. Hell, part of him definitely *wanted* to believe.

But he wasn't. Rainbows wouldn't change things between him and Alyssa, and even if he did end up single again, God forbid, it wouldn't help that Nicole would now be married--happily, he hoped.

Still, despite the water glistening on the wood and the small pockets of moisture in the cracks of the bridge, he slowly sat where Nicole had sat and tried to meditate as she'd done that day. Once again, he didn't know what he'd hoped to accomplish, maybe just to find a few moments of peace before he went back to the chaos which had become his life. He didn't know.

The only thing he knew was that for once, he found the quiet restorative, and that had to brave the coming storms.

# Chapter Eleven

Two years later

She was a whale.

Nicole tried not to look at her reflection. She'd look two months from now, after she'd had the son currently disguised as a basketball in her tummy. Right now, she was incredibly hot and uncomfortable. Pinning her long hair high on her head didn't help. Nothing helped. It was summer, and she was pregnant. What had made this a good idea, anyway?

Sighing, she leaned back against the couch and tried to get comfortable as she propped up her feet, *tried* being the magic word. She'd probably never be able to get comfortable until the growing mass inside had finally come out. Then she probably wouldn't get any sleep, or at least that's what she'd heard more than once.

The doorbell chimed unexpectedly, and Nicole glanced down at her watch, frowning. Who could that be? With effort, she forced herself to shift back toward the edge of the couch and rise, her hand immediately drifting to her stomach as though she were afraid the movement were going to disturb her baby.

"Hang on, Nick. Let's answer the door," she told her tummy, giving it a couple of soft pats as she waddled to the door.

Sarah stood on the step, a small pink gift bag in her hand. She immediately gazed at Nicole, taking her in from head to foot. "OMG," she said, shaking her head. "You're huge! You sure you haven't got twins in there or something?" She reached to feel Nicole's belly.

"Nope, just one little boy who refuses to sleep at night and keeps kicking me like he's ready for Michael to teach him the ways of football."

Nicole felt her son give Sarah's hand a kick, and her best friend giggled. "Wow! That is so cool." Sarah drifted inside.

"Well, you know, you could have one if you ever settled down, Sarah."

"Eh," Sarah said and shrugged. "I'll just spoil yours." She handed Nicole the bag.

"You do know we're having a boy, right?" Nicole asked, pointing to the pink polka dots.

"Yeah, so? Pink is just a color. You know that."

"But I'm not sure Michael does."

The two women sat on the couch, Sarah perched on the edge of the sofa as though not quite comfortable. Then again, Sarah had never totally been comfortable with Michael. Yeah, at first, she'd thought he was cute and all that. Sarah probably just didn't like the stodgy lawyer feeling that came with Michael. Of course, there was nothing anyone could do about that.

Sarah looked around and cleared her throat. "Speaking of Michael, where is he?"

"On a business trip."

Sarah pursed her lips and Nicole thought of Thumper from Bambi. her best friend was like that, sitting there, saying, "If I can't say nothing nice, I won't say nothing at all." It didn't really matter, her expression gave it away.

"Okay, spit it out," Nicole muttered, hating the way the silence between them suddenly felt so intense. She wanted to open and enjoy Sarah's gift, but that wasn't possible, not with the tension between them.

"I just can't believe he didn't stay here with you, Nic. I mean, you could have that baby any time, which means you deserve the father to be staying close, just in case." She nodded toward the bag. "Aren't you going to open that?"

"Yeah." Nicole pulled away the tissue paper and found a small, blue outfit with trains all over it, and she smiled brightly, trying to imagine her son in it. It was perfect.

"It's beautiful," Nicole finally managed. "Thank you." She started to lean over and give her best friend a hug when the baby really kicked hard and her abdomen started tightening.

Sarah frowned and watched Nicole carefully. "Hey, you okay over there? You're suddenly kind of pale."

Nicole nodded slowly. "Yeah. Nick just kicked the crap out of me." Her hand nervously caressed her belly, not liking the way it felt so tight it hurt. She couldn't be going into labor, could she?

"You sure that's it?" Sarah edged closer, one hand gripping the edge of the couch as though she were hanging on for dear life.

"Yeah, I'm fine. I'll be right back." She struggled to her feet, intending to get some water from the kitchen. As she took her first step, however, she felt an immediate rush of heated liquid whoosh down her legs and spatter the floor.

Both of them stared at it, and Sarah finally said, "Um, Nic, I think your water just broke."

For a second, Nicole couldn't answer; she just kept staring at the puddle, trying to fathom how it had happened. One moment she'd been grouchy because of being pregnant in the heat, and now she was staring at a wet floor, feeling more panicked by the minute.

"What was I thinking?" Nicole muttered, staggering back a step. "I don't know how to do this."

Sarah slipped her arm around her friend. "Can you even reach

Michael?"

"I don't know," she muttered, grateful to feel Sarah close. She didn't think she could do this alone, and the idea of calling her mother wasn't one she relished. "He took an early flight out for an important meeting." Sweat glossed her face, and she felt light-headed.

"Yeah, well, no damned meeting is more important than being here to welcome your first child. Where's your phone?"

"In my purse." Nicole pointed weakly to the counter, and Sarah rifled through the contents it until she found it. She thumbed Michael's number, but the phone went straight to messaging.

"Michael, this is Sarah. I'm with your wife—you know, the cute brunette who's very pregnant with your child? Well, she's about to be unpregnant and would like for you to get your butt over here!" She snapped the phone shut.

Nicole started to get woozy, and her knees buckled slightly but Sarah caught her arm. "Okay, I think it's time we got you to the hospital. Let's go. I'll play the fanatical driver this time."

"You're always the fanatical driver." Nicole groaned and gritted her teeth, her steps getting shorter as the pain came. "Damn, that hurts."

"C'mon, let's get you to the car." Sarah supported Nicole the whole way to the vehicle. The walk seemed to take forever, but considering the grimace on Nicole's face, Sarah wasn't about to push her any harder despite the nerve-wracking idea of Nicole giving birth right then and there. It didn't happen like that in reality, did it?

Once Sarah had managed to get her best friend into the car and make sure she was belted in, she raced around to the driver's side. As she drove she kept peering at Nic.

"Didn't you and Michael take a Lamaze class or something?" she asked, hating the way Sarah's heart rate had jacked up.

"He couldn't, not with his work schedule. He was out of town a lot," Nicole managed as her body stiffened for another contraction. "It's not his fault."

"Well, it's not yours, either." Sarah turned back to the road and found herself mentally taking in landmarks just to feel as though they were getting somewhere. She was desperate to reach the hospital. It wasn't so much that the thought of a new baby scared her as the thought of delivering said baby. Sarah hated the sight of blood, and she was pretty sure there would be lots of it when delivering a newborn.

"It never takes this long to get the hospital," Sarah muttered, suddenly stuck behind a tan minivan whose driver seemed more interested in sight-seeing than actually getting anywhere.

"That's because you're being forced to go the speed limit," Nicole said, gripping the arm rests.

"Nah--it's this stupid van." She started waving one hand around. "Hello, dipshit! Pregnant woman on board about to explode here!" She glared and shook her head. "Unbelievable."

"I don't think I'm the one exploding," Nicole gasped, running her hand over her belly. "You look like you're about to have a heart attack or something."

Nicole suddenly groaned and leaned back.

Sarah looked at her friend in horror. "Don't you dare have that baby in my car! I will never forgive you, Nic! Never!"

"Then you'd better get me to the hospital because I don't think the baby's going to wait much longer." The words came out between sharp gasps, and Sarah cursed Michael for his sheer dumb luck at being absent. This should have been his job. Then again, Nicole had often commented on how frequently Michael was gone and how hard it had been, especially once she'd gotten pregnant.

"All right. Hang on." Sarah peered around the van and saw no oncoming traffic. Instead of patiently following behind, she swerved into the other lane and veered past him in a no-passing lane.

"Sarah, what are you doing?" Nicole gasped.

"Getting you to the hospital because I'm not going to deliver your baby. I'd suck at it, and you know it, and then there's the whole traumatize-the-kid thing. No thanks."

Nicole clenched her eyes shut, waiting for the pain to pass, yet it seemed to take longer and longer for that to happen, which terrified her. She had just thought she was ready to become a mom. She'd been out of her mind.

"Nic? You okay?" Sarah asked, panic obvious in her tone as she looked at her. From Sarah's peripheral vision, she could see the hospital ahead.

"Like it or not, you might be delivering. I need to push," she grunts, gripping the arm rests with all her strength.

"No pushing!" Sarah yelled, laying her hand on the horn. By some miracle, it worked. The traffic moved, allowing Sarah to get to the entrance of the hospital and zoom through the parking lot to the emergency room entrance. "You keep that baby in there, Nic. We're at the ER." Shoving the car into park, she got out and caught a hapless EMT by the arm, dragging him as she explained the crisis.

Three hours later, Nicole lay in a bed, cradling her son against one breast as Sarah lounged in a nearby chair. Although Nicole was all smiles, Sarah looked worn out and half-dazed as her best friend cooed softly to a sleeping infant.

"Isn't he beautiful?" Nicole asked, glancing up at Sarah.

"Beautiful, yeah," she repeated, propping on elbow on the arm rest to support her head.

"Are you even listening to me?" Nicole asked, wanting to throw a pillow at Sarah.

"Of course I'm listening. I'm just tired."

Nicole snorted. "Let me get this straight. I go through the agony of giving birth, and you're tired? Really?"

Sarah forced herself to sit up straighter and shrugged. "I got tired just watching you." A shudder ripped through her. "And for the record, I'm not having any kids. Watching you in labor cured me of that desire."

"It wasn't that bad," Nicole argued. "And just look what I got out of the deal."

Sarah got to her feet. "A mini-me who squirts poo and keeps you up all night." She patted Nicole's shoulder. "That's what you got." She covered her mouth, trying to stifle a yawn.

Glancing at the clock on the wall, Nicole frowned. "Has Michael called in yet?" It was a long shot, she knew, but she really wanted to talk with him about everything that had happened. It was important, she reasoned. Surely if he had even checked his messages, he would know something had happened because Sarah never called him. Never. The two of them really didn't get along all that well, so for her to have tried reaching him should have been enough.

"Well, since we've both been kind of preoccupied with other things, I don't know. Let me check." Sarah flipped open the phone and smiled. "Yep, there's a missed call and a message."

"Thank goodness," Nicole whispered, smiling down at her son, who slept blissfully in her arms.

Sarah punched the button to listen to the voicemail, a smile on her face, too. Strangely enough, however, just a few seconds after she'd punched the button, the smile slowly died.

"Well?" Nicole asked, shifting in bed. "What did he have to say for himself?"

For a moment, Sarah said nothing. She just kind of sat there wearing a stunned expression she couldn't hide.

"An answer today would be nice," Nicole snapped. "What is with you?"

"That message wasn't from Michael. Michael hasn't even bothered to call."

Sarah's smile dwindled to nothing, and she looked down. "So I guess it was my mom who called?"

"No." Sarah pushed the hair from her face.

"Then who was it?" she asked in a voice louder than she'd intended. It made the little one squirm in her arms, and she kind of rocked him, trying to get him back to sleep.

"Jordan." Sarah started pushing some buttons.

"Wait--what are you doing?"

"Deleting it—"

"No! You aren't. Give me the phone." She held out her hand.

Sarah stood. "Nothing good is going to come from that message, Nic. We both know it." She handed her the phone.

Nicole nodded at the baby. "Could you take him for a couple of minutes. Please?"

"All right. Don't say I didn't warn you." She reached down and gently extracted Nick from Nicole's arms, instantly cooing at him to soothe the transition, then she sat in the rocker. Even though she spoke to the baby, Sarah's gaze drifted from the child to her best friend, worry in her eyes.

Nicole caught the concern. She just didn't understand it. Yes, Sarah had always been concerned about her feelings for a guy she could never have. But this? This was something else, and that troubled Nicole. It was like her best friend could see some storm on the horizon she herself could not, and Sarah was doing everything in her power to protect her best friend. But what was she protecting her from? That didn't make sense.

She pushed buttons to get back to voicemail and propped the phone up next to her ear.

"Hey, Nicole, I don't know if you remember me, but it's Jordan.

Jordan Carroway. We had that weekend P.E. class together several years back, and you stepped on a cactus." He paused for a moment. "Anyhow, I guess I could really use someone to talk to. Alyssa and I are getting a divorce, and it's just been kind of unsettling around here, if you know what I mean." Another pause. "Anyway, if you get a chance and want to call me, you've got my number. Bye."

Even after the message had reached the end, Nicole just sat there, her mouth open slightly, "catching flies," her father would have said. Yeah, well, nobody, not even her father, could have prepared her for the way she felt about Jordan even now. It hit like a bolt of lightning, and she gasped, her mind reeling.

Jordan was getting a divorce.

No matter how hard she tried to convince herself she wasn't hearing things and that this really was true, his message was real even though it definitely felt like a poor example of a joke. The humor was lost on her.

Now the irony and cruelty of timing, that was another matter.

"Okay, now would be a good time for you to say something. Otherwise you'll look like Medusa snuck in here and turned you to stone," Sarah said, rocking the baby.

Shaking her head, Nicole finally said, "I'm not sure what to say, Sarah. I'm not even sure I heard that right."

"Bullshit."

Nicole scanned all the recent calls not because she thought her best friend was lying but because she couldn't quite believe Michael hadn't thought enough about how far along she was even to call and check on her. Then again, once Michael put his head in the business clouds, nobody was going to shake him loose. Period.

"There's a sick irony to this," Nicole finally said, shaking her head. Of course right now she should've been laughing at this hand of cards she'd been dealt, but nothing felt funny.

"What do you mean?"

"My husband flies out the morning I go into labor and I can't reach him, but the guy I was crazy about in college calls me. If that isn't a sick cosmic joke, I don't know what is." In disgust, she set the phone on the rolling table near her bed.

"Yeah, well, there is that." Sarah peered at the baby. "At least you got a cute little boy out of the deal."

Nicole eyed the phone and picked it up again. As she started dialing, Sarah asked, "Oh, are you trying Michael again?"

"No." She set the phone up to her ear even as she saw her best friend frantically trying to catch her attention and tell her to hang up, as if that would work.

"Are you insane?" Sarah whispered loudly. "He's getting a divorce!"

"May I speak to Jordan, please?" She paused. "Oh, hey, Jordan. It's me."

Sarah immediately began shaking her head in disbelief. Then she whispered to Nick, "Your momma's lost the last of her brain cells, just so you know."

"I'm sorry to hear about your divorce." Nicole sounded earnest. Then again, Sarah knew it was probably because she really did feel badly for him. "Yeah, well, even if you thought it had been coming for a while, that doesn't make it any easier, and I wish you didn't have to go through that." Nicole looked down at the IV in her hand and wished they would get rid of it. She hated it with a passion because it made everything so difficult--not to mention that her hand was starting to swell from all the fluid and that if she moved it wrong her hand ached, which meant she only had one hand, really, with which she could even hold the phone.

Sarah watched her and knew the reason Nicole was avoiding eye contact was that even though Sarah didn't ask, she knew Nicole had feelings for Jordan Carroway, and this wasn't a message she needed to hear, especially when Michael decided to be lawyer of the year and leave town right now.

"Oh, I'm fine," Nicole said, smiling slightly. "I just had a baby boy, and he's awesome! So beautiful. I wish you could see him."

At that, Sarah glared at her, not quite believing what she'd just heard. Was Nicole truly that insane? Jordan didn't even have a place in her life anymore. He shouldn't even have been calling her because they were really anything but platonic friends. There had been something between them from the first, and no matter what, there was still something between them. There would always be something between them.

Nicole probably would have continued the conversation just to spite her best friend, but when she heard another call coming in, she pulled the phone back and checked out the display to find out the caller was Michael.

"Look, Jordan, I'm sorry, but I have to go. Michael is calling, and I need to talk to him." A pause. "Okay. Bye."

Nicole disconnected and handed the phone back to her best friend. "Talk to him. Tell him I'm asleep or something."

"Nic—"

"Please." There was something deep and hurt in Nicole's eyes and Sarah knew that it probably had to do with Michael always being gone and suddenly Jordan being divorced. She knew there were difficult currents, but she wasn't sure how to help her friend navigate. In the end, the only thing she figured she could do was the take the phone as she was asked.

"Hey, Michael. Where've you been?" Sarah stared at her friend as she started to pace the room, holding both the baby and the cell as Nicole looked out the window, her expression suddenly unsure and fragile. Sarah glanced at her. "No, she's asleep right now. She was in labor for a few hours, and now she's exhausted." Another pause. "Yes, Michael. She had the baby. Without you. Next time check your damned messages. Better yet, stay home."

Sarah disconnected the phone and silenced it, knowing Michael would probably call back, not that either of them felt much like talking to him. Sarah set the phone on the table and kissed the baby's head, taking comfort in his sweet baby smell. Although she wanted to say this was all about Michael being stupid, she knew better. Although Nicole and Michael had at first seemed perfect for each other, there were subtle indicators that things had gone wrong. Now, for the first time, there was a noticeable tear in the fabric of their marriage which neither of them could downplay. Sarah doubted that Michael would see the error of his ways. He'd always put the job first, but Nicole recognized that there was something wrong on a much deeper level.

## Chapter Twelve

Jordan had been driving around for about an hour and had yet to arrive anywhere. He wasn't even sure where he thought he had was going. Probably he was just going through the motions of having somewhere to be before he drove to his parents' house. He hadn't seen them in a few years—not since he and Alyssa had moved to Kansas, as a matter of fact--and that had been long before everything in Jordan's life had blown up.

His parents were expecting to find him happily married and working on starting a family, not divorced with no kids. He raked his fingers through his hair and pulled into a small coffee shop, just another way of stalling, no doubt, but he wasn't ready to face all the questions he knew he couldn't answer. Could anyone put into words the reasons for a marriage's demise? Sure, perhaps it had had something to do with not being able to have kids. Maybe that had been the fault line. But there had to be more, and there was. It just wasn't something Jordan thought he could find a way to sum up. And did the reasons really matter? Would knowing them precisely change anything? No, it wouldn't, so Jordan would rather take the cowardly way out and slip into the shop, grab some java, and read the newspaper so that when his mom decided to gossip--and she would--he would be prepared for all the details.

Jordan looked at his watch: 10:07. He scanned the empty shop, grabbed a newspaper from an empty table, and took a seat in a back booth. He'd no more than sat down when a waitress walked over with a pen and pad.

"Can I get you something?" She was an attractive blonde, totally not Jordan's type, not that he was even remotely looking for his type considering the way the last relationship he'd had had played out. Nonetheless, here she was, peering at him with big blue eyes and a smile that said she wanted more than to take his order. Of course she did.

Trouble was, he didn't.

"Could I get a cup of decaf and some cream, please?" he asked, unfolding the paper.

The waitress nodded. "Okay. Anything else?"

"Nope. That'll be it. Thanks."

He looked at the paper, pretending he didn't see her lingering there as though waiting for him to ask for her number or something else, and after a minute she eased away, leaving him to read in peace before setting a cup of coffee in front of him along with some cream.

Around him, he heard the typical sounds of any eatery—pans clanging, grease sizzling, people chatting. Normally Jordan would have been distracted by it, but today, he just kept replaying the last conversation he'd had with Alyssa—the day she'd told him she wanted a divorce. She'd said it wasn't all about not having kids, but she'd refused to go into detail. He didn't believe she was cheating on him, and he damned sure wasn't cheating on her, so what did that say for marital vows? Did anything last anymore? He wasn't sure.

He started scanning the headlines, only taking half an interest in the words he'd read before moving on to the next section. He came to the obituary section and started to flip the page when one of the names caught his eye: Edward O'Roarke.

Could there be any relation?

For a moment he blinked, staring at the picture of the bald man with intense blue eyes that peered back at him. He looked about old enough, Jordan guessed, not that he would have thought this man would have been related to Nicole. They were as different as night and day, really.

Still, the spelling of the last name wasn't all that common, and just in case it was a family member of Nicole's he felt obligated to keep reading. He was almost to the end of the obituary when he stumbled onto the connection. Edward O'Roarke was Nicole's father, meaning that even though he dreaded telling his own parents about the demise of his marriage, what Nicole was suffering through was far worse and something that demanded his attention. He could forget that the times they had spoken were few and far between, but he would never be able to forgive himself if he didn't at least go to the funeral and check on her to make sure she was okay. She did deserve that much, at least.

He scanned the obituary, gleaning the details of a life he had never known. Nicole's father had been a deacon in a church. He'd had only one child, and he had been a high school history teacher before retiring. He'd still been married to Nicole's mother, and Nicole was still married because the paper listed a son-in-law—one Michael Adams. Lingering on that thought, Jordan tried to picture someone who physically went with Nicole, yet all he kept seeing was himself. Talk about wishful thinking. He turned back to the newspaper.

Ed O'Roarke's death had been very sudden—a car wreck.

Jordan felt the pit of his stomach knotting as he realized just how much of a mess Nicole's life probably felt. As if it weren't painful enough to lose a loved one, losing him without warning seemed so much more devastating. There had been no time to get used to the loss, no chance to say all the things which needed to be said to continue on without him for a lifetime. His jaw clenched, and he hoped Michael Adams was there for her, taking care of her as he should be.

One last glance at the obituary revealed the last information that he needed to know—details of the funeral. Leaning back in his booth, he realized that either Jordan was extremely lucky or someone was watching out for him. The funeral would take place in a couple of hours at a nearby church.

Glancing down, he quickly realized he wasn't exactly dressed formally, but if he knew anything at all about Nicole, that small detail wouldn't really matter. It would be about him taking the time to attend rather than the clothes he might be wearing. He knew that because Alyssa had always been one who stood on ceremony, and Nicole was nothing like his ex.

Refolding the paper, he leaned back as the waitress brought him the coffee and cream. Her smile invited him once again to ask her out, and he shook his head, knowing he was in no way ready to jump back into the dating pool. Granted, he'd always landed on his feet before, and he'd always had plenty of girls to go out with, but his head still wasn't on finding someone to wile away time with. He didn't even feel like he knew himself anymore, and adding someone else to that mix would be was a mistake until he got things under control.

To that end, he just smiled politely at the friendly waitress and turned his attention back to the newspaper as he flipped from the obituary page to the local section. This was where his mother got a lot of rumor-fodder. Taking a sip, he read through one story about a local charity for children, the black-and-white picture there revealing three ladies, one of whom was his mother. A smile lit his face, and he wondered why his mom hadn't said anything--or perhaps she had and he hadn't paid attention when he should have. Maybe since reading of Ed O'Roarke's death, he was starting to see his own parents in a new light, as people who would at some point be taken from him. That though unsettled him, and he forced himself to read the article beneath his mom's picture so he could ask her about it. Then he scanned through the rest of the paper.

When the waitress came to give him his check, she hedged close and smiled again. "So, are you from around here?" Her fingers still held the check by the edge as it lay on the table, as though she wasn't quite ready to let it go.

Jordan shrugged. "Not really. I'm just passing through. Sorry."

She nodded reluctantly. "Okay." Her fingers eased from the check, and she said, "Well, have a nice day."

"Thanks." He pointed to the newspaper. "Could I possibly take this with me?"

"Sure. An old man just left it after he'd finished his coffee."

"Thanks."

The waitress nodded one last time and then walked away, pulling out her pad again as she spotted a couple darting into the restaurant. At that point, Jordan noticed the overcast sky had finally opened, pouring rain down, just like the last time he'd been here, causing residents to scurry down the street, hurrying toward their destinations so they wouldn't have to swim. Amazing how some things never changed.

For a moment, Jordan just watched the rain as it fell in a silent deluge. He'd always loved the rain, but he seriously doubted that either he or Nicole would love it in a few hours, when they were both at the funeral. The best thing that could be said for it was that it would effectively disguise the tears.

He purposely waited for a while longer, putting off the inevitable. He finished the paper, set out a healthy tip for the waitress, and paid for his coffee before walking out into the deluge. As he stood unlocking his door, he glanced around at all the little shops that had been there since before he'd grown up. At once, he felt grateful to be home, even though he knew his parents probably weren't going to take his news very well, not considering they had managed to hold their marriage together no matter what, and even Jordan had to admit that couldn't have been easy. Somehow they had something he and Alyssa had lacked, but even to this day he couldn't begin to say what that magic ingredient had been.

He wondered if Nicole knew.

* * *

Nicole lay in bed, staring at the ceiling as the baby slept in a bassinet next to her. She glanced over at her son, marveling at how lucky she'd gotten for him to sleep through the night at only four months, and staring at him kept much darker thoughts at bay—thoughts of her father lying in his casket, looking nothing like the man she'd grown up admiring.

Why couldn't the funeral home people get it right? Ed O'Roarke wasn't some kind of new medium to create a work of art out of. He'd been her father. He should look like the man, imperfections and all, not someone she'd never known.

Tears stung her eyes, and she tried not to think about the way the last few days had played out, all the places she'd been with her mom, trying to keep everything together. Nicole hadn't broken down once. Instead, she'd drawn the numbness around her like a thick blanket which would block out all the horrible things she didn't want to deal with right now.

Her mother had been a mess, acting like she'd been doped up when it had just been grief, and Nicole knew she never would've been able to get through putting the funeral together alone. So it had fallen to Nicole, not that Nicole minded. It had just forced her to remember things she wanted no part of, and she knew she didn't have time for her heart to break, not today of all days. She had to get through this service. All the people at Daddy's church were expecting it, and most of them had known Nicole since she'd been really young. She was a deacon's daughter and she couldn't fall apart. Period.

Her cell rang, and she resisted the temptation to simply open it and greet whomever was calling. It turned out to be a good thing, really, considering the caller was Michael. Michael in Japan. How convenient. Yes, he had explained to her that this was a critical case he couldn't miss. There were millions of dollars at stake. What could she offer that would make coming home so necessary? It was, after all, just her father, and Michael had told her she was strong enough so that his presence would be completely unnecessary.

Unnecessary, her ass--Michael was a moron.

She tossed the phone against the wall, and doing so must have broken it because the ringing stopped. Sitting up, she looked out the window at a grey, storm-tossed sky. Rain spewed from it, gently tapping at her window, and she sighed and shook her head. Yes, rain had been the perfect set-up for a funeral, but she hated the thought of her mother standing out in the cold and wet. It was bad enough that right now Nicole was sleeping in her old bedroom just to keep an eye on her mom. She was worried about when the numbness finally wore off and what would come next.

Nicole glanced at the clock and realized she had only a little while before she was expected to be sitting in a front-row pew, facing a casket she couldn't bear even to look at. Maybe that was why corpses never resembled the people who'd lived in those bodies. Maybe the funeral directors somehow thought disguising them would make it so much easier just to get through the service. They were wrong--oh so wrong.

As she forced herself to get up and go to the closet to find something to wear to the service, Nicole thought she heard noises from the kitchen below. She took one last glance at the baby and headed that way, an unsettled feeling in the pit of her stomach as she wondered what her mom was doing. She took the stairs two at a time and headed into the kitchen to find her mom standing in her cotton nightgown and robe in front of a skillet full of eggs. She had buried her face in both hands, and her normally styled platinum blonde hair fell in disarray around her face. Nicole glanced at the table and saw three place settings when there should have been two. She swallowed hard, strode to her mom, and wrapped her arms around her.

"Mom, it's okay. It's really okay."

Her mother leaned against her and sobbed loudly. Nicole rocked them both gently back and forth, hoping doing so would ease things. She didn't know what else to do. She felt tears pooling in her own eyes and kept trying to blink them away. She didn't want them to come out. After today, she'd deal with them. Just not today.

It seemed to take forever before her mother finally calmed down and slowly pulled away to look at Nicole who smiled. "That's better," Nicole whispered, kissing her forehead. "What happened, Mom?"

Margaret O'Roarke looked at her daughter and wiped the tears away with the back of her hand. "I got out of bed and came down here to fix breakfast. I was already halfway through when I remembered your father was…gone." Her voice shook with tears, but this time she managed to keep them from getting the best of her. "And now there's all these eggs." She slipped her hand over her mouth as though trying to keep the words tucked inside, where they couldn't hurt anyone.

Although Nicole had no appetite, especially for eggs, she looked at the skillet and said, "Well, I guess there's more for us, Mom. I'm really hungry, okay?"

Margaret nodded and looked at the floor as Nicole strode to the table and collected the plates. She piled eggs on one and then filled the other. "Let's eat." She set the unused plate back in the cabinet and carried the others to the table. Then she went back and grabbed her mom's arm, leading her.

Once they had both been seated, Nicole took her mom's hand and offered grace before they ate.

Jordan sat at the back of the crowded sanctuary. Yes, he was under-dressed, but he didn't care. He glanced at his watch, feeling uncomfortable in a church he didn't know, surrounded by people he didn't recognize. Then again, he reminded himself, this was really for Nicole, so his feeling comfortable wasn't really been part of the bargain.

Leaning back in his pew, he realized Nicole was coming in. Her long, dark hair had been drawn up, and she wore a loose, black dress that flowed around her as she linked arms with an older woman, probably her mother, as they walked to the front and sat. Jordan leaned forward, a frown on his lips, as he looked for other family members. Where was Nicole's husband? Why wasn't he here?

Yet even as he looked no one else came, and the service started. Although Jordan tried to pay attention, he found himself staring at Nicole, worrying more and more that she might be alone during this awful time. What kind of a man was Michael Adams? He should have been here with her. She deserved that.

The service blurred past, and Jordan followed the other cars out to the gravesite even though it was pouring, and while the church had been filled with mourners, the number quickly dwindled when it came to the cemetery. Still, Jordan knew he had to go. He kept watching Nicole, worried she might break down, but she remained in control. Others might have thought it was a lack of feeling, but he knew better. She was just trying to get through the worst day of her life the only way she could.

Jordan stood in the back even though the rain spewed toward him despite the tarp overhead. There was no keeping the storm out, and the preacher tried to speak to be heard over the rain pelting down, which couldn't have been easy. Jordan tried to keep an eye on Nicole but the man in front of him kept shifting his weight from one foot to the other, constantly forcing Jordan to move to see around him.

Jordan folded his arms across his chest, trying to ignore the wind and wet, never mind that the cold wouldn't seem to leave him alone. The graveside service was thankfully short, and when it ended, he waited until most of the attendees had already gone before he made his way to the front to express his condolences.

She was impassive as he stood before her, and only when he said, "I'm so sorry for your loss" and reached down to squeeze her hand did she look up. At first, there was only the unfocused glaze of grief in her expression, but then, recognition dawned as her fingers wrapped around his possessively, trembling. The breath caught in her throat.

He could sense she was about to say something, but the words died before they came out. Nicole looked at her mother. Her lips closed, sealing whatever she wanted to ask away, so he said, "I'm driving back to the church. I'll talk to you there."

"Okay." The response came out as a relieved whisper. He looked down at her hand, and she eased it free. The rain had picked up, and on the way back to the Jeep, he ran, not that it mattered. By the time he got there, he was soaked.

He shoved his keys into the ignition and started the engine so the wipers could clear the glass just as Nicole and her mother slowly made their way to the limo. Nicole had wrapped her arm around her mother and lead her to the open door of the limo. As Nicole's mom made her way inside, Nicole turned and looked at his vehicle. Their gazes crossed, and a small smile flitted across her face as if she were saying she was glad he'd come.

He nodded, not knowing whether she could see it then pulled away. As he drove back to the church, the rain came even harder than before—a deluge that made him drive slowly, cautiously. No matter how much he tried to tell himself not to think about Nicole and why in the world her husband had been gone during such a crucial time, he couldn't help himself. Her image came unbidden to his mind, and there was no getting it out once it had arrived. More than once, he'd checked the rear-view mirror, expecting to see the limo, yet the rain obscured everything behind him. It had a similar effect on everything before him as well, so he wavered nervously between the brake and the gas, never quite sure which he would need.

Once back at the church, he parked near the front and turned the engine off to wait for Nicole. It didn't take long for the limo to ease into the lot and pull beneath the awning where Nicole and her Mom got out. That was Jordan's cue. He yanked the key from the ignition and got out, darting toward the awning as well, just as Nicole emerged from the back seat and gently pulled her mother out by the arm.

Another woman stood there, waiting as well, and even though he didn't recognize her, she gave him a very strange look, as though she knew him. In her arms, she cradled a baby swaddled tightly in a blanket. That's when a few things clicked. Whomever the woman was, she probably held Nicole's baby. Of course, that still didn't explain where Michael was.

All the women glanced up as he darted under the awning, and while he thought perhaps it had to do with looking like a drowned rat, he was probably wrong on that score as well. As Nicole started to speak, the woman with the baby stepped toward her, trying to distract her. Nicole nodded and said to Jordan, "Hang on a sec."

She turned toward the woman. "Sarah, can you drive Mom back to the house and watch Nick for a couple of hours? Please?"

Sarah looked from Nicole back to him before finally, reluctantly nodding. "All right. Just help me get the car loaded first."

Nicole touched my arm. "Just give me a couple of minutes and I'll be right there."

"Okay." Jordan leaned against the wall and folded his arms across his chest.

Sarah gave him one last look and shook her head. She leaned

toward him and whispered, "If you hurt her, I'll kill you."

Not sure he'd heard right, he straightened and asked, "Excuse me?"

Instead of answering, Sarah gave him a withering look and carried the baby through the rain to a blue Honda. Nicole wrapped her arm around her mom and led her to the car as well. Their steps were slow, as though neither could feel the rain, and Jordan suspected they couldn't feel anything but the overwhelming grief that wouldn't release them. As Nicole loaded her mom up, more than once her gaze drifted to him, as though she were afraid he'd leave before she could talk to him.

Still, he kept puzzling over Sarah's response, unsure what to make of it even as Nicole headed back, now jogging toward him despite the strappy sandals she wore. He was tempted to tell her to be careful because the Nicole he'd known was far from graceful and probably would have fallen in the rain had she tried that.

Instead, Sarah jogged up next to him and lingered there, her breath coming out in soft, shallow gasps. As he stared at her, he could see the fine lines settling around her eyes, probably more from the stresses of the last week than actually showing her age. She seemed pale and vulnerable, which only troubled him all the more.

She took a deep breath and swallowed hard. "How did you know about my dad?" Her voice twisted at the end, as though she were barely holding the floodgates of her pain shut.

He shrugged and watched her bat her bangs back as rainwater dripped from them, threatening to fall into her eyes. "I was on my way to see my parents. I stopped to get coffee and read the newspaper. I just happened to spot the obit. Nicole, I am so sorry." He touched her shoulder.

"That makes two of us," she managed, appearing even more shaken. "Can we go somewhere? Please?"

"Of course." He stepped toward her and without realizing it set his palm at the middle of her back as he nodded toward the Jeep. "Looks like we're going to have to make a run for it again. You up for that?"

She nodded. "Ready whenever you are." The words sounded playful enough, but she seemed worn out.

"Let's go."

The two darted into the rain, and he ran to her side first to unlock her door before getting in himself. For a moment, he just sat there, dripping all over the place. Then he shoved the key into the ignition. "Gotta love this weather."

Nicole brushed the hair from her face. "If you say so."

"So where do want to go?"

"Some place quiet and dry?" She folded her arms across her chest as though trying to disguise the fact she was shivering.

Figuring the engine was still warm enough from his earlier drive, Jordan flipped on the heater. "Maybe that will help." He pulled out of the lot and headed to a small Italian restaurant where he remembered a quiet and comfortable atmosphere, probably two things she could use more than anything.

Although Jordan tried to think about what he would say to her, his mind kept coming up blank, and she stared out the window, a million miles away. When they finally pulled into the restaurant lot, he saw a handful of cars, which meant they weren't going to have to worry about overcrowding.

"You ready?" he asked, nodding toward the entrance.

"Yeah." They got out and rushed through the rain, and once they'd stepped into the foyer, they both batted at their hair. Rain spattered the floor around them, and they were grateful the restaurant was warm and dry.

Jordan laid his hand at the middle of her back and nudged her towards a sign that read, "Please wait to be seated." A short hostess walked up to them.

"How many?"

"Just us," Jordan said, watching the hostess pick up menus and silverware.

"All right. Follow me." She lead them around various tables to a booth toward the back, where Nicole took one side and he slid into the other. "Your waitress will be with you in a moment. Enjoy your meal."

"Thank you," Jordan said, picking up his menu. He realized Nicole hadn't touched hers, and judging by that faraway look in her eyes, she wasn't about to, either. "Not eating isn't going to help. It's only going make you feel more run down and help get you sick."

"I'm just not hungry," she said, closing her eyes as though suddenly seeing something she couldn't bear to look at.

Without thought, Jordan reached across the table and grasped her hand gently which forced her to look at him. "I know this isn't easy for you. I can't pretend I've gone through it because I haven't, but I'm serious. You do need to eat, even if you don't feel like it."

She gave him an almost imperceptible nod and picked up the menu as the waitress appeared to take their drink order. They both ordered water while considering other choices. Finally, when she had reached her decision, Nicole closed the menu and looked at him.

"I was surprised to see you again."

He shrugged. "Yeah, well, I was kind of surprised to be there. I'm just sorry we had to meet again under such difficult circumstances. I can't begin to fathom your loss."

Sighing, she swallowed the tears that wanted to come. "It's not so much about me, Jordan. I'm worried about my mom. My parents were married a long time, and this is going to be hard for her. She depended on him for so much, and now he's just...gone."

Even as Nicole spoke, she recognized doing so would be her

undoing. She just couldn't seem to keep it from coming out, and then the tears came flooding to her eyes, paralyzing her. She tried to cover her face but knew Jordan would still see, which made the pain even worse.

Jordan quickly scooted around to her side of the booth. He sat next to her and slipped his arms around her, burying her head against his chest. Perhaps he couldn't stop the pain, but he could at least give her a safe and private place to grieve. More than once, he waved the waitress away, mouthing that they would order in a minute, and right then and there he didn't care how long it took for Nicole to rebound enough to pull back on her own.

Jordan rubbed her back slowly, waiting. Part of him felt he had been waiting forever to hold her, while the other part kept reminding him about Michael Adams and the ring on her finger. Whatever was going on on that front, he had no business inserting himself into the middle of it, and he damned well intended simply to stay an old friend who wanted nothing but the best for Nicole. That part was true enough, after all.

When Nicole finally withdrew, her face was red and splotchy, and she brushed her hand across her cheeks, trying to wipe away the last of the tears. She looked at him with eyes that appeared a light, luminous brown.

"You okay?" he finally asked.

"I guess as okay as I can be." She shook her head. "I'm probably a mess."

He shook his head. "No, not really, but if you want to wash your face, it might help. Just tell me what you want, and I'll order for you."

"Spaghetti and meatballs, with a salad and Italian dressing."

"You got it." He slid back to his side while she walked to the bathroom, and he watched her go, amazed by how she looked so much the same as she had since the last time they'd seen one another. He shook his head. So much had changed on all fronts since that day, and more than once, he wished he could go back and make different choices. It would have been so much easier.

The waitress came, and he ordered for both of them before Nicole slipped back into the booth a bit later, her face less splotchy. He could tell by the way she was averting her gaze she wasn't comfortable with the emotions swirling through her, and he didn't blame her. He just wished he knew some way to make this easier for her.

"I ordered for us," he said, taking a sip of his water.

"Thanks."

For a moment, he debated on whether his next line of questions was too personal, but in the end, he asked, anyway. "So where is your husband? I thought he would be at the funeral."

"He couldn't get away from work," she said, unwrapping her utensils and setting her napkin in her lap. Jordan got the distinct impression doing so was more about keeping her hands busy than anything else.

He wanted to explode at that excuse. He didn't have a clue what Michael Adams did to support his family. He couldn't even venture a guess. But he knew anybody could get off for a death in the family. It didn't matter what line of work he was in. It mattered more whether he'd even wanted to get off, which clearly he hadn't.

Nicole must have felt him stare because she finally looked up. "It's no big deal, Jordan. I'm doing okay."

"Really? Because I think you might need a little help, and he should be here."

Chewing her bottom lip, Nicole knew he was right. Michael should have been here. More and more, she was beginning to feel as though she had a roommate, not a spouse, and it was getting to her, but dragging that up right now wouldn't ease the pain in her heart over losing her dad. So she focused instead on a different topic.

"So what happened between you and your wife?"

Unprepared for that, Jordan felt his whole body stiffen. "I wish I knew, Nicole. God, I wish I knew."

The waitress appeared with their salads, and for a moment there was a deep silence between them as though neither knew what to say. Then Nicole looked at her food and took a bite, suddenly more grateful to be near Jordan than she could have expected.

"Nothing has turned out quite as I expected, you know?" She brushed the hair from her eyes and focused on the salad in front of her.

Jordan unwrapped his silverware. "Join the club. This isn't the life I had in mind, either." He reached out and took her hand. "But there is something I want you to keep in mind, okay?" He waited until she'd nodded before continuing. "No matter what is going's on, you can always call me, no matter how rough things get. Okay?"

Nicole stared at him with those beautiful eyes, and for a moment, it seemed as though the rest of the world had ceased to exist.

She nodded slowly. "Okay."

## Chapter Thirteen

"It was my father's funeral, Michael. You should have been there." Nicole stared at her husband where they both sat at the prepared table. Between them were plates of eggs, sausage, and toast, but Michael was the only one eating. As usual, not much bothered his appetite, including a stressful conversation.

"The fact that it was your father's service isn't lost on me, Nicole. But I have a job that requires extensive travelling. Hell, I was travelling when we met, if you recall. As much as my absence upsets you, one of us does have to work and pay the pills. That happens to be me."

He reached out and speared another sausage link, his gaze never meeting her eyes.

Nicole scooted the chair back and strode around the kitchen. "You are amazing. Truly amazing." She shook her head and paced, her fingers wanting to grab something, anything, and just throw it to get some of the fury out. Instead, she turned to get a glass out of the cabinet so she could pour herself some juice.

For once, he looked up from his meal. "What exactly do you expect from me? You like this nice house and the life we lead. Well, that does come at a cost, and we both know it."

She whirled, her grip so tight on the glass that her knuckles turned white. "What do I expect? Are you kidding? I expect that when I'm close to delivering a baby, your baby, that you stick around just in case I go into labor. I expect that when a family member dies, especially someone like my dad, that you cancel whatever important plans you might have to be with me."

He shook his head and kept eating. "Yeah, well, with my job, you expect a lot, Nicole, and I can't always give you that. I told you from the start that I was out of town a lot."

The juice tumbled from her hand, and the small bit of control she was still exercising snapped as she hurled the glass against the wall, sensing that they had reached an impasse. Michael was more worried about his job than his marriage, and Nicole didn't know how much more she could take of it.

As she started to fly out of the room, Michael looked up and said, "You might want to get that glass up before you step on it and get some in your feet. We both know you never wear shoes in the house."

Instead of answering, she blurred past him and ran upstairs and into their bathroom, quickly locking the door. It wasn't that she expected Michael to come after her and reasonably talk this out. He didn't see the need. He wasn't the one 'given to temper tantrums' as he called them, and he would never understand Nicole's anger at his absence. How many times had they been over this and over this? Nothing good ever came of it. Michael maintained his jovial attitude the whole time he remained home as though he expected with enough time and distance from the fighting that Nicole would come to understand his far more mature view on things.

Even though she tried to keep her emotions in check, they ended up flooding down her face as she leaned against the door, grateful for the distance between the two of them. She raked her fingers through her hair and slowly slid down the door until her bottom touched the floor. Yet even there she could not escape the pain ripping through her. She brought her knees to her chest and folded her arms, giving her head a place to rest until the tears finally stopped, and even though she waited in hopes that Michael might actually come upstairs to apologize, God forbid, the moment she heard the engine of his vehicle start, she knew better. Michael just didn't operate on feelings.

She leaned back and smacked her head against the wall, one pain to take away the remnants of the other as the hurt welled up inside of her. Of course another thought came to her, one that should have come sooner but she had always rejected it before it ever saw the light of day. Trouble was it seemed to be getting more and more plausible.

Could Michael be having an affair? Is that what was keeping him so busy?

She stiffened at that thought. Could he really be that cold inside? She forced herself to stand up and peer at her reflection. The woman she saw looking back was pale, thin, and unkempt—so far removed from who Nicole had planned to be that it wasn't even funny. For months she'd been telling herself that it came with being pregnant. Now that the baby had come she found herself saying that it came with being tired. But this wasn't who she was. She knew that much.

Taking a deep breath, she brushed through her hair and tried to put herself into some kind of order before she went and dressed Nick to head to her mom's. While Margaret O'Roarke hadn't felt much like talking lately, Nicole needing some advice about Michael, and she really didn't want to talk to Sarah about this one. She knew Sarah would feel that the real reason she was having doubts had to do with Jordan which just wasn't true. Whatever there might be between her and Jordan, she wasn't allowing herself to dwell on it because it couldn't go anywhere. He might be divorced, but she was in the middle of a marriage she refused to throw away by cheating. She just wished she could say the same of Michael.

"Do you want some tea?" Margaret asked, pouring a cup for

herself. Her hand wavered slightly, probably due to all the emotions that had been running high since Ed had died, and of course Margaret believed enough tea could fix anything no matter how difficult it was.

"No, Mom. I'm fine." She pulled a chair out and sat at the dining room table, waiting for her mom to join her. Nick peacefully slept in the basinet by her feet. She figured he'd wake in a couple of hours and demand to be fed.

"So what's all this urgency about?" Margaret carried her cup and saucer to the table and sat down. Then she snapped her fingers. "Oh, I should get the shortbread cookies I bought. Would you like some of those?"

Nicole caught her mom's arm. "No, Mom. I just need to talk to you. No cookies required."

"Well, maybe I'd like some cookies." Margaret said and got up. "Sure you don't want any tea?"

Sensing that her mother wasn't going to let go of the idea behind the tea, she finally relented. "Sure, why not? I'd love a cup of tea." In reality, she hated tea. She'd just never had the heart to tell her mom that, not considering what a panacea Margaret seemed to think it was.

"Now that's a good girl." Margaret set the cookies on a small plate and carried it to the table, putting it closer to Nicole than her own chair. It didn't take much for Nicole to realize the cookies had been for her all along.

"Can you sit, Mom?" Nicole asked, feeling like the pressure building inside of her was going to spew loose at any moment.

"Just let me get your tea." She pulled down a cup and quickly filled it. "Would you like anything with it?"

"Just you." Nicole patted the seat next to her.

"Very well." Margaret carried the cup and saucer to her daughter and set it front of her. "Now be careful. The tea is really hot." Then she eased down in the chair, her trembling fingers gently curling around her own cup so she could take a sip. Then she asked, "So what seems to be the trouble, Nicole?"

*Where do I start?* Nicole thought. "It's Michael."

Margaret took a cookie. "What about him? He's got a great job, and the two of you have a beautiful baby. What more could you ask for?"

*Someone who is actually here when I need him to be*, Nicole thought. Still, she forced herself to take a deep breath. Although she knew her mom liked Michael, she kind of figured that Margaret would understand. Now she wasn't so sure.

"He's never around, Mom. He's always on the road with his job, and here lately I've begun to wonder if it's more that."

Margaret took another sip and frowned while staring ahead, lost in her own thoughts. "What are you saying, Nicole?"

Up until now Nicole hadn't actually said anything. Saying it meant that it could be real, and that was the last thing she really wanted to think about. Yet she wasn't stupid enough to believe the whole out-of-sight, out-of-mind thing. Averting her eyes, Nicole finally just plunged into the conversation. "I think he might be having an affair and that's why he's gone so much."

Although Margaret was taking another cookie, the moment she heard her daughter's words, her fingers fumbled and she dropped it. "An affair? You really believe Michael could do that?"

Studying her mom's face, Nicole quickly realized that while she could believe it about Michael, Margaret was a bit more skeptical. Then again, her mom had a track record for always giving people the benefit of the doubt. It was like a compulsion with her. This only made Nicole second-guess her own thoughts more. Like she really needed that.

"He's gone a lot, Mom, especially during important times, times when he should be here." She looked down at her hair, checking the ends to see if she needed to get a trim.

"He has a job. That does limit how much he can be around, Nicole. You knew that when you married him." Margaret picked up her tea cup and took a sip, carefully avoiding eye contact with her daughter.

"Maybe I did know that he worked a lot," she admitted. "But everybody has days they can take off when a wife is expecting a baby or someone in the family has died. Yet Michael never takes off. Our relationship is somewhere at the bottom of his list, and I hate it."

Unable to take just sitting anymore, she got up and paced the room. Her mother watched her walk around the room. "Wearing the carpet down isn't going to make anything any better, and you know it." She took another bite of cookie. "Have to talked to Michael about any of this?"

Nicole whirled. "You mean have I accused him of cheating?"

"Well, yes."

Nicole strode back to the table. "Mom, I might be nuts, but I'm not going to say anything unless I have proof. If I do find proof then I will definitely confront him."

Although Nicole was really angry about her husband's less than attentive behavior, the thought of actually confronting him made her head spin. If she did catch him, it was going to mean starting divorce proceeding, and the last thing she wanted to be was a single mom with a son.

Margaret stood and walked to her daughter so she could wrap her arm around her. "Baby, maybe you are just overreacting. Maybe Michael really is just working so hard and that's why you never see him."

Although Nicole wanted to argue with her mom because her gut told her that Michael was cheating, she felt her resolve caving in as her mother wrapped her arms around her in a gesture of comfort. It would be so much easier for everyone if she were wrong. Maybe she was just really angry at him for missing both the birth of their son and her father's funeral. Perhaps that was clouding everything.

"It just feels like everything is off."

Her mother gave her one last reassuring squeeze and released her. "Your daddy just died, Nicole. Did you expect that everything would feel normal after that?" She nodded to the table where their cups sat. "Maybe we should get back to our tea. It's getting cold after all."

Without waiting for Nicole to say anything, Margaret walked back to the table and sat to enjoy her tea. Nicole glanced at her mother, struck by how Margaret seemed to be so happy with the smallest things. That was one thing Nicole's daddy had really loved about her mother. It made it so easy to get a smile out of her. Of course that just made Nicole wonder if she were just being too hard on her husband, that maybe considering his work schedule that she was expecting far too much from him. She just didn't know.

For the rest of the day Nicole drove around. She went the park, to the mall, to the arts and crafts store. Anywhere but home. Her last words to Michael had been cast out in anger, and she really didn't feel any less angry at him. She had thought perhaps talking to her mom might ease the fury, but it hadn't.

As she carried the a small sack from the drug store, Nicole tried to think of another time they'd fought like this, but she couldn't. Of course perhaps that might have been because Michael was gone so much. It took both people being present or at least corresponding over the phone to argue so it only stood to reason that perhaps the reason their marriage had been so peaceful was because of absence and distance not love and devotion.

Nick cooed at her, another sign that even he was tired and had had a long day.

She shook her head, glancing at the blackness around her. Even though she'd been gone for hours without ever telling Michael where she headed, he hadn't called to check on her. Was he having an affair? Or was he just so sure that he was right about everything that he never doubted their marriage could start to fall apart when both of them failed to nurture the life they'd forged together.

Glancing upstairs, she saw that the light was off. Michael, a creature of habit, had probably gone to bed already, completely convinced that wherever Nicole and Nick were, they were both fine and would return home soon. How did anyone have that kind of faith. She worried non-stop whenever Michael traveled and yet he slept so soundly when she hadn't come home by eleven.

Nick started to fuss a little, a sure sign that he was probably hungry so once she slipped into the foyer, she headed into the kitchen to fix him a bottle to help him drift to sleep as she sat in the rocker, gently moving back and forth. It didn't take long for him to drift away.

A sudden yawn confirmed just how exhausted Nicole truly felt and how grateful she was to carry her son to the crib and gently lay him down. Standing there, she stared at his peaceful face, liking the way the moonlight poured down around him. He was so beautiful and amazing. Still, she thought, looking at the paper sack from the drug store, she still had one important thing to get done before she turned in.

In the bathroom, she pulled out the lone content of the sack—a pregnancy test. Even looking at it made her grit her teeth. It wasn't that she didn't want to have another baby. She did. Nick was the brightest spot in her whole world. But right now things were so upended with Michael, and she felt adrift, especially at the thought of him having an affair.

Granted, maybe her mother was right. Maybe it was just a lot of long hours that he worked keeping him away from home all the time, but Nicole didn't feel that was right. When they had dated, Michael hadn't had nearly the trouble with traveling as he did now.

Still, she mused, one thing at a time. And the first thing was peeing on a stick. Once that was accomplished, she sat on the toilet and waited for her future to develop into one or two lines. At first she thought the results were negative, but in the last couple of seconds, a faint second line appeared. Nicole slumped against the back of the toilet and kept staring, as if that would make the second line disappear. She didn't need a baby right now, not with all the stress between her and Michael.

A soft knock at the door made Nicole jump.

"Nicole? You in here?"

*Who else would it be?* She thought savagely. "Just a minute. I'll be right out." She crammed the test, the box, and the directions back into the sack from which they'd come. Trust Michael to find her while she was doing a pregnancy test.

A moment later she emerged, expecting to find Michael standing in the hallway. Instead, he had probably gone back to bed. Shaking her head, she tossed the bag into the trash and headed to her bedroom.

"Hey, you," Michael said in a sleepy voice as he held his arms wide. "C'mere."

Stress tensed her back and shoulders. Still, she forced herself to walk over to the bed and lie next to him, not nearly so comfortable with the dark and his proximity as she had once been. Not five minutes after he wrapped his body around hers, Michael drifted back to sleep. She could tell by his easy exchange of breath. She envied him that. Then again, who's to say what Michael dreamed of.

## Chapter Fourteen

Seven months later.

Jordan had been lying in his apartment for the last hour. More than once, he'd started to drift off, only to jerk awake again. He could blame it on any number of things—trying to get settled, dreams about Alyssa and the divorce. Just plain stress, but somehow it seemed simpler than that, as though an answer was right in front of him. He just didn't know what it was.

The air conditioner had kicked on and off, but the room was incredibly hot. Maybe that was why he just couldn't get settled, no matter how he tried. Shaking his head in disgust, he threw the covers back and strode to the window. Peering out, he spotted a full moon low in the sky with clouds to either side.

It was a beautiful night. Of course, Jordan definitely would have preferred to be sleeping right now because getting to work at eight tomorrow was going to suck. Then again, he hadn't slept well for some time, probably not since he and Alyssa had finally split. Part of the world felt out of kilter. Maybe it was sleeping in a bed big enough for two people. Invariably, he kept waiting for someone to fill the other side, but it wasn't going to happen--or maybe it was just losing both his wife and his best friend at the same time.

It really didn't matter what the reason had been.

As he propped both hands on the sill and looked out into the moonlight, he heard his cell begin to play a Bon Jovi song—"Never Say Goodbye." He glanced at the display: Nicole.

He glanced at the clock. Two-thirty. Could it be things were off in her world as well? There was only one way to find out. He flipped the phone open. "Hello?"

"Jordan?"

He frowned at the sound of Nicole's voice. It had been months since they'd spoken. "Hey, how are you?" he asked, stepping slowly back to the bed so he could ease himself down on the mattress.

"I'm…okay." Her voice wavered slightly, and he sensed that, whatever she might be, okay wasn't it.

"So what made you call at 2:30 in the morning?" He raked his fingers through his hair, unsure what to ask or how to ask it but sensing she wanted to talk just the same. The air conditioner kicked on again, and he glanced toward it.

He heard her inhale sharply. "Oh, my God. I didn't even realize it was that late. I am so sorry."

Without thought, he raised his hand to reassure her, even though he knew she couldn't see it. "It's all right. I was having trouble sleeping, anyway, so you didn't wake me." He took a deep breath. "So I guess I'd like to know what's keeping you up this late." Perhaps he could have said it better, but she had this way of always keeping him on the edge of everything, so he wasn't sure what to say.

"It's just been kind of a rough day." More wavering. Was she crying? He flopped back on the bed as his stomach tightened nervously.

He swallowed hard, not sure how to proceed. "In what way?"

"I should go." She was definitely crying. He could hear it now. "I shouldn't have even called."

"It's okay," he insisted. "Just breathe and talk to me. I don't want you to hang up when you sound this upset."

A pause. He wondered if she would hang up, and if she didn't, he hoped like hell he could figure out what he was doing.

"It's Michael. I think he's…having an affair."

Jordan cringed. Trying to get his reply together, he rubbed his forehead. "What makes you think that, Nicole?"

"He's always gone--always, even when he should be here because it matters." Her voice almost died away at the end, and Jordan could hear her sobbing openly.

"Take a deep breath. Let's think this through, okay?" He rose slowly and started to pace. "How much is he home?"

"Not much--and he's definitely not interested in me when he gets here."

*Crap*, Jordan thought. One was a coincidence. Both of them were kind of pointing to the same thing: an affair. Reluctantly he said, "Well, that does sound kind of suspicious. Is it possible he's just tired?"

"Maybe. I don't know." Her tone shifted slightly, as though she were trying to regain control of her emotions.

"Look, Nicole, I'm not trying to downplay what you're feeling. There's a chance you could be right. I just want you to approach this rationally, and considering how much emotion is invested in your marriage, that isn't so easy to do." He took a deep breath, hoping he'd said at least something right because he sure didn't feel it.

"Yeah, you're definitely right. Maybe I'm the one who's too tired. Jordan?"

"Yeah?" he asked, closing his eyes and trying to imaging her sitting there, her long, dark hair flowing around her face and wide eyes, luminous with pain and tears.

"Sarah and I were going to take a road trip this weekend. I wanted to know if you might be able to meet up with us."

Jordan's shoulders sank, and he tried to tell himself not to even think about this because the last thing he needed to do was insert himself into the middle of a troubled marriage, and it was more than a little obvious by Nicole's tears that her marriage was in trouble. He just didn't know how much, and probably neither would she until it was all said and done.

"I'm not sure that's a good idea, Nicole. It sounds like you've got some things going on, and the last thing I want to do is cause problems."

"We're going to Sunset Beach, North Carolina. I've never been to the ocean."

Jordan smiled. "You're going to love it. I've often thought of moving to one coast or another."

"Will you come?" she asked, her voice painfully soft, subdued by fresh tears. "We're going to be staying at the Causeway Inn. I could book you a room." Her tone was pleading, and he knew he shouldn't accept, but he couldn't seem to help himself.

"Okay. I've got some time off coming. I'll be there around five on Friday. Will that work?"

"Yeah, it'll be great." For the first time since he'd picked up the phone, he thought he heard her smile which made him smile.

A couple of moments later, he finally hung up, but only after he'd felt confident Nicole was in better spirits. He knew he should've said no, but he figured, what the hell? It wasn't like they were going to be alone. They weren't even going to be staying in the same room, and Sarah, her best friend, would be with them. What could go wrong like that?

"You what?" Sarah asked as she pulled into the Causeway Inn's parking lot. Her foot stuttered on the gas as though even it couldn't believe what Nicole had just said. Sarah glared at her best friend, not feeling a bit sorry for her, even in this ninety-degree heat. Yeah, she was eight months pregnant. She had also done something unthinkably stupid.

"I invited Jordan to meet up with us for the weekend." She looked at her watch. "He should be getting here in about thirty minutes or so if he doesn't get held up in traffic."

Shaking her head, Sarah edged into a parking space. "Are you out of your mind, Nic? You said you needed a stress-free weekend, which this was supposed to be."

"Jordan doesn't stress me out." Nicole dabbed at the sweat beading on her forehead.

"No, but he definitely might stress Michael out." Sarah grabbed the key from the ignition and stored them in her purse, still shaking her head in utter disbelief.

"Well, maybe. If he knew. But he'll never find out." Nicole eased herself out of the car, immediately tired from carrying around her daughter, who was due to enter the world next month.

Sarah strode around the car and grabbed her best friend's arm. "Are you insane? Why are you meeting a guy you fell for in college when you're married and about to shoot out baby number two?"

Nicole glared at her and jerked free. "There's nothing wrong with meeting up with an old friend, Sarah. If I were planning on doing something, this would have been a solo trip, and you know it. Besides, why don't you ask Michael about his little extracurricular activities? I'm sure that might clear up a few things."

Nicole didn't wait for Sarah to catch up. Instead, she strode into the lobby and pulled out her credit card. She could see Sarah walking in behind, and as she paid for the room, neither spoke to the other. It appeared they had reached an impasse of sorts, but Nicole didn't care. Sarah was her best friend, not her keeper, and if Nicole wanted to invite Jordan to meet up with them, she was an adult. She knew what her vows were, and she wouldn't break them even if she didn't believe

Michael had kept his intact. Still, that didn't mean it wouldn't be nice to have a little company around. Surely she deserved that much.

Once she'd finished paying, she turned to say something to Sarah when movement at the corner of the lobby drew her attention. She glanced over and found Jordan standing there, both hands shoved awkwardly in his pockets. As their eyes met, they both smiled, and she rushed to him.

"Jordan!" She embraced him quickly, and even though he wasn't totally prepared, he caught her easily enough, held her for a moment to enjoy the feel of her in his arms, and slowly pulled back to take a look at the swollen belly he'd felt when they'd hugged.

"Oh, wow." He smiled broadly. "When are you due?"

"Next month."

He spotted another woman coming toward them, a frown toying at her lips. When she stood beside them, she cleared her throat and glared meaningfully at Nicole.

"Oh," Nicole said, gesturing to Sarah. "Jordan, this is Sarah. I think you've met her."

Jordan shrugged and nodded. "Yeah, we've met. How are you doing?"

"Fine." Her tone was frosty, and Jordan sensed Sarah didn't much care for him.

"Have you checked in already?" Nicole asked, nodding toward the front desk.

"Oh, yeah. I got in about an hour ago, so I was just hanging around, picking up brochures and waiting for you two."

"Fancy that," Sarah said, plucking the plastic card key from Nicole's hand. "I'm going to get changed and hit the beach. Are you guys coming or what?"

"You want to?" Nicole asked, brushing a stray hair from her eyes.

Jordan swallowed hard as he stared at her eyes, wondering if he'd ever really noticed the golden flecks swimming amid the brown irises. He couldn't remember, but they were stunning, just like Nicole. "Sure. I'm game. I've got to change as well. Then we can head off. What room are you in?"

"220."

He nodded. "Well, good. I'm in 221. I'll meet you on the balcony when I get my suit on."

"Sounds great." She offered him a smile, and he nodded toward the door.

"Shall we head that way?" he asked.

"Yeah."

As they started walking, Jordan slid his hand to the middle of her back and rested it there. It was an unconscious movement, and it was only when they'd reached her room that he moved his hand.

She turned to face him, offering another smile. "I guess we're here."

"Yeah." He spotted a strand of hair in her eyes and brushed it back. "It's really good to see you smile. I was kind of worried about you."

Her hand drifted to her stomach, and she rubbed it. "I'll be fine."

"Okay. I'll be right back."

Jordan stood there, watching as she went inside and closed the door. As Nicole sat on the bed, she saw her best friend come out wearing a white t-shirt over her bikini, a towel draped around her neck.

"I brought your bag in." Sarah gestured toward the corner at the duffle there, then she started walking again.

"Are you angry?" Nicole asked, going to the corner and pulling her bathing suit from the bag.

"This is crazy. You just invited someone you barely know to hang out over the weekend."

"He's a friend, Sarah. That's it."

Sarah folded her arms across her chest and glared. "No, Nic. I'm a friend. He's something else entirely." She started toward the door.

"You can be angry all you like, but be angry at me. I invited him so it's not his fault."

Nicole waited for a response, but none came, frustrating her all the more. Instead, Sarah opened and closed the door, leaving her to change. Nicole quickly shimmied out of her clothing, at least as quickly as her huge belly would allow. As she peeled on the suit, she caught a glimpse of her reflection and blushed. *Was* she in her right mind? Her belly was big and unflattering; then again, it didn't matter. He was just a friend. Isn't that what she'd told Sarah?

She glanced away from the mirror and grabbed a towel, thinking, *besides, I wouldn't even have called him if I didn't think Michael was cheating on me--not that I'm planning to* go *there.*

Taking one last deep breath, Nicole stepped out onto the balcony, where Jordan stood. He'd propped both arms on the black iron railing and leaned against it, a towel suspended next to one hand. He wore no shirt, revealing a nice tan on a very muscular body. At present, there was a small dip in the area between his shoulder blades because of the way he was standing.

"Been waiting long?" she asked, stepping up to him.

"No, not really." He nodded to the beach as he grabbed his towel from the rail. "You ready?"

Nicole scanned the sandy area and felt her nerves kick in. She hated being pregnant, especially this pregnant. She felt massive, and massive didn't belong on a beach with all the tanned and slender bodies out there. Still, she forced a smile and nodded, "Ready."

As they walked, Jordan asked, "So what's with your friend? It seems she doesn't like me."

Nicole shrugged. "Sarah's pretty hard to explain. She's a really good friend. Very protective."

Jordan smiled. "Yeah, and I'm the kind of guy you need to be protected from." He shook his head. "I didn't know if I should have come or not."

Batting a hair from her eyes, Nicole asked, "Why? Didn't you want to?"

"Sure. But I know you and Michael have a lot of things going on, and I don't need to be a distraction, Nicole. We both know that."

A flush crept into her cheeks, and she reached out and grabbed his hand. "You're not a distraction, Jordan. You're a really good friend, and I need as many of those around me right now as I can get."

Jordan opened his mouth to say more when they both spotted Sarah just ahead. She'd pulled off her shirt to apply sunscreen and had barely glanced their way--or if she had given them both "the look" as Nicole called it, Nicole couldn't tell because of the sunglasses shielding her eyes. Of course, it didn't take much for Nicole to realize her best friend was ticked. She really thought Nicole was being disloyal to Michael, and maybe, in some strange way, she was, but Jordan was just a friend.

Reaching Sarah's spot, Nicole unfolded her towel and gently laid it on the sand. She knew it probably wasn't the best idea to lie down because at some point in the not-so-distant future she would actually have to get up, and that might be a problem, what with her beached-whale syndrome and all, still, she thought, sinking to her knees, the sun felt incredibly warm and inviting, so she was going to enjoy every moment.

Knowing there was no way Nicole was going to be able to lie on her belly as Sarah was doing, she rested on her back, and although the sun was bright, if she closed her eyes, it didn't matter, and the warmth did feel exquisite. She planned on getting wet once she felt a little too warm to keep lying here.

"I'm going to hit the water," Jordan said, dropping his towel near hers.

“Don’t have too much fun,” Nicole said, smirking.

“Don’t worry,” he said cheerfully.

Once he’d reached the water’s edge, Nicole glared at her friend. “You know, you could be nicer. It really wouldn’t hurt you.”

Sarah lifted her hand to shield her eye as she looked from her best friend to Jordan who now dove into the ocean spray. “Maybe not. At least I know why you like him. Eye candy.”

“That is *not* why I enjoy his company!” Nicole snapped. “We’re just friends and you know it. I’ve never done anything close to wrong in my marriage.” She furiously batted the hair from her eyes, but it was a losing battle against the wind, which immediately blew it back.

“Just keep telling yourself that, Nic, especially when studly there makes a move on you.” She nodded to where Jordan now stood in the surf, his dark hair now sodden against his face, only making him look that much more attractive as he raised both arms and raked the hair back.

“Look, we’re just friends. Can’t you just leave it at that? I just wanted to talk to him about Michael--you know, pick his brain.”

“I’m your best friend. You could’ve picked *my* brain.” Sarah turned onto her side and propped one elbow into the sand to rest her head in her palm.

“Yeah, well, you’re not a guy. I wanted a guy’s opinion to help me figure out if Michael's cheating.”

Sarah’s eyebrows arched higher, and she exhaled loudly. “You really think that’s it, Nic? I mean, maybe you’re mistaken.”

Shrugging, Nicole said, “Okay, maybe I am. But I do think Jordan will probably have ten times better intuition about it than either you or I, so he’s the perfect person to ask--or he *would* be the perfect person to ask if you’d stop being so grumpy at him because he’s male.”

“Point taken,” Sarah said, slowly getting up. “Don’t look now, but your lover boy is coming, so I'm going to go for a little swim and let the two of you talk things out." She adjusted the bottom of her suit and walked toward the water just as Jordan, still dripping, made his way to Nicole and eased down onto his towel.

"So, are you enjoying your road trip?" He raked his fingers through his hair, pushing the dripping strands from his face.

"Yeah, so far," she said, smiling.

"Have you talked to Michael yet?" He drew his knees to his chest and slid his arms around them.

"No," she said, "not yet." A twinge in her abdomen drew her attention, and she ran her fingers over it, suddenly not feeling as good as she had been.

He nodded. "I can understand that." He looked at her belly. "After all, you are just about to bring a new life into the world. That should be your focus."

A tightening in her abdomen drew a soft gasp from her. About to bring a new life into the world was right, she thought. The twerp just needed to wait until she got back from this road trip. It wasn't anywhere near her due date, for crying out loud.

Jordan leaned closer. "You okay? You look pale."

Pasting on a smile she didn't feel, she nodded. "Of course, I'm fine. Just a slightly pregnant." She started to her feet, and he scrambled to his so he could offer her a hand up and study her face more closely. "You really don't look like you feel well."

She gave him a dismissive wave. "I'll be fine. I think I'm going to go lie down and get a little rest. The baby's been pretty active, and that makes it hard to sleep."

"Then I'll walk you to your room." He touched her elbow protectively, his fingers gently easing around it so he could guide her.

While she found the gesture sweet, part of her felt frustrated by the tightening in her stomach, very much like weak contractions; she just kept telling herself she was nowhere near her due date, so this had to be Braxton-Hicks. She was not going into labor in Sunset Beach, North Carolina. No way. Michelle, as she had taken to calling the daughter still neatly tucked away in her abdomen, needed to learn patience and stay indoors until they got home.

"You okay?" Jordan asked, leaning closer as though he were ready to carry her if necessary. "You were breathing funny just then."

"I'm fine. Really. You don't have to follow me."

That made Jordan more stubborn, and he leaned closer. "Uh-uh. No way. You're not walking back to your room alone. The last thing you need is into go in labor, gather a crowd, and deliver this baby on the beach by yourself. You'd never live down the title Beach Baby, if you know what I mean."

She burst out laughing, and for just that instant, it felt like it had when they were on that physical education trip so many years ago. "You can relax, hot shot. I'm not about to give birth on this beach. Really."

The stairs to their hotel rooms loomed just ahead, and even though she wanted to get there, Nicole felt herself moving more slowly than ever and leaning on Jordan more than she'd intended. She suddenly felt tired, and the pain was getting to be a little more than mildly annoying—not a good thing.

"Should I go get Sarah?" Jordan offered, sliding his arm around Nicole because he was afraid she was going to fall.

For a few seconds, Nicole stared straight ahead and chewed her bottom lip. "I think I'll be fine. I just need to lie down."

"Okay," Jordan finally agreed, eyeing the hotel room door just ahead. Even though Nicole felt as though she didn't need help, he damned sure planned to get Sarah once Nicole was settled. "Got your key?" he asked as they stepped right in front of the door.

Nodding, she pulled it out and handed it to him so he could unlock the door. Nicole took a deep breath and let it out, trying to control the chaos spinning inside her. She kept trying to tell herself the contractions weren't real, that she wasn't really in labor. The trouble was, this felt like real labor.

Jordan unlocked the door and opened it so he could lead Nicole to the bed and watch her ease onto it. "Is there anything I can get for you? Something to drink or eat?" He hovered nearby, not sure what else he could do.

"No," Nicole finally said, struggling to get comfortable as her back began to hurt, which was far from a new symptom.

"I really don't like seeing you like this," he said leaning close. He thought she might answer--that her closed eyes might flicker open--but it seemed that Nicole had suddenly drifted toward unconsciousness, which might be a good thing for her. Of course, he wondered if she were in the early stages of labor. Surely Nicole would recognize them because of her other child.

He started to walk away so she could rest, but his hand drifted to her hair, his fingers gently stroking the long strands that felt like silk. Standing there, so close, he felt mesmerized by her, and he kept silently slamming her husband for being such an idiot. The truth was that her husband was more than likely having an affair, and no matter how much everyone might want to put everything back in the box as if it had never been disturbed, that wasn't going to happen, no matter what he did. Her world was never going to be the same. He just wondered what she was going to do if she figured out he was having an affair. Would she stay with him because of their kids? He just couldn't see that somehow.

She stirred slightly and he quickly pulled his hand back, somehow embarrassed to think of being caught in such a gesture of familiarity. He doubted Nicole would mind, but he couldn't seem to help himself somehow.

He finally forced himself to close the door and head to the beach, back to the spot they'd occupied earlier. Sarah was now lying on her back on the towel, her eyes closed as she drank in the sun's warmth.

He strode over to her and knelt, intending to say something, but she beat him to it. "You're blocking my light."

"Maybe so. But I think Nicole might be going into labor."

"What?" Sarah sat up quickly. "Where is she?" She scanned the beach, searching for Nicole.

"Easy." Jordan laid his hand on her shoulder. "I helped her back to the hotel. She was pale and seemed pretty tired. Although she said she wasn't going into labor, I have my doubts."

Sarah didn't wait for him to say anything else. Instead, she hastily started to gather her things, and Jordan quickly joined in. As she stood, she grabbed them from him and started to turn away.

"Why do you hate me so much?"

"Because you're not good for her. You've never been good for her." She started to walk away, but Jordan caught her arm.

"I don't understand what you mean. I've never done anything to hurt her. Ever."

"Haven't you?" She shoved her sunglasses on to block the light. "She was crazy about you, and you waited until the last possible moment to tell her you were engaged. I'd say that's pretty crappy." She whirled and headed to the hotel, leaving Jordan standing alone, stunned.

## Chapter Fifteen

"I need to push!" Nicole screamed, struggling to sit up.

Sarah quickly eased her back down. "No, you don't. The doctor will be here in a moment."

"Where's Jordan?" she asked, her voice thick with pain.

"He's out in the hall." Sarah eyed the door, praying the doctor would just come and get this over with. Her best friend had been in labor for twelve hours, and she was exhausted--some vacation for both of them.

"Can you get him?"

"You want him to see you…like this??" Sarah shook her head in disbelief.

"He's just a friend, Sarah--and it's not like Michael is suddenly going to arrive to welcome his daughter." Even before Nicole had stopped speaking, her face turned pale as another contraction seized her, and she closed her eyes, trying to focus on breathing. "Please get him," she managed through clenched teeth.

"All right. All right." She slipped into the hall where Jordan sat on a bench. He looked up as she approached. "She wants you."

"Me?" Jordan stood slowly, unsure. "Why would she want me in there?"

"'Cause there is no way in hell Michael will get here in time for the delivery. He missed the first one, too."

Jordan's eyes bulged. "You're kidding? He wasn't there? No wonder she thinks he's sleeping around. Jerk." He took a deep breath and slipped into the room to find Nicole lying there, staring out the window.

"Hey, you," he said, ambling over. At first, he thought she was just turned away, but then he realized she was also crying and trying to hide it. "What's the matter?" He pulled a chair up beside the bed and took her hand.

She drew a shaky hand across her face. "Look, this isn't your problem, and if you don't want to stay, I completely get it. I just know Michael is MIA on a business trip, and I don't want to have to do this alone again, so I wondered if you'd mind sitting with me."

His jaw clenched as he thought of what Sarah had revealed to him on the beach, and ever since that moment, his regrets had piled themselves into a mountain and he wished he had called his wedding off. Had he really believed Nicole had been in love with him, he might have. It was hard to say. But right now he knew his presence wasn't helping her think clearly.

"Nicole, I'm probably not the best person to be here with you. Perhaps Sarah—"

"Why? We've always been good friends, Jordan. Why does this have to be different?" She looked up at him with glassy eyes, her expression pleading. "All I'm asking you to do is stay with me until this baby is born. That's all I want. I know my marriage is in trouble, but this is something separate. Please." She squeezed his hand, and as he stared into her plaintive eyes, he found himself unable to refuse.

"All right," he said. "I'll stay. But you do realize I don't have a clue what to do with a baby."

She might have answered had another contraction not latched onto her, stealing her breath and stiffening her body with agony.

Seconds later, a doctor popped into the room, and everything blurred as Jordan sat beside Nicole. Sweat sheened her face, and she struggled to breathe and push as he helped support her back, gently coaching her in a way that felt strangely intimate and yet right, as though she was the missing part of him for whom he'd always searched.

After about thirty minutes of Nicole trying to push, the doctor said, "The head is crowning," and a few pushes later, that baby suddenly appeared. Sitting there, Jordan felt chills go through him as he watched Nicole smile and relax against the bed while hearing the newborn cry.

"It's a girl," the doctor said. "You have a daughter."

"I knew that," Nicole replied, looking at Jordan and dazzling him with the most serene smile he'd ever seen. She was beautiful, and he reached out and touched her face before he'd thought to stop himself. He just didn't understand how everything could feel as though he was supposed to be with her, and this should have been his child.

"How did you know that, Nicole?"

"Sonogram, dopey. I'm not psychic or anything."

They both laughed, and the nurse gently handed the baby to him. "Your daughter."

"I'm not—"

"It's okay. Take her," Nicole said. "Really."

The nurse looked from one to the other, and Jordan gently reached out and accepted the little thing wrapped in pink, and the whole time he stared at her he found himself amazed and grateful to have witnessed this. "What are you going to name her?"

"Michelle Maddison." Nicole smiled at the way he seemed to bond instantly with the baby.

A nurse brought Sarah in, and she glared enviously at Jordan. "Hey, how come he gets to hold the baby?" She perched at the end of the bed.

"Because I'm the delivery coach," he joked, still mesmerized by the tiny sleeping face.

"Okay, Delivery Coach, smile." Sarah held up her phone and snapped a picture of the three of them. Then she glared at Nicole.

"Come on, Nic. I'm your best friend," she whined impatiently, hovering close to Michael so that if he wanted to give her Michelle, she'd be ready to take her.

Nicole shook her head. "Okay, Jordan, you might want to let Sarah hold the baby before she has a meltdown and teaches Michelle how to throw a temper tantrum."

Sighing, Jordan slowly eased the baby into Sarah's arms yet still hovered just in case Sarah didn't completely "have" her. When he looked back at Nicole, he found her eyes had grown heavy and that she was drifting toward dreamland.

"I think she's pretty wiped out," he said, folding his arms across his chest.

"Yeah, I don't doubt it." Sarah rocked the baby slowly back and forth to settle her to sleep.

"Where is Michael? Does he even know that Nicole went into labor?"

Shrugging, Sarah looked at him, a flush covering both cheeks. "I haven't been able to reach him, just like last time, so, no, he doesn't have a clue Nicole had their daughter."

Jordan eyed Nicole's chest, confirming by its easy rise and fall she had drifted away. "You do realize he's probably having an affair, right?"

"I'm guessing." She eased the sleeping baby into the glass basinet by the bed before leaning against the windowsill. "And it's only going to make Nicole try harder to keep the marriage together, for Nick and Michelle's sake." She gritted her teeth, wanting to throttle Michael.

"You know she deserves better." Jordan nodded at Nicole.

"And are you what's 'better'? Is that what you're trying to say?"

She waved her hand dismissively at him.

"No, that's not why I'm trying to say at all. I don't have anything to do with this. I just want her to be happy, and this jerk can't even make sure she's okay and stick around long enough for her to have their baby. She doesn't need this."

Sarah's cell rang, and she looked at the display. "It's Michael."

"Yeah, well, it's about damned time." He walked off, intending to get some fresh air to cool off.

He strode into the hallway, trying hard to regain control of the emotions that swirled darkly inside. He knew he had no business being pissed, but he also knew Nicole was right on the money about her suspicions: Michael was in the middle of an affair. Nothing else explained his absences.

Pacing the hall, he wondered just what the hell he was really doing there. He should've been flattered to know just how much of a thing Nicole had for him, but knowing had only tangled his emotions that much more because he'd always had a thing for her as well. Right now, seeing what her idiot husband had right in front of him that he didn't seem to want only made Jordan that much angrier.

He turned to pace in the other direction and almost collided with Sarah. Stepping back, he averted his gaze. "Sorry. How's Nicole?"

"She and the baby are sleeping."

And what about Michael?" Although he tried to keep his tone neutral, even he could hear the resentment festering in it.

Sarah folded her arms across her chest. "He'll be out of pocket for the next few days which means I'll be driving Nicole and the baby home so we can pick Nick up from her mom. This was supposed to be a last relaxing trip before the baby came, but I guess that didn't quite pan out."

Jordan's shoulders tensed. "He's not even flying in to check on her?" His voice echoed loudly enough for two nearby nurses to peer over at them.

"Lower you voice," Sarah hissed, a bright red coloring her cheeks. She brushed the hair from her face. "This isn't new behavior for Michael. Of course, this might just be the straw that actually breaks the camel's back. But I'm guessing he's got it coming."

"Yeah, he does," Jordan agreed, starting toward Nicole's room.

"What are you doing?" Sarah asked, catching his arm.

"Saying goodbye. The last thing she needs is me brooding about her husband, and any advice I might give her wouldn't exactly be neutral. We both know that."

He pulled from Sarah's grip and headed into Nicole's room. As Sarah had said, she was sleeping, so he forced himself to walk to her bed and kneel beside her. Without even thinking about it, his hand drifted to her face and lovingly stroked it. At the feel of his touch, her eyes fluttered open.

"What're you doing?" she asked, her voice groggy with fatigue.

He pulled his cell out of his pocket. "I've sort of got an emergency back at home, so I need to leave."

"Do you have to? Right now?" Nicole started trying to sit up but Jordan settled his palm on her shoulder to keep her down.

"Yeah, I do. Besides, I think you've got more than enough distractions to keep you from focusing too much on Michael."

A disappointed frown tugged at her lips, and she motioned for him to lean close, which he did. A second later, she kissed his cheek and wrapped her arms around him. "Thank you for coming with us. It meant a lot to me."

"It meant a lot to me, too." His voice sounded deep and gravely, probably from all the emotions he was trying so hard to bury. Sometimes, though, there was no real way to bury things.

Swallowing hard, he slowly eased from her embrace and slipped away, giving her one last smile before he vanished.

# Chapter Sixteen

Four years later

"Don't you think I know what's going on?" Nicole stood in the kitchen, leaning against the counter as she crossed both arms over her chest. "I'm not stupid, Michael."

"I never said you were," he replied calmly, reading the morning paper. He leaned over to his bowl and took a milk-sodden bite of bran.

"You do this every time," she said throwing her hands up. "Why don't you just be a man and admit it?"

He set down the paper and glared at her. "Admit what, Nicole? You're the one thinking I'm having an affair."

Nicole made a sort of growling sound and went to her purse. She pulled out an envelope of pictures she threw onto the table in front of him. The envelope wasn't sealed, and the glossies spilled out, flashing images of Michael with a lanky blonde, both of them naked, their bodies tangled on a bed.

"What the hell?" Immediately Michael jumped up and tried to gather the pictures into a neat pile. Unfortunately, his trembling fingers kept fumbling. "Where did you get these?"

"Does it matter?" Nicole asked, leaning back against the counter again and glaring at her husband.

"Hell yeah, it matters." He finally managed to stuff the photos back into the envelope and fold it shut. "Where did you get them?"

Nicole's eyes grew bigger in outrage. "I have proof you're screwing some blonde, and all you can do is demand to know how I found out?" She pointed to the pictures. "I want to know who she is. I think I've earned that right."

Michael glared at her. "How the hell did you get these pictures?" His tone was icy, and Nicole found it almost amusing that he was more protective of his mistress than he'd ever been of her.

"I hired a private investigator, Michael. You see, I didn't even think anyone could find you, let alone your little girlfriend." She stepped toward him. "Just tell me--were you screwing her the day of Dad's funeral? Or maybe when I gave birth to your kids?"

Michael pointed at the pictures. "You leave her out of this." He kept staring at the envelope, and Nicole wondered if she had ever known her husband at all.

"I'd love to leave her out of this, Michael. Truly. But you dragged her into to our marriage, and now I want to know her name and how long you've been sleeping with her."

His shoulders sank, and he rubbed his forehead as though a headache had blossomed there. "I've been seeing her for five years."

One of Nicole's knees buckled, and she sagged against the counter. Michael reflexively reached to steady her, but she said, "Don't touch me." She walked around the kitchen, trying not to look at their home--trying not to remember when they'd bought the vase on the kitchen counter or when the photos on the walls had been taken. The house was loaded with too many memories, but now they threatened to overwhelm her. "So tell me why, Michael. I loved you. I devoted my life to you. And we have kids. What didn't I do?"

He bowed his head and his shoulders sank, and for the first time, she saw his eyes soften in pain. "Because I fell in love with her. I didn't mean to. It just happened."

"So what's her name?" she demanded. She didn't know why it

mattered. It just did.

"Kelsey. Kelsey Roberts."

Tears pricked her eyes and she tried to keep them from flowing down her face, but they came, anyway, as she realized how pointless it had been to try to salvage this marriage. It would take both of them wanting that--that, and a few miracles. Even if she could count on the miracles, Michael didn't want this.

"I never meant to hurt you," he began, and stepped toward her.

"It doesn't matter what you meant, only what you did. Get out."

She waited for him to argue, to plead his case--she'd expected it--but instead he walked past her. It was only when she heard the front door open and quietly close that she knew it was over--really, really over--and for the first time she was terrified. The tears came hard and fast, blinding her as she fumbled for the kitchen table and fell into one of the chairs as the sobs consumed her.

She rocked back and forth as the emotional storm ripped through her, and even though she tried to tell herself she'd known this day had been coming, it didn't help. She'd thought he would at least have apologized for breaking their vows. Instead, he'd been furious at having been caught.

Had Michael ever truly loved her? She didn't know what to think. Her head hurt from all the tension, and she couldn't seem to stop the pain and tears exploding through her. She constantly brushed her hand across her face, trying to wipe them away.

"Mommy?" a small voice said.

Nicole looked up to find Michelle standing in the doorway, her long, brown hair falling toward her face, not quite hiding fearful brown eyes that seemed so large amid her thin face.

That forced Nicole to take a deep breath, wipe her face one last time, and paste on a smile she didn't feel. "Hey, Baby. Did you wake up from your nap?" She patted her lap so her daughter would walk over.

"Did you get a boo boo, Mommy?" Michelle asked, taking slow, cautious steps toward Nicole. Her daughter had always seemed older than she was, probably because of those soulful brown eyes.

"A boo boo? What makes you think that?" Nicole asked, wrapping her arms around her daughter and giving her a hug.

"Because you're crying." Michelle touched Nicole's damp cheek, her small fingers gently brushing against her mother's skin.

At that moment, Nicole wanted to burst into tears again because the last thing she wanted her child to know about was the uncertain future ahead of them both, yet instead of giving way to her emotions, she gently drew her daughter close and kissed her forehead. "Everything is going to be okay. Mommy is just tired."

That seemed to satisfy Michelle, and Nicole cuddled with her a few more moments just to be sure her daughter didn't feel the undercurrents that lingered in Nicole's mind. Then she gently patted her daughter's back and suggested she go play.

Michelle eased up from Nicole's lap and gave her mother one last look before skipping from the room. In that instant, the fake smile Nicole had been forcing into place abruptly vanished. With a trembling hand, she reached into her purse and pulled out her cell. Taking a deep breath, she dialed Sarah's number and waited for her best friend to answer.

When she heard her best friend's chipper voice, she said, "I was wondering if you could come over? I really need to talk. It's about Michael."

That was all Nicole had to say before disconnecting the call and waiting for Sarah to show up.

* * *

Sarah kept shaking her head as she stared at the photos, and the only real giveaway about how angry she was getting was that with each progressive image, she smacked the photo against the counter harder and harder.

"I don't know what to do," Nicole said softly, resting her elbows on the table so she could cradle her head in her hands.

Another photo smacked loudly against the counter. "You don't know what to do?" Sarah raised her voice, but Nicole gestured for her to be quiet. Then, as if on cue, Michelle walked in. When she spotted Sarah, her eyes grew big, and a smile lit up her face. Sarah glanced at the photos in horror and flipped them over to hide Michael's indiscretion from his daughter.

"Aunt Sarah!" The little girl flew toward Nicole's best friend, and Sarah opened her arms wide.

"Wow, Squirt, you're getting so big!"

As the two embraced, Nicole got up and started a pot of coffee. Although she liked coffee, right now she wasn't doing it because she actually wanted something to drink; she was just trying to keep herself busy, her hands moving.

"What'cha doing over here?" Michelle asked and then squealed as Sarah began tickling her.

"I'm visiting your mom, silly." She kissed Michelle's forehead.

"Are you gonna make her feel better? She was crying a little while ago." Both Michelle and Sarah turned to her.

"Yep," Sarah said, smiling as she tousled the little girl's hair. "That's exactly what I'm here to do, and I bet if you run over and give her a big hug, she'll feel even better."

"'Kay." Michelle hopped down and rushed to throw her arms around her mother and squeeze her as hard as she could.

"I love you, Mama." She peered at her mother with luminous brown eyes Nicole could never resist.

Stroking her daughter's face, she said, "I love you, too, Michelle. Why don't you go play in the back yard while Sarah and I talk, okay?"

"'Kay." She gave her mother one last squeeze and slipped away, leaving Nicole staring at the coffee pot as though doing so would somehow make it work faster.

"So how did you get these photos?" Sarah asked as the coffee finally started flowing into the pot.

"I hired a private investigator." She tried to keep her tone even, knowing that another emotional meltdown wasn't going to do anyone any good.

Sarah flipped the pile of pictures back over and finished going through them, the whole time shaking her head in disbelief. "Well, not that this is going to make you feel any better, but you definitely got your money's worth."

"Yeah, there's that," Nicole said in a distracted tone as she rubbed at one of her temples, trying to still the throbbing within.

"So what are you going to do now?" Sarah asked, walking over to the counter to peer out at Michelle, who was busy playing on the swing set out back. It had been a pointed question, she knew, one Nicole had managed to avoid earlier, but right now, in a kitchen filled with too many memories of Michael and a marriage which had just shattered into a thousand pieces, Nicole had to think about the future. It didn't just involve her and Michael. They had two beautiful children to think about.

"I don't know," Nicole said softly, grateful the coffee pot had finally filled so she could top off two mugs and hand one to Sarah. Perhaps this would finally make her be quiet.

"Surely you can't be thinking about staying with him, Nic."

Nicole's hands trembled, and she worried about spilling the coffee. Still, she refused to put it down because she needed to keep her hands occupied. "I don't think that's an option, if you want the truth. He tells me he's in love with her."

Sarah sputtered on the coffee and whirled to face her best friend.

"In love with her? I don't think the man knows the first thing about being in love with anyone. Except himself." She made a sort of growling noise and shook her head. "He has some kind of nerve."

Sarah wordlessly walked over to the table, set down her mug and sank into a chair. As she looked at the table in front of her, she spied her wedding ring. She inhaled sharply and jerked it from her hand before casting it across the room.

"So where is the loser?"

Nicole shrugged. "Who knows? I told him to leave. He could always be with Kelsey, which is what I think he really wanted." A chill swept through her as she put the name to the girl in the picture--blonde, petite, and nothing like Nicole. Gritting her teeth, she felt anger coursing through her body.

Sarah joined her at the table. "What about the kids?"

A huge lump seemed to block Nicole's throat, and no matter what she did to swallow it, it refused to budge. Tears burned her eyes as they pooled and overflowed. "I don't know what's going to happen with the kids or anything else. I'm not even sure I know my own name anymore."

For a moment, Sarah just sat there, unsure of what to do to help. Was there anything she could do? Then she thought of Michelle, and she knew that Nicole needed some time to get her head wrapped around this situation, and she wasn't going to be able to do that with the kids around.

"Hey, why don't I take the munchkins to the movies and keep them over at my place for the night? I think you probably need some time to unwind, and if Michael comes back tonight, it's probably not going to be pretty."

Nicole opened her mouth to argue, but she knew her best friend was right, especially the part about things turning ugly if Michael came back. "Are you sure? Nick can be such a handful."

Sarah set her hand on her Nicole's shoulder. "I think I can handle him, Nic. Really."

An understanding look passed between them, and Nicole finally nodded. Sarah stood. "I'll go tell the munchkin about our play date."

* * *

Hours later, as night hedged in, Nicole tried everything she knew to distract herself, from watching television in the recliner to reading a book at the kitchen table. She even went about the task of making dinner, only to realize there was way too much food and that she really had no appetite.

Part of her thought Michael might return. She wanted him to tell her it had all been some elaborate practical joke even the private investigator had been in on, that none of it was real and capable of breaking her heart. Thinking it wasn't real was so much better because the last thing she wanted was a life alone. That thought haunted her like nothing else.

Still, as the day pressed, she realized her husband wasn't coming back even to get some of his things—well, at least not tonight, anyway. He'd probably pick a time he knew Nicole wouldn't be there as a way to minimize his guilt. Of course, that assumed Michael even had any feelings of guilt.

When none of the distractions worked, she paced the room. The house felt as though it were closing in around her, and she couldn't breathe. She needed to talk to someone. Sarah was out of the question, as she was distracting Nick and Michelle. There was no way in hell she was calling her mother. She could just imagine what a catastrophe that would be, considering just how much her mother loved Michael. She hadn't really even believed Michael could cheat on Nicole. It was unthinkable. Now if her father were still alive, he would have believed Nicole.

Of course, if her father were here, she would have him to talk to, and he would know what to do. Since he wasn't, she felt she had only one choice left—Jordan.

Jordan sat on the couch at his parents' house, sipping a beer. Although his mom had already gone up to her room to read before bed, his dad sat in the recliner nursing his own beer. Kimmie, his slightly younger sister, had curled up reading *Cosmopolitan.* They'd watched a football game between OU and Baylor a few hours ago and the television had filled all the awkward silences that might have made things difficult. Now the two men sat, both staring off into space. David Carroway was the first to break the silence.

"Have you been dating at all, Jordan?"

Kimmie looked up, cocking her head to one side as she, too, waited for the answer. In fact, she rested the magazine against her chest and gave her brother her full attention.

A flush crept across Jordan's face, and he felt his whole body tighten. "That's a no, Dad, and considering the way things went with Alyssa, I'm not sure I really want to think about a relationship this soon."

"This soon?" Kimmie said, shaking her head. "You've been divorced for years, bro--or hasn't that sunk in yet?"

"I know," Jordan snapped. "Thanks for your concern there, Kimmie."

She lifted the magazine from her chest and began reading again. "Anytime, Jordan. You can always count on me."

David drained the rest of his beer and thumbed toward the kitchen. "I'm going to get a refill." He nodded at Jordan. "You want another?"

Jordan shook his head. "No. I'm going to get on the road early in the morning. The last thing I need is another beer."

"Okay." David started to get up. A grimace transformed his expression, and he groaned softly.

"Dad? You okay?" Jordan leaned toward him, concerned by his father's sudden change of expression.

David started to say something, but all that came out was a gurgling sound. Jordan watched in horror as his father slowly tumbled to the floor, striking his head on the table as he fell.

"Dad!" Jordan jumped up and raced to his father. In the distance, he heard his cell ringing, but all he could think about was getting to his dad, who was unconscious, probably from hitting his head on the table. Jordan could see the blood, and it should have alarmed him. It would have had David been breathing.

In that instant everything seemed to freeze. Jordan heard the hammering of his heart and felt himself shift his father's body so he could start CPR. He even heard his sister answer his phone, repeatedly saying, "hello" before she hung up.

"Call 911!" he shouted before leaning over and breathing for his dad. His voice sounded stretched and deep, slowed like everything else.

## Chapter Seventeen

Jordan sat on the beach, staring out at the tide, watching it slowly roll in and recede. He'd been sitting there for hours, and even though his hands and ears were so cold, he couldn't seem to force himself to move. The strong north wind blew his hair back, yet he sat unmoved by the sound of the ocean and the feel of the world around him.

He'd been staring at the water for so long he could've closed his eyes and still would have seen it, yet it would be better than replaying the last moments of his father's life. He kept telling himself he should have realized sooner his father was having a heart attack. He should have seen the signs before his father had collapsed. If he had, there might've been time to change the course things had taken.

There were so many times he wanted to undo the past--to unburden himself from this pain--but there was nothing that could take it from him. Although he'd hated making this trip by himself, he'd known that Kimmie really needed to stay with his mother—she hadn't taken the David's death particularly well.

Looking around at the empty beach, Jordan frowned in puzzlement. He'd thought he'd known his father well, but his last wishes in the will had come as a surprise to everyone in the family. Cremation and a scattering of the ashes along a beach. He'd always thought of his father as reliable and constant—someone who'd want a grave, not this impulse to be one with a listless ocean and beach where gulls circled lazily overhead, crying out to one another.

It didn't so much bother Jordan that this last request had seemed to come from out of the blue. No, what had unsettled him was the idea that perhaps David's love of the beach had been far from the last unknown Jordan would run across. Still, there would be no more opportunities to find out about the hidden sides of his father and to understand who David Carroway had truly been besides his father. Perhaps there were details only his mother knew, but she'd said so little, and the last thing Jordan wanted to do was remind her of a past which could bring neither joy nor relief.

A pair of gulls swooped low and landed on the shore not far from where Jordan sat. He watched them peck at a piece of paper half-buried in the sand, the edge of which waved in the breeze. His father, had he been there, would've laughed and pointed at them. "Look at those birds," he would have said, shaking his head. "Just like two women fighting over a sweater during a sale."

Jordan smiled in spite of the lump in his throat and the enormous weight that had settled on his shoulders, threatening to bury him. He wished his father were here--how he wished that. Gritting his teeth, Jordan shifted his feet, making a ridge in the sand, some of which spilled across his feet, speckling his shoes.

He raked his fingers through his hair, trying to resettle it against the cold breeze that smelled of ocean tang. He wondered whether his father had had any regrets. Surely he had. Didn't everyone? Sighing, Jordan stood and ambled toward the water's edge, peering at the ground. At the sight of a flat, smooth stone, he bent and picked it up then stretched out his arm and tossed it out over the water. The stone skipped three times before sinking, and as Jordan bent to grab another stone, it occurred to him what his own biggest regret was.

Nicole.

That thought caused him to falter in his throw, and the stone ended up plinking into the shallows not far from his shoes instead of sailing out. He took a couple of steps back, trying to wrap his mind around that thought, but still not sure what to do with it. He'd known he'd had feelings for her for a long time. He'd just assumed they would die at some point, considering a future with her wasn't possible, not so long as she was married, anyway.

His frown suddenly shifted to a scowl as he thought of her husband, and he wished things had turned out better for her. She had definitely deserved better, not that Dweeb, who had been too busy cheating on her to even to deign to come to her father's funeral or appear at the hospital when his children were born.

Jordan forced himself to take a deep breath and not react. Reacting wasn't going to fix anything for anyone, least of all himself or Nicole, unfortunately.

He tried to imagine what his life might have been with her by his side, yet all he could seem to think about was that it felt empty without her. Losing his father was probably one of the most important moments in his life, and the only person he wanted to share it with was a woman he'd met during a chance encounter years ago--a woman he'd never been able to forget or stop measuring others against--and if he really wanted to be truthful, she'd been the reason he hadn't tried dating again. There was no point in dating when someone already possessed your heart. He was smart enough to know that.

He was in the process of picking up a third stone when he felt someone watching. He turned just in time to find a couple starting onto the beach. The woman had long, flowing hair, much like Nicole's, and if he tried hard enough, he could probably morph her features to match. That wouldn't do him much good, and the last thing Nicole needed was some guy telling her after all this time he'd finally realized he was madly in love with her.

The couple strolled down the beach, holding hands as they walked.

Jordan waiting until their figures were small blots on the horizon before taking one last breath and heading back to his Jeep. There was no point in putting off the inevitable. While he might love the beach, there was a reason he'd come here, and it had nothing to do with taking a cold swim.

He opened the back of the Jeep and pulled a thick bag of ashes from the floorboard. As he hefted it into his arms, he wondered again how a human being could be reduced to this; it just didn't seem possible. Nonetheless, this was all that was left of his father, and fulfilling his father's last request had fallen on his shoulders.

"All right, Dad," he half-whispered. "I guess it's showtime."

Carrying the bag out onto the beach, Jordan tried to find a perfect place, one he felt would be tranquil enough for his father. It was a stupid idea, he knew. Considering the reckless wind toying with his hair, Jordan recognized his father's aches would be quickly scattered and that would be the last Jordan saw of David Carroway.

Part of him wanted to just drive away and keep the ashes in some kind of urn. It didn't have to be fancy or anything, but the idea of casting what was left of his father out unsettled him, as though parts of him, too, would be forever riding the wind. His mother must have felt something similar because she, too, had been against this final wish. It had broken Jordan's heart to have to go against her, but he'd respected his father's wishes, no matter how hard they might end up being.

For a few seconds, Jordan just stood there, holding the bag. He knew what he needed to do, and he kept telling himself to just do it, but no matter where he looked, it didn't appear to be the right place. Then again, he wasn't sure he knew what the right place would look like; nothing had felt right since his father had died.

Taking a deep breath, he opened the seam which sealed the bag. Every muscle in his body ached--had had been aching since he'd driven up here, as though this small bag carried the weight of the world.

Gritting his teeth, Jordan finally forced himself to jerk the bag upwards so that some of the ashes fluttered through the air and dissipated. He repeated the motion until the bag was almost empty, then he turned it over and let the final remnants cascade from the bag into the wind, which carried them away quickly. Although he kept staring ahead, thinking his vision should still be hazy due to the ashes, he could see the bright glare of sunlight on the ocean. Still, he didn't want to close his eyes, not until he had to. He wanted to memorize the moment for what it was: the instant his whole life suddenly seemed to change, to tighten around a single truth he would never be able to deny.

He'd never worried about wasting his life. He'd always just assumed it would go on as it had, and that there would be more until suddenly it was over. Now he couldn't shake the *over* part. What if he died tomorrow? What had he left behind that mattered? A failed marriage? A career that really didn't matter besides the income it provided?

Jordan crumpled the bag and shook his head, dazed by the life he'd realized he'd slipped into without intention. He'd taken the path of least resistance, and now it haunted him because he kept thinking about what did matter, and all he could think about was the missed opportunity with Nicole and the fool he'd been to assume such a chance came every day.

As the rolling surf soothed him, Jordan struggled to figure out what to do with the bag. Part of him thought it was meant for the trash. Part of him felt like it had become the last link to his father, so he just held it, took a few steps back from the ocean, and sat in the cool sand.

Farther down the beach, the man chased the woman, and the sound of their laughter echoed back to Jordan. Although he knew it wasn't wise, he thought about Nicole and wondered if things had been different if that might've been the two of them instead of two strangers. The man caught the woman by her waist and swung her around until they both tumbled to the sand. Then they kissed as though Jordan didn't exist, and maybe he didn't, not to anyone besides his mom and sister. Maybe that was a part of what bothered him—not just the loss of his dad, but the feeling that he had ceased to matter, that he'd become a ghost of sorts, and that he was alone in a way he'd never in his life expected to be.

Stowing the bag beneath his leg, Jordan pulled out his cell. For a moment, his fingers just hovered over the buttons as though he'd suddenly frozen up and couldn't remember the number he wanted to call. In truth, he was debating whether he should or shouldn't call, and while *shouldn't* was definitely winning, it didn't mitigate his drive to push the buttons, anyway. In the end, he justified following through with it because his father had died and the emptiness was eating him alive. It was at best an excuse, but if that were all he had, he'd take it.

He punched her number from his speed dial and waited. It took three rings before she finally picked up and answered in a sleepy voice.

"Hello?"

"Hey, Nicole." He forced a smile onto his face, hoping she wouldn't hear the raw cut of pain he couldn't drive away. He dug one of his shoes deeply into the sand.

"Who is this?" she asked, yawning.

The smile died, and he suddenly wondered if he'd made a huge mistake. "Ummm, it's Jordan Carroway. Perhaps you don't remember me." At that moment, his mind flashed back to the delivery room when he'd stood in for her loser husband. "Maybe I should let you go." Again his finger hovered over the buttons.

"No, wait, I remember." Her answer was much quicker. "I'm sorry. I was just taking a nap, so I wasn't fully awake."

Jordan chuckled. "Napping in the middle of the day? Are you getting old, Nicole?"

She, too, laughed. "Some days I feel like it."

"That's what kids will do to you." He thought of the baby that the nurse had thrust into his arms. How right it had felt, even though the little girl hadn't been his. He'd never forgotten the way Nicole had looked at him when held her daughter.

"I'd have to agree with you there," she said. "So what's up?"

Jordan heard rustling in the background, and he assumed Nicole was sitting up in bed. "It's been kind of a tough couple of months. My dad passed away."

A moment of silence. Then Nicole said, "I'm so sorry, Jordan. I remember what that's like."

"Yeah, that's why I called. I just wanted to talk to someone who'd been through it." He swallowed hard and noticed the wind had eased the bag from beneath his leg and threatened to blow it away, so he put it back and applied more pressure to keep it still. Of course, he was lying to Nicole. He could have talked to his sister or his mom. Instead, he'd wanted to talk to her because something about her voice seemed to make everything more bearable. He'd never understood that, but he accepted it for what it was.

"How long ago did he die?"

"About a month," Jordan said, trying not to think back to that moment, but no matter what, Jordan found himself reliving those last few moments when his father had been alive, lying on the carpet as Jordan administered CPR.

"I'm really, really sorry," Nicole said, her voice sounding slightly breathless. "Is there anything I can do?"

"No." He looked out at the rolling ocean, amazed by its size. Just one more way he felt insignificant in the grand scheme of things. "I was just sitting on the beach where my dad wanted me to scatter his ashes."

As if in response to his words, the breeze tried to lift the bag once more, but Jordan kept it flat against the ground because the last thing he wanted to have to do was get up and chase it.

“That’s interesting. “My dad wasn’t half so adventurous,” Nicole replied.

Jordan shrugged even though she couldn’t see him. “Yeah, well, that adventurous streak didn’t set so well with my mom. She about had a bird when she read the note he’d stapled to his will stating that he wanted to be cremated. I thought she was going to have a heart attack herself, right there on the spot.”

That, too, was a tough image for Jordan to get out of his head, and he felt that in honoring his father’s last wish he was somehow betraying his mother, which really didn’t make sense. Then again, not much in his world had made sense since his father had died. He kept waiting for something logical to happen, but it never did.

“Is your mom there on the beach with you?” Nicole asked.

“God, no,” Jordan responded without thought, shifting position so he could lie down. Although he knew this would get sand all over his clothes, he didn’t care. Life was far too short for caring about sand. “She wouldn’t have handled watching me deal with the ashes very well, so she stayed home. It really was better that way. How’s your little girl?” he asked, suddenly feeling too raw to keep talking about his father.

“Michelle? She’s getting big and definitely keeps me on my toes.”

Jordan laughed, and it felt good to leave his world behind for a moment and think about Nicole’s. “Is she anything like her mother?”

“Yeah, quite a bit, actually. She looks a lot like me, but she’s quieter. No idea where that came from because Michael’s not.”

Jordan frowned. He thought he heard a sudden tension in her voice when she said her husband’s name, and he wondered how they were getting along. Then again, there were some questions he knew better than to ask, and that was definitely one of them.

Looking down the shore, he spotted the couple in an intimate embrace, and his stomach clenched. He knew that no matter how many times he called Nicole, it wouldn't change the overwhelming sense of loss he felt.

"Hey, Nicole, I should probably go. I told my mom I'd start the drive back today, and since my dad's death, she's been paranoid about everything."

"Oh…okay." Her tone sounded slightly off. He just didn't know if it had to do with talking about her husband or his sudden shift. Maybe it didn't matter. "Be careful, okay?"

"Will do."

Jordan snapped the phone shut and looked once more at the tide gently rolling to the shore. It was funny how the ocean and death tended into put things in perspective. Now if he only felt like laughing.

He walked back to the Jeep one last time and unzipped a backpack in the passenger's seat. Although it took him a few minutes to find what he was looking for, his fingers finally latched onto Nicole's old camera and he pulled it out. It had taken him so long to get all the parts, and now that it was finally supposed to be back in working condition, he figured he'd test it.

He turned back to the beach and started snapping pictures, imagining Nicole was right there with him.

## Chapter Eighteen

Twelve Years Later

"Learn to drive!" Nicole snapped, watching someone weave into her lane, cutting her off. It was a miracle of brakes and swerving that kept her from clipping the tail of the Buick, and she didn't realize she'd held her breath until she exhaled loudly and felt a cramping in her shoulders from all the tension.

It had been one of those days, and frankly she was glad it was also a Friday so she and Michelle could curl up on the couch and watch a chick flick like they did every weekend. It wasn't that her daughter didn't like to go out--Michelle was very outgoing and very social--but she was choosy in her friends and even more choosy in the guys she expressed an interest in, yet another trait she'd gotten from her mother. In fact, she'd gotten a lot from her mother, including a frustration for her weekend-warrior dad, who didn't understand that everything wasn't about having fun when they visited. Besides, there was still his girlfriend, whom neither Nicole nor Michelle had ever been able to stand.

Nicole pulled up in her driveway and slowly got out, hoping the crick in her neck would ease itself out overnight. It would definitely help if she didn't attract idiot drivers, though. The front door was open, telling Nicole her daughter was at home. Michelle usually rented the movies, while Nicole took care of ordering pizza, which was actually more for Nick than either of them, but they had to offer him something besides the chick flicks. Granted, sometimes he popped his head into the living room, but Nicole often thought it had more to do with trying to understand women than really wanting to watch any movie that they'd rented--a movie that often made no sense to him-- and even though he looked a lot like his dad, he, too, was much more like his mother. He just tolerated the weekend-warrior dad a little better.

Of course, the girlfriend was another matter. Nick couldn't stand her, either.

Nicole entered the house and set her purse and keys on the table in the entryway. "Hey, Michelle, did you rent our movies?" She reached up and pulled at the comb holding her hair up. Immediately, the long, wavy strands fell around her face.

"Not yet." Michelle's voice came from the living room, so Nicole headed that way.

"Why not? All the new releases are going to be gone." She stepped into the room and spotted her daughter sitting on the sofa. Her long, dark hair also spilled around her face, and everyone who had ever seen the two of them together had said they looked more like sisters than mother and daughter. Then again, Nicole had always been fortunate because she didn't show her true age.

"What are you doing?" Nicole looked at the scrapbook in her daughter's hand and assumed it was Michelle's baby book. For some reason, Michelle loved to look at scrapbooks, but she had no interest in creating any.

"Hey, Mom, who's this?" She pointed at a picture Nicole could hardly see from a distance, so she had to sit on the couch as well.

As she looked at the glossy photo, Nicole gasped sharply, and her whole body went rigid. She opened her mouth like she wanted to speak, but nothing would come out.

"Mom? Are you okay?" Michelle looked down at the photo,

trying to figure out what had made her mother react. It was a simple photo taken in the delivery room where her mother lay on the bed. Standing beside her was a tall man she didn't recognize. It was her baby picture, she realized from the pink on the infant. The stranger held her.

"Mom, who is he?" she prompted again, her finger touching the stranger's chest just above where she, as a baby, lay.

Nicole swallowed hard before answering. "Your godfather," she whispered softly.

"Well, if he's my godfather, shouldn't I have heard of him before?" Michelle asked, looking more closely at the picture.

"It doesn't matter, Michelle." Nicole's tone was sharper than she'd intended as she gingerly took the scrapbook from her daughter's hands, closed it, and resettled it back on the shelf.

"So aren't you even going to tell me who he is?" Michelle asked, rising. Even as her mother put the scrapbook away, she stared at it, suddenly even more interested than she had been, and Nicole quickly realized it was because she was reacting when she shouldn't be. It was just that she hadn't expected to suddenly see an image of Jordan, and certainly not one that had made her daughter ask questions, not that Nicole had anything to hide.

There were just some things people never got over. Jordan had been one of those. He always would be.

"A name, Mom. At least tell me that much," Michelle said as she whisked her way into her mother's path. Michelle looked up at her with dark eyes that matched her own, and Nicole knew that the bigger the deal she made of this, the more her daughter would pursue it, and that was the last thing Nicole needed.

"His name is Jordan Carroway, and he's a friend. Not much more to tell." She side-stepped her daughter to go deeper into the living room, where the phone book had ended up on the table. "Perhaps you should go get those movies now while there's still a selection."

"All right. I'm going." She slipped from the room, and Nicole waited for a few seconds before she pulled out the scrapbook and flipped back to the page where she could look at Jordan's smile. Without realizing it, her finger had crept to his image and touched his face. It had been so long since they'd met, and while she'd never meant to fall in love, she had. Now she just couldn't take it back.

Of all the things she'd expected, a warm pooling of tears hadn't been among them, and even though she tried to wipe them away, suddenly there were too many and they spilled down her face, forcing a quiet sob to escape as Nicole once again thought of how things should never have gone that way. Never.

But it didn't matter what she thought. There would be no revising the past.

* * *

Michelle stood in the entryway, hidden just enough so her mother couldn't see her as Nicole slowly went back to the shelf and pulled down the scrapbook. As Michelle watched, she saw her mother flip through pages until she'd come to the one Michelle had pointed out. When Michelle saw her mother's expression soften at the sight of Jordan's picture, she frowned, wishing she could make sense of what she was seeing. What was it that seemed to disarm her mother the way no guy, including her father, had ever seemed able to?

Then the tears came, which caused her to take a step back and wonder at her mother's words. If Jordan Carroway had been just a friend, Nicole wouldn't be crying, so she knew the story her mother had given her had been false, and though she just didn't have a clue why the secrecy was so important, she sensed a sort of urgency in her mother as she struggled to keep it secret. Still, if there were one person who could untangle her mom's secrets, it would be Aunt Sarah. She knew everything, and she would talk, even if Michelle's mom didn't want her to.

At one time, Michelle had believed she knew everything about her mom, but the older she got, the more she realized her mother had had a life, and there were so many years that hadn't included her. Still, this was the first time she'd seen some glimmer of a life that might not have included her dad, and that definitely made her curious, especially since Jordan had done something that now made her mom cry at the sight of his photo.

* * *

Sarah was sitting outside by the pool when she heard her cell ring. She slowly eased one eye open and glared at the phone, hoping that would effectively silence it. No go. A third ring followed and then a fourth. Of course that was when it went straight to messaging so she figured it was all good. Until the phone rang again.

"Oh, all right," she muttered and reached for it. "Hello?"

"Aunt Sarah?"

Sarah frowned and sat up. "Michelle, is that you?"

"Yeah, it's me." In addition to Michelle's voice, Sarah also heard the wind around her, telling her Michelle was outside.

"What's wrong? Is your mom okay?" She looked out at the blue-green water that beckoned her and figured that once she'd finished this call, she'd dive in and cool off. Suddenly the sun felt way too hot for comfort.

"I think she is, but there're some things I want to ask you. Can you meet me at Burger King by my house?"

Frowning, Sarah nodded. "Okay. I'll be right there." She disconnected the call and gave the pool one last longing look. "So much for a swim," she muttered, and headed into the house to slip on a pair of shorts and a shirt before sliding her feet into flip flops. This done, she grabbed her purse and keys and flew out the door, driving like a demon.

Michelle was already there when Sarah arrived, and she quickly slid into the booth opposite her best friend's daughter. While she sort of expected Michelle to be upset or something, the teenager only sat calmly, sipping a milkshake.

"Okay, Michelle, out with it. What's so important?" Sarah brushed the hair from her face and took another sip of the drink she'd just bought.

"Who's Jordan Carroway?"

Sarah choked on the drink and sputtered. "Where did you hear that name?" She grabbed a napkin and wiped her mouth, suddenly wary of where this conversation was going.

"Mom told me. I just want to know what you know about him."

*Of course you do*, Sarah thought, suddenly unsure what to say that wouldn't upset her best friend. Surely, if Nicole had wanted her to know, she would have told her, right? She opened her mouth and closed it more than once as she tried to figure out how to answer Michelle's question. "Why does it matter who Jordan is, and how did you find out about him? I know there's more to this story than what your mom told you about him so if you want info, you tell me what happened." She leaned back and folded her arms across her chest.

"Okay." Michelle leaned close and told her the story about the scrapbook. When she'd finished, she asked, "Now are you going to tell me about Jordan and why a picture of him could make my mom cry like that?" She propped an elbow on the table and stared at Sarah expectantly.

Taking another sip, Sarah considered her options. She could tell the truth, or she could say that Michelle wasn't old enough to understand. The problem with option number two was that Michelle was mature for fifteen, and if anyone would understand, Michelle would. Besides, Nicole had never compromised her marital vows. That had all been Michael. She would even have fought to keep their marriage intact had Michael had the slightest glimmer of loyalty.

So she finally nodded at Michelle. "Okay, here's the deal--but if you tell your mom, I'll have to kill you, and it will be a slow and painful death before I feed you to my Chihuahua. Got it?"

Michelle started laughing and shook her head. "You are so insane, Aunt Sarah. You don't have a Chihuahua, and you know it."

Sarah nodded coolly and took another drink. "Well, yeah, but I'll buy one just for the occasion. Do you agree to be eaten by a Chihuahua if you tell your mom?"

A huge smile lit up Michelle's face as she realized Sarah was about to give her what she wanted. "Yes, I promise already. Now tell me!"

And Sarah did. She started with the weekend PE trip when Nicole had first fallen in love and went through all the moments she was aware of her best friend being around Jordan, and Michelle sat with stars in her eyes, eating it all up until Sarah reached the end.

"So why doesn't Mom call him now? She's divorced. And it's not like she doesn't deserve some happiness. Besides, while I like our movie nights, it would be really good to see her go out every once in a while, if you know what I mean."

Sarah nodded. "Yeah, I know what you mean, Michelle, but this has to be your mom's choice. Besides, I think she did try to call him. A woman answered the phone, and Nicole figured he had remarried."

Michelle let out a sigh and shook her head. "But that doesn't mean she knows he's remarried. She's guessing. She should just call him and ask him or something."

Sarah frowned. This was the same conversation she'd had with Nicole, and her daughter was right, but Nicole had just believed without proof he was married and was willing to let that be the end of it, which had troubled Sarah to no end. Still, Sarah knew her best friend wasn't going to give on this, so she held up her hand.

"Listen, Michelle, I know you mean well, and I know you want what's best for your mom, but this is something she needs to do. We can't do it for her. However things work out for Jordan and your mom, it's not up to us."

Sarah might have said more, but her cell rang and caught her attention. She checked the display and smiled. "Hello, hot, sexy, and dangerous." Then she nodded to Michelle. "I've got to take this."

"Of course you do," Michelle sighed. "I need to go rent movies, anyway." She gave her aunt a parting wave and disappeared.

## Chapter Nineteen

Nick stood in the basement, sorting laundry, figuring that if he wanted workout clothes, he was going to have to wash some. He'd finished loading the washer when he looked in the corner and spotted his mom's easel standing there, the canvas turned from him.

"So what are you painting these days, Mom?" he muttered, his curiosity getting the best of him as he walked to the easel and turned it to face him.

Nick really didn't know what he'd expected to find, but the naturalistic landscape in front of him wasn't it. He frowned at the center of the work. Whatever was supposed to be there, he wasn't really sure. It was clear, however, his mom had tried to draw many different things and changed her mind, probably at least one of those that Nick could tell was a couple. That's when Nick spotted the picture taped to the side of the canvas. Yes, the woman in the picture was his mother. That was clear enough even though she was much younger than now. But who was the dark-hair stranger sitting next to her on a bridge?

The mystery of it all intrigued him, and Nick thought he'd ask his mom later, maybe tomorrow. He gave one last look at the washer to make sure everything was okay before he trudged upstairs. Nicole and Michelle were about at the end of *Autumn in New York* when Nick poked his head into the room, his hand propped on the door molding.

He stared at the screen for a few seconds.

"Okay, *now* what are you two watching?" His dark hair glimmered auburn under the florescent lights. He frowned and once he saw Richard Gere's face quickly headed toward the kitchen while calling out, "Any pizza left?"

"The box is in the oven," Nicole yelled. "You could sit with us."

Nick reappeared, pizza box in hand, and sat in the recliner. He opened the box and began eating. As he saw both his sister and mother begin tearing up, he quickly shook his head. "That's it. Too much estrogen in this room." He pointed to the screen. "It's just a movie. Nobody's really dying!"

Michelle picked up a couch pillow and swatted her brother with it. "*You* might be if you don't shut up so I can hear. You chew like a cow!"

Nick got an evil glimmer in his eye and took a hefty bite of pizza before he leaned close to Michelle's ear and began chewing as loudly as he could.

"Eww, gross!" she yelled, shoving at him. "Get away from me."

Nick nodded as though his mission had been accomplished, and through a full mouth, he said, "I'm going to my room."

"Thank God!" Michelle and Nicole said in unison.

The silence didn't last, though. Just as quickly as Nick had vanished to his room, the front door opened again, this time admitting Sarah. She, too, took one look at the television and shook her head.

"Oh, depressing movie night. How classy." She leaned close and gave Nicole a kiss on the cheek.

"Hey, Sarah," Nicole said, scooting over so her best friend could sit. "Don't you have a date?"

"Later," she said, skimming her hands over the pillows on the couch. "Right now I'm crashing your movie night."

Without warning, she grabbed one of the larger decorative pillows and slammed it upside Nicole's head. Nicole just sat there and shook her head. "Did you really have to do that?"

"Yep." She brushed the hair from her face, then swatted her again.

"All right. That—" Nicole started, but a quick swing of Michelle's pillow cut her off. Nicole shook her head. "What is this? Two against one?"

"Nope," Michelle replied, swatting Sarah on the head. "It's every girl for herself."

"You'd better run," Sarah said, rising. "'Cause you know what they say about paybacks."

The room exploded into three females bashing each other with pillows and giggling. More than once, somebody tripped over the couch and the other two quickly capitalized on that opportunity, and toward the tail end of the pillow fight, when the three had almost completely exhausted themselves, Nick came out of his room and stepped into the perimeter.

"What is going on?" he asked, holding his hands in the air in a questioning manner.

The three girls looked at each other, and a silent agreement passed among them as they charged Nick, all of them swinging until Michelle just threw her pillow down and wrestled him to the couch so the other two could smack him.

"So not fair. Three against one."

Nicole started laughing. "I'm your mother, Nick, and if I say it's fair, you'd better believe it's fair." She wiped her hand across her forehead. "I don't know about anybody else, but I could use something to drink."

Sarah nodded toward the doorway. "Yeah, that makes two of us. I need something before I go. I don't want to go into this date dehydrated."

Eyes wide, Nicole slammed her elbow into her best friend's stomach.

"Oof." Sarah took a step back. "What was that for? I was just saying."

"Yeah, you were." Nicole agreed, giving her a dirty look that convinced her not to keep talking about future activities with Mr. Hot, Sexy, and Dangerous.

Michelle's cell rang and she said, "Mom, it's Bethany. I need to talk to her." Then she ran off to her room as the other two maintained a course to the kitchen, where Sarah plunked down at the table and Nicole pulled out two cans of soda. She gave one to her best friend and opened hers.

"So how are you?" Sarah asked and took a long drink.

"I'm okay."

"Really?" Sarah leaned back in the chair, still slightly out of breath from the pillow fight. "'Cause that's not what Michelle thinks. She said you were upset over a picture of Jordan. So what was that about?"

Nicole shrugged. "It's just a rough time to be alone. I mean even Michael has his wonderful girlfriend--you know, the same one he was in love with when we were married. Go figure. Seeing that picture just reminded me there's nobody to come home to."

Waving toward the back of the house, where Michelle and Nick's rooms were, Sarah asked, "And what does that say about your kids?"

"Nick's a junior. He's seventeen, Sarah. Michelle's not far from that. Then the house really will be empty, and there's nothing I can do about it."

Sarah reached out and squeezed her best friend's hand. "You could call Jordan."

Nicole shook her head. "No. I used to want that more than anything, but something about us just doesn't make getting together possible. He's engaged, I'm not. I'm married, he's divorced. I'm divorced, he's probably re-married. I know when to say *when*, Sarah."

"So why do you keep the picture, then?" Sarah insisted. "If he doesn't matter anymore, why not just throw it away?"

Nicole took a deep breath. "I really don't know." She licked her lips and tried not to think about it. The last thing she wanted to think about was anything to do with Jordan. Sometimes memories were just too difficult. Perhaps Sarah was right. Maybe she really just needed to completely let go of the past haunting her.

"Nic, I know you. You've been hiding for a long time, and you keep thinking it's going to get easier to get back out there and let yourself feel, but it never does. You just have to be willing to jump in no matter what and force yourself to swim."

For the first time in a long time, Sarah saw tears forming in Nicole's eyes, and she wondered what she could say that might help. Over the years, she'd said so many things, from "You need to move on" to "It'll be okay." Nothing worked.

"You know that I never really liked Jordan. Never. But this is me telling you to call him, Nic. This is me telling you it's not supposed to be like this."

* * *

*A full moon hung low in a black velvet sky which night had brushstroked with large, rolling clouds. Nicole was lying on her back, staring up at the heavens from between large branches, and the world smelled like moss and damp leaves, two things that always comforted her.*

*As she sat up, she looked down at her body and found herself in a beautiful gown she'd never seen. The bodice was black velvet and tight, something she might have worn when she was twenty or so. The full sleeves and skirt were made of a white gossamer and almost glowed in the moonlight.*

*Puzzled, she slowly rose to her feet and brushed her hands down her dress, worried about how the ground might have stained such beautiful fabric. She looked around her and saw a beautiful, ornate mirror, something out of a fairytale, but even the frame held little interest. No, it was her reflection that made her hold her breath.*

*She was younger, so much younger. She was twenty, the person who hadn't married Michael or had two kids. She was beautiful, and Nicole shook her head, trying to make sense of what was right in front of her. What did it mean?*

*In the mirror's reflection, she saw someone else standing there--a man with dark hair and eyes. Jordan. He was young there, too, and he wore a suit, almost as though both of them were guests at a wedding or something. But why were they in a forest?*

*She whirled and found him there, looking at her.*

*A smile touched her lips and she reached for him. "We can still be together, Jordan. We can do this. We can!"*

*She waited, knowing he would take her hand. He looked at her, his expression unchanged.*

*"Jordan, please!" She stretched her hand out closer to him as he smile died.*

*Slowly he turned and walked away.*

Nicole jerked upright in bed. Her heart was pounding furiously, and she felt hot tears streaming down her face as pain thundered through her.

Why was she dreaming this now? Why didn't it ever get any easier. She wiped the tears from her face and forced herself to get up. There wasn't much point lingering in bed alone. Besides, the one thing she counted on to get her through the rest of the day was the coffee. She was shaking so badly from that dream that she almost tripped twice on her way to the kitchen. She was in the middle preparing the pot when she heard the knock at the door.

“Who would that be?” She raked her fingers through her hair, trying to pat it into place before she opened the door. She hoped whoever it was wouldn't see the effect of the dream. That was the last thing she needed. Although she thought it might be Sarah or perhaps her mother, she did not expect to find Michael there--Michael in jeans and a sweater, looking as informal as she’d ever seen him, and that was what unnerved her more than anything.

“Michael, what are you doing here?” She leaned against the door and tried to calm her racing heart.

He nodded toward the house. “You mind if I come in?”

Nicole numbly stepped back and waved him inside, the trepidation inside mounting with each passing moment. Michael never came over here. Never. So why now? She closed the door and started toward the kitchen.

“Do you want some coffee?”

“Sure.” He followed her into the kitchen and sat at the dining room table, looking at the walls. Although this had been their house years ago, the décor had changed at least two or three times, and Michael no longer seemed to fit in, or at least that’s what Nicole kept telling herself.

“So what brings you to my neck of the woods?” she asked, filling a mug for him.

“There’s something I wanted to talk to you about.” He took a sip.

Nicole suddenly laughed and filled her own mug. “Well, that’s rich considering just how much we never seemed to talk about during the course of our marriage.” She gritted her teeth and forced herself to walk to the table, even though that was the last place she wanted to be at present.

“Still bitter, I see.” Setting his mug on the table, Michael turned his full attention to her.

“It’s not bitterness. It’s anger, Michael, and I have a right, considering how things went.” She took another sip even though the coffee was way too hot to drink. She needed something to keep her trembling fingers busy, and right now holding a coffee mug was about the best she was going to get.

“Yeah, well, that’s kind of what I wanted to talk to you about.” Leaning back, Michael stretched out his long legs and took a deep breath. Nicole marveled at how he could seem to relax no matter where he was or what he was doing. It was truly amazing, and she wished just once she the power to unsettle him as deeply as he’d unsettled her on more than one occasion.

“Okay, I’ll bite,” she said, looking at her mug instead of her ex.

“Kelsey and I are getting married.”

It was a good thing Nicole was sitting down because the air seemed to suddenly slip from her lungs, and her whole body went weak. Grateful for that one small miracle, she closed her eyes and tried not to let her emotions go haywire. It was the "m" word, the one she never expected to hear from Michael. He wasn’t exactly the marrying sort, and she rather figured that while he might live with "her," he would never completely entangle his life with another human being's. Marriage wasn’t in his best interest.

Now she knew the truth. Marriage with her hadn’t been in his best interest.

“Damn it, say something, Nicole,” Michael growled, leaning toward her. His hand slid over the top of hers.

"Gee, did you get her pregnant?"

Michael looked away. "Yes, she's pregnant, not that it matters."

She looked down and tried not to feel the rage building inside. She pulled away. “Congratulations, Michael. Is that what you want to hear?” Glaring, she stood and walked over to the window in the kitchen, wishing she were anywhere but in this room, where it felt like the walls were crumbling around her. It was hard to breathe, and she couldn't bear the pain.

Finally, something dawned on her. It made no sense for Michael to come all the way over here, something he never did, and make this announcement--not unless there was something he wanted. She slowly turned and folded her arms across her abdomen. "Okay, Michael. Out with it. I'm tired of waiting for the other shoe to hit the floor."

"I don't know what you mean." He took another sip of coffee.

"Really? I'm the last person you'd ordinarily talk to about 'her,' for obvious reasons." She waved at the table. "Yet here you are, telling me about all your future plans, including a wedding, I presume. Why is that?"

She waited for him to answer, but he just calmly sipped his coffee, seemingly oblivious to the tension between them. He had to feel it. He had to. She couldn't be the only one almost drowning in this painful sea.

"All right," he finally conceded, his eyes meeting Nicole's. "There is something I need you to do."

Every muscle in her body tensed, and she forced herself to walk back to the table and sit across from him. "So make this easy and get it over with. What do you want?"

"I need you to talk to the kids." He took another sip of coffee, and it took a moment for Nicole to digest what he'd said because his tone was pleasantly formal, as though she were one of his clients or something.

"About what?"

"Kelsey."

At the sound of her name, Nicole burst out laughing. He had to be joking. Didn't he? One look at his face revealed that he was serious. "You can't really expect me to do this, Michael. I'm your ex-wife, and you left me for her."

"That doesn't mean we can't be civil when it is required." Another sip of the coffee. Right about now, Nicole wanted to throw her mug at him and watch the coffee splash all over him. He'd deserved it. Then again, scalding him would hardly improve the current ability of his brain cells to fire adequately.

"Civilly? You want to talk about being civil?" Nicole heard her voice rising, but she couldn't seem to control it. Michael had that effect on her. "If you wanted things to be civil between us, you never would have slept with her in the first place." Now she was screaming, and that immediately got a reaction from Michael. He hated when anything shattered his appearance, and if screaming did nothing else, it did that entirely too well.

"Take it easy, Nicole." He stepped toward her, and she knew he was going to try to calm her down. It was his freaking lawyer voice, and she didn't want to be calm, not in her own house.

"Don't patronize me!" she shouted, her hands settling on her hips, challenging him to touch her.

"Do you really want the neighbors to hear our business?"

"I don't care what they hear!" she yelled. "I'd much prefer the truth to image, Michael, and those kids are never going to love your mistress even if you marry her. They're smart enough to know the truth."

Michael started to say something else when he saw movement in the corner of his eye, forcing him to turn to see Michelle and Nick standing there. Michelle wore her robe over a nightgown, and right at that moment, she appeared the spitting image of Nicole, her arms folded across her abdomen.

Nick leaned against the doorway, wearing a navy t-shirt and grey knit shorts. His hair stood on end. Both of them blinked at their parents. That's, of course, when Nicole felt tears burn her eyes because what she saw in their faces was her own vulnerability—the realization that all the mysteries of their parents' divorce had been revealed.

Nicole felt deficient and useless.

She closed her eyes and tried to summon the calm, but it refused to come, refused to answer with her heart pounding so furiously it was all she could hear. So at last she turned to Michael and said, "Well, there they are. Perhaps you might explain to them why they should be so enamored of their stepmom to-be." She shook her head. "This is a low blow, even for you, Michael."

She turned slowly and cast her eyes at the floor as she passed close to her children. Nick sensed the pain and fear radiating through his mother and tried to grab her arm so he could find some measure to calm her, but Nicole ducked away from his touch and kept walking, heading to the bedroom.

"What does she mean, Dad?" Nick asked, staring after his mother, an unpleasant frown on his face.

"It's nothing," Michael said.

Nick stepped closer. "Yeah--that's why she was upset. Try again."

Michael took a deep breath and looked out the window. "Well, Kelsey and I are getting married, and I—"

"Thought Mom would just say all the right things to us," Michelle finished for him, shaking her head. "Well, she doesn't have to, Dad. I don't like Kelsey. I've never liked Kelsey, and that's that." She turned and headed back to her bedroom.

"That makes two of us," Nick said before his father could say anything. "I know you left Mom for her, and Kelsey is nothing like Mom, so I guess the two of you deserve each other. Just leave the rest of us out of your demented happily ever after. I think you can see yourself out."

He also walked away and spotted Michelle standing at their mother's closed door, where she lightly knocked. "Mom? You okay?"

"I'll be out in a little while, Michelle," Nicole said, her voice muted by the door. But even that couldn't hide the way the tears had thickened her voice.

Michelle frowned and started to say something, but her brother caught her arm. "I know you want to help, but right now she probably needs space."

"Dad is such a jerk," she seethed and whirled to go to her own room, leaving Nick standing there, shaking his head.

"Yeah, he is," Nick finally agreed.

* * *

As much as Nicole wanted to say she hadn't been hurt by Michael's news, she knew better. In all the years since she and Michael had split, she had gotten used to the hole in her heart her ex-husband had left. He made no sense to her, and she'd finally realized the best she could hope for from him was a long and wonderful life with his two children. Michelle and Nick were the best parts of both of them, anyhow.

She'd waited until Michelle and Nick had gone on various errands before she finally slipped out of her bedroom. Walking into the kitchen, she marveled at how normal things seemed, not fractured the way Michael had left them.

The bastard.

Unable to stay in the same room which had not only been the place Michael had finally admitted his affair but also the place where he'd finally told her he was getting remarried, Nicole headed into the living room, where she walked around like a stranger in her own house. She touched the framed pictures on the fireplace mantel and scanned the bookshelves as though she really didn't know what was there, and it was only when she ran across the few scrapbooks she kept that Nicole knew she ought to turn a blind eye to the past. Nothing good lay there except the life she had led with her children. Still, the scrapbooks had the same allure as Pandora's box had, and they would probably have the same effect if she weren't careful.

She was beyond careful these days, she realized as she picked up the middle scrapbook. Wrong move, she realized, as she flipped it open and saw a large photo taken at her wedding. The breath caught in her throat, and no matter how hard she tried to look away, she found her eyes drawn to Michael's face. He wasn't looking at the camera. No, he was peering at the Nicole who had ceased to exist beyond these pictures--the smiling, happy Nicole who'd believed that love always worked out and that there was nothing else worth fighting for, the Nicole who'd learned firsthand that sometimes love was a casualty of life no matter how hard you tried to keep it alive, and that there was always one person who loved the other more. She had been that person, and she had paid dearly for it.

A sad smile crept across her face as she wished she had known how to keep that Michael with her, the one who'd promised he would never hurt her. How could he have slipped so far away? Tears burned her eyes, and she closed the album. It took three tries to get it back into its spot because her vision was so blurred. A sob cut through her, and she knew better than to keep playing this game, but something wouldn't let her cut her losses and quit.

She reached for a different scrapbook, determined to find memories that wouldn't sting so badly. Her trembling hands flipped open the book, and she came face-to-face with another, different blast from the past, no less breathtaking but for very different reasons. She saw a small picture that had been taken of Jordan and at the end of the PE trip when they'd met. The instructor had taken different shots of students. Jordan had been sitting cross-legged on the bridge, in the exact same spot where she'd been right before she'd fallen off and she was right beside him.

Once again, she found herself asking why things hadn't worked out between the two of them. If things had even been slightly fair, they would've because he would never have broken her heart like this. Never. Somehow she knew that much. Staring into his dark eyes and at his inviting smile, she found herself lost and broken.

A wave of pain rushed over her, and she started crying. It wasn't just about Jordan or Michael. It was about all the things Nicole had believed in which had crumbled into a million pieces and now lay at her feet. It was about losing her father and about her kids growing up and about all the fears she could never contain or shake. She'd never felt so alone and so *diminished* in her entire life.

Sobs ripped through her, and she couldn't stop crying. She couldn't even move, and the only thing she could see was Jordan. Tears rolled down her face and spattered the slick sheet protecting her memories, and they just kept coming in wave after wave of pain and emptiness. The only sound she could hear was her heartbeat thumping throughout her body.

In that instant, she wasn't expecting to feel arms around her, and she started to pull away until she realized it was Nick. He'd come back, and he held her tightly to let her spend her grief. Nick, the son of Michael—a man who afforded her no compassion and no regrets, a man who had loved her easily and then, just as easily stopped.

But Nick was nothing like him. She knew that much as he held her until she'd stopped crying. He frowned, and his expression was troubled. "You okay, Mom?" He eased down in the chair next to her.

Brushing her hand across her face, she nodded. "Yeah. It's been a long day."

"Dad's a jerk. I know it, Michelle knows it, and you know it, and it doesn't matter if he marries that bimbo. She's never going to be you."

Swallowing hard, she offered a wan smile. "Thanks."

"You're welcome." As he stood, he glanced at the scrapbook she'd been looking at.

"Hey, who is that?" he asked.

"No one," she whispered. "Just a friend from long ago."

"Oh." He shrugged and walked away.

Nicole took one last look at Jordan's picture and closed the album, sealing the past in place once again.

## Chapter Twenty

Nick waited in his room until he heard Michelle run upstairs to her room and turn on some music.  Sitting on his bed, he'd been staring at the walls, wishing he could knock some sense into his old man.  Although he and Michael didn't see eye to eye on a lot of things, he tried not to fight with his dad, but this--this was stupid.

His dad was actually going to marry that woman, the same one who'd been the reason his dad had left his mom in the first place.  And his dad actually wanted them to like her?  *Seriously*?  And what the hell was the deal with the picture on the canvas and in the scrapbook?  That photo had to mean something to his mother for her to have duplicated it and been trying to paint it, as well. There were so many pieces that didn't fit, and even if Nick had been good at understanding females, he wasn't sure even he would be able to put the pieces together on this one.  Whatever was going on, he needed to do *something,* so he did the only thing he knew—he barged into his sister's room.

Michelle was sitting on her bed with the phone pressed to her ear when he opened the door.  She glared at him and said, "Ever heard of knocking?"  Then she gestured for him to leave.

"We need to talk," he said and sat in her rolling chair, his arms folded across his chest.

"Look, Jenny, my brother has invaded my room.  I'll have to call you back."  She shook her head and snapped the phone shut.  "Now what?" She looked at her brother's tee-shirt, at the sweat stains around his neck and under his arms, and she squinched up her nose. "You've been sweating. Did you even think to take a shower?"

"Damn it, Michelle, this is important!" Nick growled. "I just got back from my workout and when I came in, Mom was crying, and she had her scrapbook open to a picture of this her with this guy I've never even seen. If that's not enough, she's got that same picture taped to a canvas on her easel. She's been trying to paint it. What the hell is going on?"

"Dad's probably made her feel crappy, and the picture is of a guy named Jordan," Michelle said quietly. "Aunt Sarah told me about him." And then she went on to tell him the rest of the story. All the while, Nick sat there, propping his elbows on his knees so he could rest his chin in his hands, a distant look in his eyes.

When she'd finished, she shook her head. "I wish we knew where to find this guy. I mean, it's been years since they knew each other, and even though Mom never quite got over him, she was great to Dad. And then he dumped her."

Nick stood and stretched. "Well, what the hell would we do if we could find him? I mean, he might be married with a family by now."

Michelle looked at up at him. "But he might not."

"True," her brother agreed. He still had a faraway look in his eyes. "So what now?"

Thinking for a moment, Michelle asked, "How about I call Aunt Sarah and you get mom out of the house so we can hatch a plan?"

"Where do you want me to take her, Michelle?" He stared at her in utter disbelief.

"How about the movies? Say it's an early birthday present. She'll never know."

"All right." He headed for the door. "I guess I'd better get a shower."

Laughing, Michelle nodded in agreement. "Yeah, I'd say you stink, all right."

"Thanks." He went out the door, and Michelle threw a pillow at it.

* * *

"Your mother would kill me if she knew I was even considering this with you," Sarah said, sitting on the couch. "Yes, she is still crazy about Jordan, but she doesn't even want to try because I think she's afraid of being rejected."

"It can't hurt," Michelle argued, pacing the room with her arms folded across her abdomen. "I just want to know how to find him."

"Well, if you can get your mom's phone, I think she's still got his number."

"Genius!" Michelle said and began looking around. Sure enough, Nicole had been so flattered and in a rush to go to the movies she'd actually left her handbag sitting on the dining room table. Michelle grabbed the phone from inside and headed back to the living room.

"Throw it here," Sarah said, holding her hands open to catch it. Michelle tossed it, and Sarah flipped through the numbers and held it up for Michelle to see. "Bingo. We have a winner."

Squealing, Michelle grabbed the phone and said, "Here goes." She pushed the button as Sarah stood.

"Whoa, what are you doing?"

"Fixing things," Michelle said, and gestured for Sarah to sit.

* * *

"Nothing like a hotel room," Jordan muttered, "a nice, expensive hotel room in France, and I'm staring at the walls." He shook his head and looked around the room, starting with the muted television that ran an old *I Love Lucy* episode--badly dubbed, of course. His gaze ended with a watercolor painting of a woman who reminded him of Nicole. He'd wrapped up his business, and tomorrow he'd fly stateside. This painting would be a welcome memento from his trip abroad, especially since he'd given up on the real thing.

He'd seen the painting earlier that day, and it had cost him 1000 euro, not that he'd minded parting with it. It was a beautiful image of a woman on the beach, her long, dark hair swept over one shoulder.

Shaking his head, he knew he should have been over Nicole long ago. Funny how the human heart had its own timeline and intentions. He'd started to guess he would never get over Nicole, and he really didn't mind. It helped to have something consistent in his life.

He started over to the painting to look at it in greater detail when his cell rang. Puzzled, he shook his head, not sure what to say. Who would be calling him here? His mother, perhaps?

He picked up the phone and found Nicole's name on the display. A smile tugged at his lips. He quickly pushed the answer key and said, "Well, speak of the devil. I was just thinking of you and wondering how you were."

"I'm fine," she said. "How about you?"

"Well, I'm in France, and it's beautiful." Yet when he said the word *beautiful*, his gaze didn't look out the window but at the portrait instead.

"Wow. Is your family with you?"

*What a strange question*, Jordan thought. "My family? Nicole, I live alone. I haven't remarried. I thought you knew that."

There was a pause at the other end. Then, finally, she said, "Oh, my."

"Are you all right?" Jordan paced the room, suddenly feeling as though something he couldn't quite put his finger on wasn't right.

"I'm fine."

"How's Michael?" He didn't know what else to say.

"He's an ass who's about to get remarried."

"What?" Jordan stopped pacing. "I didn't even know you were divorced."

Another strange pause. "Yeah, I guess I should have told you. So, when are you flying back?"

He paused for a moment and looked at the display. In all the conversations he'd had with Nicole, this was by far the strangest.

"Tomorrow."

"There's something I want to ask you." Her tone suddenly seemed nervous, and another nervous flag went up.

"What's going on? Are you okay?"

"I'm…fine. I just wanted to meet with you so we could talk. It's kind of important."

The pacing resumed, and he looked at his watch, as doing so would get him home more quickly. "Nicole, this doesn't sound like you. I'm worried."

"Don't be. Just meet me. Please?"

"All right. I can be there in two days, and I can meet you at the Denny's by the church where you had your dad's funeral. Would two o'clock be okay?"

"I'll be there."

They both said goodbye and hung up, yet even as the phone went silent in Jordan's hand, he still kept hearing her voice, but this time, he was worried. Perhaps the divorce had cut too deeply and she needed a friend. He didn't know. He just knew that, no matter what, he had to be there for her.

* * *

"Oh my God!" Sarah squealed. "You did not just *do* that."

Michelle nodded and said, "Oh, yes, I did--and I'm going to do you one better: Nick is going to meet him at Denny's and tell him what's going on. You and I are going to take her camping at the park with that bridge where the two of them first met, and Nick will bring him later. I can tell he has the hots for Mom. He's never remarried, and he still thought she was married, which is why he never asked her out after she divorced Daddy."

Michelle started doing this weird happy dance, and in that moment, Sarah got up and followed her lead, both of them laughing uncontrollably. They were so lost in laughter they didn't hear Nicole and Nick enter.

Nicole walked up and asked, "Okay, what are you two on, and where can I get some?"

While she'd expected one or both of them to answer, all she got was more giggles as her daughter threw her arms around Nicole and forced her to join in their dance.

"Okay, this is one of those weird female things." Nick stood there and shook his head. "I draw the line here." Then he walked off and headed to his room.

A few moments later, the three of them stopped giggling and fell to the sofa. Nicole glanced at the ceiling and thought of her son. "Should we let Nick know it's safe to come back down? That the estrogen has cleared the room?"

"Nah. He likes to brood alone, Mom," Michelle said, twining her arm around her mother's. "So how was the movie?"

"It was good, but I still think he took me because you're planning something." Nicole leveled an accusatory glance at her daughter.

"Me? Planning something?" Not likely. I never plan anything."

Nicole leaned against her daughter. "Yeah, right. That'll be the day. Let's just hope it's not a grounding offense."

Sarah and Michelle looked at each other and burst out laughing again.

* * *

Two days later, Jordan sat in the parking lot at Denny's, trying to figure out what the hell he was doing there. Yeah, he was meeting Nicole, but there was something strange about this. Nicole hadn't sounded like Nicole, not by a long shot.

He glanced down at the clock and realized he had about ten minutes before he was actually supposed to be at the restaurant. He debated whether he should go in early and how it would look. Of course, why the hell should it matter after all these years? He didn't have a clue, but it did.

Before he pulled the keys from the ignition, he ducked his head slightly and peered into the rear-view mirror, checking to make sure he was presentable. The longer he stared, the more he fixated on the tiny wrinkles around his eyes. When had he gotten those? Never mind. He hadn't worried about them before. There was no point in suddenly thinking about his age. One last glance, and he finally decided to get out of the Jeep and amble toward the entrance.

Although there was still a small crowd left over from lunch, there were plenty of empty tables, so he was seated without waiting. He scanned the room, wondering if Nicole had arrived before him, but he certainly didn't see anyone who looked like her, and he figured she probably hadn't changed so much he wouldn't recognize her. Realizing she wasn't there yet, he turned his focus to the menu.

As he opened it, he pondered why she'd wanted to meet him. Could it be just a matter of her wanting to get together for old times' sake? He shook his head. No, he hadn't gotten that impression when he'd been on the phone with her--not that he knew what to do with the impression he did get when they'd last spoken.

"Figure out what you're having," he muttered, forcing himself to stop going over things in his head. It wasn't going to do him any good. Whatever reason Nicole had had for wanting to meet with him, he'd know soon enough.

"Excuse me."

Jordan looked up to find a teenage guy standing there. His dark eyes and hair seemed familiar, but he couldn't quite place him. "Yes?"

"Do you mind if I sit here?"

Jordan took a hasty look around again. "Well, I'm actually supposed to be meeting someone, and there are other unoccupied tables." He frowned, suddenly wondering why the kid wanted to sit with him. It didn't make sense.

"Yeah, I know you're meeting someone. It's just not who you *think* you're seeing."

Jordan's eyes widened, and for a second he was speechless. Then he shook his head. "Come again? Are you sure you have the right table?"

"Are you Jordan Carroway?"

"Well," Jordan began, "Yes." He scrutinized the kid, that familiar feeling nagging at him, and then it dawned on him: he had Nicole's eyes. Her son, perhaps? "You're Nick, aren't you?"

Nick nodded, surprised and sat across from him. "I didn't know if you knew about me."

Jordan laughed and set the menu on the table. "The last time I saw you, you were still in diapers right after your grandfather's funeral, so it's been a while, but yeah, I definitely knew about you." He looked around the room, trying to find Nicole. "Where's your mom?"

"Not here." He leaned back.

"Is she all right? She sounded strange on the phone."

It was Nick's turn to laugh, and since the waiter appeared at that moment to take their orders, Jordan had to wait to find out why. When the waiter finally walked away, he asked, "What's so funny?" Then he grabbed his water and took a drink.

"That wasn't my mom you talked to on the phone, actually. She was at the movies with me while my sister and Aunt Sarah called you."

The pit of Jordan's stomach seemed to lurch as though he were on a roller coaster and had just gone over a large hill. "But Sarah hates me."

"Not as much as she hates my dad--and you haven't seen my mom lately. She's been a wreck. Sarah even told her to call you, but she wouldn't listen."

A flush crept into Jordan's cheeks, and he took a deep breath. "Well, I guess that explains why she sounded the way she did. At first I couldn't put my finger on why her voice was so different but since I was talking to a teenager, I'm thinking now she sounded like one. I just didn't get it at the time."

Jordan stared at Nick, kind of amazed at how much he really did look like his mother. It seemed as though he should have known immediately when he'd first spotted Nick; that's how uncanny the resemblance was. Still, there was no way he could've known, really.

"Yeah, well, Michelle was pretty pleased with herself that she was able to convince you she was Mom and get this whole meeting set up."

Jordan set his glass down. "But why wouldn't your mom just call me herself? Why have your sister do it?"

A bit of color drained from Nick's face. "Mom doesn't have a clue Michelle even called, and it's better that way. Really it is."

The waiter brought out a salad for Jordan, and once Jordan had unwrapped his silverware, he tried again to wrap his head around a conversation he couldn't believe he was having with someone he couldn't even believe was this old. Where had the time gone?

"Okay, so what's going on with your mom?" He looked at the salad but suddenly didn't have much appetite.

Nick took a deep breath. "I'll tell you. But first I want to ask you a question. It might seem a little personal, but you gotta understand. This is my mom we're talking about. It's important."

Jordan's back tensed, and he suddenly felt unnerved. What was going on? What had he stumbled into? "Okay, I'll do my best."

"Do you love my mom?"

Jordan blinked, trying to believe he'd heard right. As he struggled to answer, a couple passed by them on their way out.

"Why?"

"It's a simple question. Do you love my mom?"

Jordan took a sip of water just to give himself some time to form an answer to a tough question he really already thought he knew the answer to. Saying it was a different story, though. His gut reaction was to keep his feelings locked up, to play it safe, but something about the way Nick sat there, his eyes delving deeply into Jordan's, made lying impossible. "I care very much for your mom, but up until two days ago, she was still married in my mind, Nick. Up until now, I've never had much chance to explore them. I'd like to, but I can't just say I love her without a foundation we haven't had a chance to build." He toyed with his silverware. "I know maybe that isn't what you want to hear, but it's the best I can say."

Nick smiled and nodded. "Well, you didn't lie, and that's what's important. My dad could stand to take a few lessons from you on how to treat women."

Jordan shoved his fork into the salad. "You're a lot like your mom, Nick."

"Thank you."

The waiter returned with Nick's order, and for a moment the two men busied themselves eating. Then Jordan finally looked up and set his fork down again. "So what are you expecting from me? I mean, your mom doesn't know I'm here, so why bother?"

Nick swallowed the bite in his mouth. "Well, the thing is, my asshole dad has decided to marry his girlfriend—the same one he cheated with during his marriage to my mom--and it's been really tough for her. Aunt Sarah's been trying to get her to call you since the divorce years ago, but Mom figured you were remarried, and she didn't want to complicate your life."

*She's never complicated my life*, Jordan thought. *Never.* He arched his eyebrows at the mention of Sarah again. "You sure Sarah tried to get her to call me?" He shook his head in bewilderment.

Nick pointed his fork at Jordan. "Take my word. You put Sarah and my dad in a room, and there're fireworks. Guaranteed. Besides," he said, slipping his hand around his glass of soda, "you haven't seen my mom since my dad made that boneheaded announcement. She's been crying a lot and thinking about the past. Once Sarah told us about how Mom met you, both Michelle and I decided we had to do something."

Jordan leaned back, suddenly aware he was finally about to get to the point where he fit into a plan he'd known nothing about. "Is your mom okay?"

"Yeah," Nick finally said. "I guess. She's pretty upset, and we didn't know what else to do."

Jordan took a bite of his chicken and asked, "Okay, it sounds like you, Michelle, and Sarah have cooked up a game plan. How about letting me in on it?"

Shaking his head, Nick said, "Okay. Here's the deal: I was going to take you to meet Mom. Right now Michelle and Sarah are setting up a campsite with Mom—"

"Wait." Jordan held up his hand, stopping the conversation as he leaned forward. "Please tell me your mother isn't camping."

"Well, yeah, she is. Why?"

Jordan starting shaking his head as he imagined all the disasters which were about to befall Nicole. "Have you ever taken your mother camping before?"

Nick fiddled with his hamburger. "Well--no--my dad didn't much care for the Great Outdoors."

"Then let me enlighten you about what happened the last time your mother decided to spend some quality time with Mother Nature. I was there with her when she fell into a river, tipped a canoe, and stepped on a cactus. By that point, I think the only reason she didn't get into more trouble was that I was carrying her. The world is not ready for your mother to go camping, Nick."

Shaking his head, Nick said, "Then we should get to the campsite before something bad happens?"

Jordan set down a tip and stood, grabbing both checks. "That would be my guess."

Nick also stood. "I'm following you."

Jordan stepped up to the register and handed the cashier the checks.

"You don't have to pay for my meal."

"I know," Jordan said, grinning. "But I don't mind." As the cashier handed Jordan his change, he turned back to Nick. "Now perhaps we should go rescue your sister and aunt."

## Chapter Twenty-One

"Tell me again why I let you guys talk me into this? You know I hate camping." Nicole glared at her best friend while holding the poles of their tent in her hand. She'd tried to tell herself she was intelligent enough to make sense of how a tent should go up. The tent, however, seemed to be getting the upper hand, and all Sarah could do was sit on her butt and laugh.

"You came because your kids asked you to, and you know that in a few years they'll be in college and you'll wish you'd had more moments like this." Sarah turned her focus to the tent poles in Nicole's hand. "Okay, well, maybe not exactly like *this*, but you know what I mean."

Nicole waved the poles in the air in exasperation. "How is it I can have a bachelor's degree and still not know which pole goes where?"

Sarah chuckled and held her hand out for the poles. "Here. Give me those before you hurt someone. How did you ever get through that weekend P.E. trip with Jordan?"

Immediately Nicole's shoulders stiffened, and she closed her eyes as though she didn't want to see what was right in front of her. "I was a disaster, that's how," she finally managed in a weak voice.

"Have you talked to him lately?"

Nicole gritted her teeth and glowered at her. "I think you know the answer to that."

Looking away, Sarah began assembling the tent. "You could

always call him. I'm sure he'd be glad to hear from you."

"Yeah, well, considering how my last relationship went, I think I'll pass just the same." She plunked down in one of the folding chairs to get a great view of her friend fighting with the tent. Unfortunately, it seemed Sarah was a bit better at assembling the tent than Nicole had been.

"Nic," Sarah began, her hands pausing so she could look up at Nicole. "We've been over this, hon. What happened between you and Michael wasn't your fault. He was a dick, and you got hurt. Your kids will tell you that, even though you'd never ask them because you try so hard to make things equitable." She shook her head. "Well, do something for you. Just this once make things equitable and enjoy your life. You aren't married, and you're free to call whomever you want. Jordan is a big boy. If he's in the middle of a relationship, which I doubt, he'll be the first to speak up, I'm sure."

Sarah went back to shoving the poles into place, and to Nicole's frustration, the tent began to take shape--and it even looked right, unlike what she'd done earlier. Chewing her bottom lip, Nicole reached into the ice chest and pulled out a bottle of water.

"You seem certain Jordan isn't in the middle of a relationship. Why?"

Sarah straightened and stretched; half the tent was done. "Well, let's face it. You never got over him, and I'm willing to bet he never got over you. Yeah, he married Alyssa, but that didn't last very long. You married Michael, and even though you did everything you were supposed to, it fell apart. Who's to say that what you and Jordan had wasn't meant to be, and that both of you were just too stubborn and stupid to know better?"

"Thanks for your vote of confidence, Sarah. I can't tell you how much I appreciate it." She sighed and took a drink before wiping her hand across her forehead. "Besides, even if I did call Jordan and we wanted to go out, I'm not sure what the kids would think, and the last thing I want to do is upset them the way their dad is upsetting them."

At that, Sarah actually threw one of the smaller tent poles. Even though Nicole tried shifting out of the way, the pole dinged her shin. "Ouch! That hurt! Why are you throwing things at me?"

"You're a grown woman, Nicole Adams, and you deserve your chance to go out and have fun just like the rest of the population. I think your kids are smart enough to recognize that." She began to assemble the last part of the tent. "You just can't put a tent together to save your soul.

Nicole squirmed in her seat, knowing her best friend was probably right, but that didn't make it any easier to think about. It was bad enough that both her kids had seen her break down during a weaker moment even though she'd fought so hard to avoid it. She didn't want to have to explain about going out on dates, too. Then again, if she hadn't believed so strongly that Jordan had remarried, she probably would've tried to get together with him, if for no other reason than to rule out this infernal feeling of being incomplete without him. That was really beginning to get on her nerves.

Nicole glanced around the campsite and shook her head. "By the way, have you seen my two wonderful teenagers—you know, the ones who thought this would be such a great experience for mom?"

Sarah shrugged. "Nope. Then again, Nick in particular knows just how well you put things together, so my money is on him wandering around, and Michelle has probably found the part of the river where all the cute guys are swimming and is reluctant to leave."

She snapped the last pole into place and then gestured to the tent, a proud smile on her face. "The tent is up."

"Have I mentioned you suck?" Nicole growled standing. Part of her wanted to find some kind of fault in how the tent was standing but couldn't. Sarah somehow knew just where everything went. It was sickening, really. "So where did you figure out how to put up a tent?"

"It's not hard." She picked up a flyer from the other folding chair. "They're called instructions and they tell you everything you need to know about putting the poles in the right places. You should try using them sometime." She waved them at her best friend and started laughing.

"Well," Nicole said, looking at the tent. "It's hours before we need to think about dinner. So what are we going to do?"

Sarah's cell began to ring, and she shrugged. "Hold that thought. Let me answer this." She flipped the phone open. "Hello?" A pause. "Oh, yeah. The usual spot is definitely where it needs to be. Thanks." She flipped the phone shut before turning back to Nicole.

"What was that all about?" Nicole asked, frowning.

"Mom's keeping an eye on the house because Greg is out of town. I was telling her to put the mail in the usual spot." She stretched her arms over her head. "So how about we take a little walk to stretch our legs?"

"All right. But I'm kind of getting a little nervous about Nick. He should have been here already."

Sarah gave her shoulder a squeeze. "I'm sure Nick is fine, Nicole. He's got a good head on his shoulders."

The two of them headed down the road, and even though Nicole thought the landscape seemed familiar, she really couldn't place it. Although it was warm enough for swimming and she figured there would be more than a few people hanging around, there weren't, which actually made it nice. The two kept walking until Nicole spotted her son's truck , and she jerked her best friend toward it.

"Now you get here," Nicole said, watching as her son rolled the truck window down. "I could've used some help putting up the tent!"

Nick grinned. "Yeah, well, I'm sure you could've."

Sarah threw her hands up in exasperation. "Hey, I helped.

Otherwise, the tent would still be on the ground in pieces. Your mother so needs tent assembly lessons."

Nicole shoved her elbow in Sarah's side, which immediately quieted her. "So where have you been?"

Nick shrugged. "I had to pick up a friend."

Scanning the empty passenger seat, Nicole frowned. "Okay, if you really want me to buy that, you should have someone sitting next to you."

"He's on the bridge, Mom." Nick's dull tone suggested his mother really should be more observant.

"On the bridge?" It was then that Nicole remembered the park from years ago, when she'd first met Jordan. The sun was bright and she had to shield her eyes even to look at the bridge, which was when she saw a man in jeans and a denim, button-down standing at the center in pretty much the same spot she'd stood that day. He held a bouquet of daisies.

"Who is…." Nicole's voice died as she took in his dark hair and build. It was Jordan. Her mouth opened, and she meant to call his name as her feet started moving. At first, it was a slow canter, but a few steps later, she was running full force and didn't stop until she'd launched herself into his arms.

"It's you! It's really you!" she whispered breathlessly.

Jordan thought about answering, but for the moment all he could do was just hold onto her the way he'd always wanted since they'd met. She wrapped her legs around him and buried her head against his neck, the silence broken only by the sound of dragonflies buzzing through the air and the sound of their hearts.

"I thought you'd remarried," she said.

He pulled back to look into her eyes. "And I thought you were still married. Just goes to show what happens when you think instead of feel." He smiled, and in the instant their eyes met, he knew he had to kiss her. His head bent low, and their lips touched at last.

For a moment the world seemed to spin. Jordan could swear to that because suddenly they both listed to the side--and fell over the edge, the arms of the one never releasing the other. They surfaced, laughing.

“We have to stop doing that,” Nicole said.

“Let's do it every year.” Jordan pulled her close, and they kissed again.

From the bank, Nick yelled, “Hey, Jordan,” I think I got it.” He waved the camera.

“Oh my God--is that my camera?" Nicole asked, incredulous. "The one that fell in the river?”

He nodded.

Nicole swallowed hard and felt tears glimmering in her eyes. He’d thought of her all those years and kept part of her close. “But I told you to get rid of it.”

Jordan smiled. “Some things just take time to fix.”

Maria Rachel Hooley has been featured in numerous publications such as Green Hills Literary Lantern, Westview, and Kimera. She has written over thirty novels in numerous genres. Her first chapbook of poetry, A Different Song, was published by Rose Rock Press in 1999. She is a high school teacher and lives in Oklahoma with husband and three children, one of whom is on the autism spectrum. She is an advocate for education about autism.

Made in the USA
Las Vegas, NV
03 February 2025

17419473R00135